D1531203

Modern Jewish Literature and Culture

ROBERT A. MANDEL, SERIES EDITOR

Mitzvah Man

Mitzvah Man

John J. Clayton

Texas
Tech
University
Press

This book is typeset in Adobe Minion Pro. The paper used in this book meets the minimum requirements of ANSI/NISO Z39.48-1992 (R1997). ∞

Library of Congress Cataloging-in-Publication Data
Clayton, John Jacob.
    Mitzvah man / John J. Clayton.
        p. cm. — (Modern Jewish literature and culture)
    Summary: "After a tragic event, Adam Friedman sets out to change the world with small acts of heroism as Mitzvah Man"— Provided by publisher.
      ISBN 978-0-89672-683-3 (hardcover : alk. paper)
  1. Jewish men—Fiction. 2. Jews—Fiction. 3. Jewish fiction. I. Title.
    PS3553.L388M57 2011
    813'.54—dc22

                           2011008974

Printed in the United States of America
11 12 13 14 15 16 17 18 19 / 9 8 7 6 5 4 3 2 1

Texas Tech University Press
Box 41037 | Lubbock, Texas 79409-1037 USA
800.832.4042 | ttup@ttu.edu | www.ttupress.org

For my wife Sharon Dunn, for my children
Aaron, Sasha, Laura, and,
as always, Josh

Mitzvah Man

1

Adam Friedman wasn't always the Mitzvah Man. He was once a personal success.

Shouldn't victory, success, be climax to a story, resolution of a pattern? So this story begins where a story should end. Of course the victory is merely in his own eyes—and in the mental snapshots he's clicking to bring his wife. *Oh, will Shira laugh!*

This victory, how did it come about? In January 2005, Adam Friedman received in the mail an invitation from the Chase Day School in New York to a twenty-fifth reunion of his prep school class. How did they get his address? For years their alumni office would call him for donations, but that was before he moved to Boston. Well, it was their job to find him; his, to ignore their calls, their letters. And when that didn't work, he'd told the development guy on the phone: "Look, friend, when I think about Chase, all I remember is pain and humiliation. It's become a decent school—so I hear, and so you say. In my day, mid-seventies, it was at its nadir—a school for rich, vulgar brats. I was physically tortured at Chase; worse, I was bored. The headmaster was a frightened lush, the teachers were shockingly ignorant. None of that's your fault—you're just doing your job. But please don't ask me for support."

You'd think that would do it.

But beginning January 2005, letters from the class twenty-fifth reunion committee. A parade of letters, names of the men who'd signed up. Deadheads, all—except for his old friend Ben Licht.

His mother hadn't wanted him to go to a public school where he'd face tough boys, anti-Semites, God knows what. She was full of fantasies. *My son,* she drawled in her fancy fake-Brit accent, *attends one of the finest preparatory schools in the country.* Some *finest.* He went to Chase because, unlike Horace Mann, Chase gave him a full scholarship. His father made *bupkus* as a salesman; his rich uncle refused to help. He was poor boy in a rich boy's school. The other kids, also Jewish, came from families in the dress business or on the stock exchange.

They somehow got wind of his scholarship, laughed at his hand-me-down wingtip shoes, his father's old shirts, collars frayed. This was just after the end of the war in Vietnam, but you'd think the student revolt had never happened. It was one of the last all-boys schools in New York. Politics, music, art were not cool at Chase; foreign movies, not cool; near-shoulder-length hair, not cool. Even being active as a Jew, taking it seriously, not cool. What was cool? Jocks were cool, guys who got laid were cool. It was cool to have season box seats at Yankee Stadium. Then there were the uncool—like Adam, like Ben Licht. Which turned out to be a blessing, though not experienced as a blessing, for it's what led Adam and Ben to music and art. It let them feel contempt for "the animals." They wrote stories, they attended concerts mostly as demonstrations of a different way to be. Later, literature, music, became a real part of their lives.

Together, after school, talking, talking, talking, Adam and Ben walked across Central Park to the Metropolitan Museum or sat cross-legged on the floor of Ben's living room while Adrienne Licht, Ben's mother, played Chopin on the seven-foot grand or put on records of violinists—first Menuhin, say, then Stern—playing the same passages. Adam remembers mooning over Ben's mom. He loved her eyes. He loved it that she'd get him a ticket to High Holiday services so Ben would have someone to sit with. He loved going to the Metropolitan Museum with them.

Was art worth getting tortured over? He would have been better off in a school full of gang kids. It was okay if he got pushed around. Snapped with towels? Bearable if not pleasant. But this one guy, Phil Cole, six-three, well over two hundred pounds, waited for him on the stairs between classes. If you ignored him, he'd say, "Adam, Adam, I'm insulted. Aren't you going to say hello?" If you said, "Hello, Phil," he'd say, "Adam, I'm insulted, Adam. Aren't you going to shake my hand?" Bastard! If you shook his hand—well, sometimes he'd just smile his evil smile and send you on your way. But most days, smiling, smiling, he'd squeeze, squeeze until you thought the bones of your hand would snap. Or he'd twist an arm behind Adam's back. Higher, higher. "Uncle! Uncle!" Screw "uncle." *Uncle* wouldn't cut it. "Got to get to class," wouldn't cut it. At the point you were sure your hiss of breath was going to turn to a scream, he'd let go.

And if you screamed? He screamed; no one paid attention. But if a teacher was close by, he and Phil would wind up in the headmaster's office. The headmaster, a morning drunk, hardly knew what was going on; mumbling, he'd mildly chastise, and for the next week Phil would squeeze murderously, twist murderously, and say, "Aren't you gonna yell today, you little faggot?"

But Phil, strong as he was, was an outsider, too; who liked him? And after a couple of years, Adam learned to keep his mouth shut and, as in a prison, suck up to the boys in charge—buy protection with homework. One day, Gary Mankin, bull of a guy—Adam wrote a paper for him—stayed out of sight on the landing above. Cole made his move; Gary leaped down the steps four at a time, slammed Cole once, twice in the face, once in the gut, and when he doubled over, bloody, grabbed his throat, warned him—*You keep the fuck away from Adam.* It's not fair to say Gary helped him only because of the paper. He had a sense of justice; he liked smacking a bully.

Early March, clearing after a late winter storm. Adam decides to take the train in from Boston, and, after the reunion, stay over at the Westbury, take a meeting in New York in the morning, and fly the shuttle back.

Why is he attending this reunion of a class he despised? It's not just seeing Ben again. It's to measure the distance he's come—isn't that it? To put himself in the midst of guys he once feared, hated, envied—now that he's gained strength and position. To break a spell.

"But it's not kind," he says to Shira. "You know? It's boastful. It's contemptuous at the core. And why do I care? How strong can I be if I need that?"

Shira laughs. She grins at Lisa, who's doing homework at the kitchen table. She puts her arms around Lisa's shoulders. "We believe Dad's strong, don't we?"

"Dad's a tiger," Lisa drawls, not bothering to look up. It's her new amused, cool fourteen-year-old style. Her feet, in white socks, are hooked around the legs of the kitchen chair, leaving her skinny legs jutting at odd angles. She seems all knees and elbows. "Like grrrr, Dad."

"You, you are my beautiful tiger," Shira says in a whisper, for him alone. "No—you really *are*. And do you always have to have noble motives?"

So. A fresh shirt and underclothes in his briefcase, light enough load that he can walk up Seventh Avenue to the Stage Deli for, ah, a hot pastrami sandwich and half-sour pickles. And instead of grabbing a cab, he takes the subway up to 86th, remembering in the rocking of the car the old fear everyday on his way to school. But there's comforting nostalgia for him, too, in smelling the subway, standing up in the familiar dance, abjuring pole and hand-hold—free-style skiing, dry water-skiing—as the car jiggles and rocks. And the walk along Central Park West and down West 87th. The school itself has changed—it's a beautiful new building, three times the size of the old school. Inside, dark wood paneling, panache of an upper-class, old New York that has nothing to do with these kids or their families, most of them Jewish.

"Adam *Friedman*?"

He pins his name tag on his jacket when the portly, powerful, balding man at the table, looking at the name, stands up slowly.

"Gary Mankin? Hey, Gary. Nice to see you." *You once saved my ass,* he doesn't say.

"Adam *Friedman?*"

All evening there would be a moment of doubt; then, in Adam's brain the face and body would undergo a mutation; you'd see, yes, of course, it's the same boy, twenty-five years added on but the same. Extra weight, most of them, puffy faces, age lines, fine suits. But within a minute, not all that different. The same shmuck who copied his math answers, the funny kid who was in the school play with him. But that's not the way *Adam* is seen. All evening this is the victory he'd antici-pated: to see himself reflected in surprised looks. Gary is the first. "You—you were a plump little kid. Wow. Look at you. What hap-pened?"

"Oh. I'm a late bloomer," Adam laughed. "I was a year younger, and besides, I grew up late. I grew ten inches in sixteen months—it began late in my senior year."

Gary can't get over it. "Hey, Les? Look at this guy. You know who this is? It's *Adam Friedman.* Remember Adam? Our valedictorian? He looks like a movie star."

Not really. He's tall, long-boned, black hair tightly curled; he sports a wiry Pan-like beard. He looks more like a Norwegian fishing captain than a movie star. Still, he enjoys the comparison. *Hey, Shira, you mar-ried a movie star,* he tells her in his head. Shira leans invisibly against the glass-fronted bookcase, grinning.

Les, once the tallest boy in the class, a foot above Adam, is now shorter. He takes Adam by the shoulders: "Amazing. *Adam?* You really *Adam Friedman?*"

Adam laughs, "Yeah, yeah. You guys! Come on. Let me see the list. Is Ben Licht here?"

"In the social room."

"And what about that . . . Phil Cole?"

"Also," Gary says, pointing a thumb. "And still an asshole. Sixty per-cent of the class. Great turnout. Go get yourself a drink." Gary calls, "Artie—see this guy? It's *Adam Friedman.*"

As he walks away, he hears, "ADAM?" Hears it again, again, that's the cry, more question than exclamation. *ADAM?* Unbelieving. And you look at these guys. Something about their eyes—eyes of dull, rich men. Adam has done business with so many men like these. Decent enough men, as he's sure these are decent men. He pumps hands, slaps shoulders, listens again: "You were this little guy, fat, short. Hey, you look terrific." And from one man, Myron Belsky, himself lean and handsome, one of the only interesting guys in the school, he hears something better: "You were always too smart for most of these guys. Good to see you, Friedman. So what do you do?"

"I'm in business. Software." And he leaves it at that. The fact is, he's become something of a star. During the nineties he built a trio of software companies, all helping corporations integrate their computer systems, systems that had developed hodge-podge as need and technology arose. He sold the companies while the selling was good. Now, in 2005, he's on a couple of boards, makes a very good living consulting. So by the time of the reunion, this son of a salesman, scholarship boy at school, has become as rich as, maybe richer than, anyone from his class.

And his marriage—that's part of his victory. It seems half the men he talks to are divorced, most of these remarried. He and Shira, well, quarrel and gripe. But dear God, she's in his bones; in his mind her skin is always warm silk. The intimate silliness—for instance, the standing joke, told when they first knew one another and even now, was that there must have been a past life when they were together—in a palace overlooking the Tigris or the Ganges or a sea on a distant planet, another galaxy. They stood at Sinai together listening to Moses. You're just too familiar, he said to her. Obviously, she said, we've known each other in life after life. World after world, he said. They still said these things, liked saying them in front of Lisa, even if she rolled her eyes.

Dear God, thank you for my life.

He drinks a little too much; alcohol is meant to loosen his checkbook when the development people speak; but the buzz helps him accept the glow of victory, it blurs out responsibility for his contempt for his old classmates. ("So what business are you in?" "You remember," the man says, "the family business. Paper products." A grin. "You don't

remember? We used to kid about it. *Toilet* paper." "So? That's great.
What the hell's wrong with toilet paper?" Adam asks.)

Adam wanders around looking for Ben. A paneled room with high, multipaned windows, urban pastiche of Brit boarding school elegance. What would the windows look out on if the drapes weren't drawn? Just 87th Street. At the drinks table he sees Phil Cole. The guy's gained another fifty pounds. He's grotesque—he's dumpy, an oaf—but wears a very expensive suit. Phil's father ran a BMW agency somewhere in Connecticut. Phil probably took it over.

On the way down in the train Adam imagined confronting Phil. This ox.

At first Phil doesn't notice him. Glancing over, he sees the name before he sees Adam, grunts "Hi," goes off with a whiskey. Suddenly he lets out a guffaw and turns back. "You. Sure, you're Adam. I remember you from the staircase." A grin. "Remember the staircase, Adam?"

There are ten, fifteen guys in small groups in the room, holding drinks. He knows they're not paying attention to Phil, but he flushes; at once, the old storm in his stomach comes back!

"Remember, Adam? 'You want to shake hands, Adam?'" Phil doesn't intend to hurt him; he's only making a joke, a parody of what he once did. Mostly it's a way of saying *Hey—sorry, Adam. Hey. That was high school.* But isn't he also saying, *I'm still a big guy—and don't forget it.* Something like that. Adam laughs, puts up his palms, waves them and smiles, backs away past suited shoulders, clearing an aisle for his dance with Cole. Phil keeps coming, presses past a couple of men, slowly puts forth a hand; it's the grin—the grin and that old, hostile slowness that does it. *Oh, yes? All right, then.* Adam opens his hand. As Phil goes for it, smirking, Adam slips his own hand past, outside Phil's arm; stepping in, he hooks his arm around Phil's throat and guides him effortlessly over his hip, down to the polished wood floor: *thud.*

The men, drinks in hands, pull back from the thud. As Phil goes down, Adam half-holds him to break the fall. The big guy still lands hard; luckily he's padded. In an instant Adam's got a knee on the bastard's chest, hand at his windpipe, demonstrating, but holding back the force of the thrust—*it would be easy to finish you*. His old classmates circle them. He gets up, turns to look down at Phil, who's lying there, all two hundred twenty pounds of him, dazed. "Want to shake again, Phil? Next time you won't get off so easy."

"Are you crazy?" Phil is choking. "You must be crazy." He looks for support among the other men, but no one accepts his glance.

Quietly, in modulated tone: "Hmm. Crazy," Adam says. "I could be. Want to come see? Want to shake again? Next time, I promise," he says slowly, *"I'll snap your arm at the elbow."*

"This isn't fucking high school." Phil says this as a speech for the benefit of his classmates. Now he brushes himself off and retreats, crabwise, to the drinks table in front of the tall windows.

Adam spots Ben Licht, chuckling. He grins back. Ben is just old Ben, a little plump, with glasses, a sweet-faced man. A sweet-hearted man, Adam is sure, as he was a sweet-hearted boy. How can this nice guy work in New York as a lawyer? "Hey, Ben." Ben, he embraces.

"It *is* 'fucking high school,' isn't it?" Ben's wearing a soft, dove-gray suit and blue silk tie; otherwise, within seconds, he's again Ben, his face the face of kindness Adam took refuge in. Now, he takes refuge in Ben's good humor, but as waves of indignation recede, Adam's not laughing.

"That's right," he says, deadpan, almost grim. "In some sense, I guess it always will be."

"Did you come here knowing you'd take Cole down? I mean—were you hoping for the opportunity?"

"No, I don't think so. Well," he grins, "yes, I think I *considered* it. You know, Ben, maybe all my training—I mean years and years, aikido, karate—ever since college—maybe it hasn't been to achieve balance and serenity. It's so I could put that poor pathetic piece of crap down on the floor. Some damn fool, huh?" They link arms and head for the drinks table. He hears, behind him, Phil complaining, men laughing.

The man from the toilet-paper family pats Adam's shoulder. "Hey, I saw that. Nice move."

Adam nods, smiles, and puts him aside, walks off with Ben.

"So what have you been doing?" Ben asks.

"Business. Hi-tech businesses. You?"

"Law. But you know that already. Estate law."

"Good," Adam says. "Good." This has become private talk. "Tell me." Adam puts his hand on Ben's jacket. "We always liked each other. I don't get it—why did we lose touch?"

Ben is a ponderer—always has been. He sits with the question. "I think it's because of who we were at school. We were a reminder to each other of a bad time, when we were a couple of losers—that's what I think. If we'd stayed friends, it would've been harder to become other people."

"Or stay the same people but feel okay about it. Not feel like losers."

"That's right. Say. Why don't we slip away early? You're the only guy I came to see. Come home with me, meet my wife, meet Margaret. I told her I might drag you over. Your wife in town?"

"No. She's a violinist, part of a trio, and they're practicing tonight. And she's a pediatrician—she's working in the morning. Okay. Sure. I can stop in for a couple of minutes."

Adam visits the bathroom. It's not the old school bathroom with bleach-smelling hexagonal tiles and warped wooden doors on the stalls, a room smelling of marijuana and deodorizer. It had a little translucent window with wires through the glass, always filth in the corners of the panes. Kids pitched quarters against the wall—but quarters didn't let them feel they were really cool, so they pitched quarters for dollars. It was a place he used to fear. Who'd be in there waiting to overturn his book bag, toss his papers into a toilet bowl? Now, it's a bright, clean restaurant bathroom; for this alumni event they've put out cotton, not paper towels.

Why does he feel hollow, depressed, in this nice room? What's happened to his victory?

He turns on his cell phone and checks for messages; there are a couple, but he doesn't listen. It's ten o'clock. He's disappointed Shira hasn't called; she must be back by now. Maybe there'll be a message at the hotel.

They leave and nobody knows it. They leave before the guy from the alumni office can make his pitch, and they walk down to Broadway. "I wish you could meet Shira," Adam says. "Well, you will. Let's plan on it. If I've become a decent man, Ben, it's mostly because of her."

"I can't get over you with that beard," Ben says. "You look like a million dollars."

At the Apthorp, 79th and Broadway, a massive, elegant building which, like the Dakota, surrounds a large court, Ben points up one, two . . . five stories, to where they live and where his wife lived as a child. "I used to stand down here and look up," Ben says, "and sometimes Margaret would open her window ten stories up and look down and wave. Like Juliet—except her parents and my parents were crazy about each other. Still are. They take vacations together. They're closer than we are, Margaret and I. Well. You know what marriage is like. I mean it's tough."

"It can be. You've known Margaret that long? I met Shira in my late twenties."

A call comes on Adam's cell. "I'm sorry, Ben. I'll turn it off."

"No, no. Take it."

So Adam tilts his head into the phone. He listens. "Where?" He listens. "And what's happening with my daughter?" He listens. "I'll be there as soon as I can make it."

And that's the end of the victorious part of the night, the victorious part of his life.

2

In Boston Shira is at Peter Bent Brigham on life support. A car full of young men, surely drunk, swung around the corner and, skidding on a patch of frozen snow, smashed her as she was opening the door of the car to come home from rehearsal. She was pinned against the open door; held up by ripped door panels, she couldn't fall. Lois, cellist in the trio, waving goodbye from the steps of her house in Brookline, saw everything. Saw the faces, saw the car take off, swerve, stop, back up, almost hitting her, too, as she ran across the street—and take off again. Rough shriek as it scraped another car and fishtailed down the street.

By now, Shira's coat had ripped away from the dangling door, and she'd slumped, rag doll, to the street. "A rag doll," Lois told Adam at the hospital. "At first I thought, 'Omigod, her hands, her violin,' that was my worry, but when I saw her fall . . ."

Lois knew not to move her. Neighbors started coming out next door, across the street. "Call 9-1-1," she yelled. She ran inside for a blanket. The police were there within no more than two minutes; an ambulance a couple of minutes later. Shira was lifted into the ambulance. Lois followed in her car—her husband stayed with the kids.

By the time Adam gets to the hospital by shuttle and taxi from Logan, Shira has been operated on to stop internal bleeding. She's fallen into a coma or a coma has been induced to conserve her strength. "If we can stabilize her, we'll go in again, but for now the

John J. Clayton

bleeding's stopped and the pressure is off her lungs. We've got lung tubes in place. The car broke her rib cage."

He sits by her bed in the ICU. Her face is purple; there's a bandage on her forehead. But it's what he can't see that's terrible. "Lots of internal damage," the doctor says. "Her spleen may be ruptured." They walk out. "Rupturing inside. And of course concussion; how bad, well, we don't know. If she makes it through the night, we have a chance. She'll be in rehab for months."

"And her back? You spoke to our friend about her spine."

"We just don't know yet."

"But she *is* going to make it? Through the night? You think?"

"You'd better stay—stay overnight. You can sit by the bed, but don't disturb her."

A nurse tells him what the numbers mean. Oxygen absorption, blood pressure, pulse, heart lines, breathing lines. A pulse of 130? Is that possible? He asks a second nurse, a man, what would be good numbers, what would we want to see? He sits, trying to pass peace and energy her way, trying to bring himself into a state of being in which he can magically change the numbers. Or maybe it's not magic. Maybe it can be done. He has no doubt there's energy that isn't limited by the isolate body, that can be shared. If he can learn.

He watches the numbers. He breathes as calmly as he can, trying to change the numbers.

The numbers don't change. They go up, they go down. They don't change for the better.

He goes to the lounge to see Lois, questioning, questioning, hungry for the tiniest shred of information, making interpretations of pauses in the doctor's words, nuances of tone, tiny discrepancies between what this doctor has told him and another doctor has told Lois. Making up a story. *It'll be months. We'll take such good care of her. Lisa—Lisa will sit with her, Lisa will read to her. Thank God I can work from home, but we'll have to get someone in to help. . . .* "So was she coherent when you covered her with the blanket? Was she conscious? She was conscious, wasn't she?"

If he believes absolutely, absolutely, that she'll recover, then she'll recover. But that means even the slightest doubt is dangerous. *Faith*, he thinks. He mumbles in English because he only knows a few words of the blessing in Hebrew, a *mishaberach* for healing.

He's heard that if you talk to someone in a coma, at some level they hear. He'll sing her favorite songs to her.

"I have to call Shira's mother. Please, Lois, you go home now. You've got to get sleep. There's no point." He stands at the window holding the cell in his hand. It's almost one o'clock. Midnight in Minneapolis. He holds the cell. A seventy-five-year-old woman, wake her up at this hour, and what for? Or Shira's brother Max?

Lois puts on her coat, notices him holding the phone like a statue, lays her arm over Adam's shoulder, kisses his cheek. "Suppose anything happens, God forbid, and you haven't called?"

"I'll call. Good night."

"I'll call you here in the morning. She'll be okay. I'm sure of it."

"Thank you. Yes. Good night, Lois. Thanks for everything you did."

He can't call. He sits in the lounge. Should he call Max in Minneapolis, her sister Ruth in Boston?

The family of a cancer patient at the edge of death huddles in the opposite corner, talking in a Slavic language. He sits. If he hadn't gone to New York tonight, he'd have been home with Lisa, and maybe Shira would have been more relaxed leaving, maybe she'd have stayed at Lois's another minute, another ten seconds for godsakes. Just another ten seconds. Or she'd have called him before she left to say, How's Lisa? Did you miss me? Or she'd have gotten to the car ten seconds earlier, wanting to be home with them. The car door would have had a scrape.

He tells himself a story: she's going to be okay, but *months*, the doctor will say. And it'll be such an ordeal, making Lisa feel good about taking care of her mother, not worry, not show worry, tell her, *Mom's growing stronger and stronger, and you're helping so much.* And she *will* help. She's a great helper. She'll make a huge difference. Adam sees her sitting in their bedroom on a rented hospital bed. Helping her do rehab, walking through the house. He sits. He tries to trick himself out of remembering to call Nina, Shira's mother. He hears an ambulance siren—someone else being brought in. He'll pray for that person. He mustn't be selfish in his prayers.

Of course her accident has nothing to do with his childish sense of victory tonight. But it feels like punishment. Of course it isn't.

He doesn't want to bother the nurses but is hungry to sit by her bed. Tentatively, he raps at the swinging doors of the ICU. If he tells them Shira is a doctor, a pediatrician, will they pay more attention? No, of course not. No one comes to the doors; he walks in. There's a curtain all around Shira's bed. He sees legs under the curtain, hears blurred talk. A male nurse rushes out, over the intercom, blurred words. He hears "code blue." Running, the nurse pushes a cart into Shira's area.

The doctor he spoke with hurries through the swinging doors and past him. Not stopping or looking his way, he calls, "Please—please stay outside."

If he's good, if he listens, she'll make it.

Why did he need that damn victory? God's joke. He says this the way you'd touch a tongue to a cavity, knowing the accident has nothing to do with the reunion, his arrogance. *Mom's been in a terrible accident. She's never coming home, she's staying with God.*

My wife almost died—stupid, drunk teenagers. Lois said they'd stolen the car, a joyride. They left it at Cleveland Circle and ran. Sons-of-bitches. *My wife almost died.*

"Mr. *Friedman*." The doctor's slow walk tells a different story before the doctor says a word. He looks down at his chart, looks into Adam's face. "I'm very sorry, Mr. Friedman."

He spends a few minutes with her. He doesn't want to remember her like this, but he's hungry for moments in her presence. She's still in the room, he believes that—the living core of her still here. Is she, as a separate being, conscious of him? He lays a hand on her breast and whispers the Mourner's Kaddish. *Y'it'gadal v'yitkadash shmey raba.* . . . (May His Great Name be exalted and sanctified. . . .). Like any Kaddish, it's a prayer to be said in a minyan, a quorum of adult Jews. But it's all he knows to say; his own words don't come. Her name in Hebrew, *song*, is all he can say to her. "Shira . . . Shira. . . ." A nurse, a woman, enters the curtained-off area. "Mr. Friedman . . ."

The first days he's supported by grief and ritual. The rabbi is called, Rabbi Klein, the *chevra kadisha*—burial society—takes Shira's body; the women wash and sit with it, chanting psalms all the next night. Adam doesn't know the chants, but he reads psalms aloud at home, then over the closed coffin at the funeral home. The service and burial take place the following morning. He covers mirrors, sits shiva.

Almost always one of them was home in the evening. But when her mom was practicing with the trio and her dad was away, Lisa would go to sleep without them. So when he came in that first morning, he sat in the kitchen until she woke and made her bed and got ready for school and asked, "Hi, Dad. Where's Mom?" For a moment he thought about not telling, breaking the news in bits: Mom is hurt; Mom may not make it; Mom is gone. But he's never been someone to withhold truth. It comes out of his mouth. He took her hand and said, "Sit down with me for a minute, we have to talk." And holding her, he told her, when she shook her head, he told her again, and when he saw the blankness of her look told her again. *Your mom, your beautiful mother, isn't coming home. She had an accident last night, somebody hit her with a car, and your mommy's not coming home. We're going to pray for her a lot, honey. And she'll pray for us.* He spoke to her as if she were seven or eight, and her face was broken open to the little girl beneath.

As it entered her, she cried, *No, no, no,* and then she howled and screamed. *Daddy? Daddy? No, Daddy!* And he held her and told her again, and she held onto him. Waves of weeping, howling, and then quiet, and then again. At the grave she held onto his hand and wouldn't let go.

At the evening service at home, the rabbi, a young man working for their new congregation part-time, leads the service. Adam likes him. Rabbi Klein is ten years younger than Adam but really knows so much, has studied Talmud and the commentaries every day since he was a child; and he knows how to be with people, how, without touching them, to make people feel held in his kind awareness. Most of the little congregation is there or has left a message with the rabbi. Shira's sister Ruth sits on a pillow on the rug, the rose-colored Bijar that Shira so delighted in, sits next to their mother Nina. Ruthie holds her mother's cheek to her shoulder. Ruthie's husband Leo looks out of it. Lisa sits beside them, a stone. Her long, pretty face with those big eyes of hers— no life in them. Her hair, usually a mess, has been brushed and tied back. That saddens him; it's a sign of what's going to happen to her.

After the service Adam knows he's expected to speak to friends, to fellow congregants. He brings out photo albums. Shira loved to document everything in their lives. He imagines her standing off to one side tonight and snapping pictures.

He opens the albums; they sit on his lap, get passed around the room. He shows pictures of Shira, Shira as a child, as a bride, as a mother. He talks about Shira, his love for Shira, how impossibly good she was. Everything he says, although it's true, feels slightly false. Then Shira's mother, unable to bear it, starts to keen, to howl. He can't continue speaking.

That night Adam sleeps in Lisa's room on the narrow trundle bed for when her friends stay over. He remembers the night she had the croup; the nights of nightmare; the nights Lisa would come in and announce, "I can't sleep," and one of them would sleep across the room from her. Now he lies in that bed, not fully sleeping, slipping into sleep, out again.

His friend Bob Mirsky leads the morning service; it's a smaller group, but even the family itself is more than half a minyan. Jerry Rosenthal comes in and hugs Adam, thumps him on the back and hugs; and there's Shira's brother Max and wife Evie, who flew in from Minneapolis with Shira's mother; they're staying in the guest room. And Shira's sister Ruth and her Leo. As an Orthodox woman, Ruth, fiercely *frum*, observant, won't count herself in the minyan, though Adam, a Conservative Jew, counts women. But it doesn't matter. By the time of

the first Kaddish there are ten men, and by the end of the service, fifteen—as well as twenty women.

Ruth pulls him aside. "After a while," she says, "if you want us to take
Lisa to live with us, with her cousins who love her, just say so. If that
feels like an intrusion, I don't mean it to be."

"I know you mean well, Ruthie, but it would be like taking the rest of
my life away."

He says this blandly, without emotion, a fact.

Shira wore her Judaism lightly, more comfortably than Adam; she
took it for granted, though she was serious about revering Shabbat,
preparing for Pesach, making sure Lisa was immersed at Hebrew school,
at summer camp. Her sister Ruth, who married into an Orthodox
family, is more intense about her Judaism. She wants to send Lisa to
Maimonides—a Hebrew day school—with her own kids. For a moment,
Adam hates her, then becomes calm—she has no authority. It's not going
to happen. For better or worse, Adam thinks, Lisa's got just me.

It's not only congregants who stop by all week; it's friends—Shira's
friends, so many. Circles, some overlapping, most separate: the com-
plexity of a life. Friends from music, the orchestra she'd joined, the trio.
Lois, who saw the car smash into her, comes often and can't stop weeping. Adam feels it's he who has to comfort her. Friends, patients, from
her practice as a pediatrician. The Rosenthals—Talia, a doctor in the
same practice as Shira, and Jerry, Adam's tennis buddy—sit a few minutes every day. Fellow congregants whose kids were in Hebrew school
with Lisa. Her running partner. Cousins, more cousins. Shira's is a large
extended family, with deep roots in the Boston Jewish community.

Ben Licht calls. On the third day he flies up to Boston and sits with
Adam one whole afternoon, then flies home. *Thanks for coming.
Thanks, Ben. . . .* They sit together. Adam's soothed by seeing him, by
not having to speak, but then the gap between the other evening and
today weighs him down.

His mind isn't clear. At times, thinking about putting away excess
food, a thought flits through him, *Shira will take care of that*—and then

he wakes up. The food piles up. Lisa is the one who puts it away. Already she's calm. In her room she spends time in crying jags, but when she's with her father or company, she's fourteen again; no—older. When people come to the house, she remembers to ask them to remove their shoes and boots, she stacks them by the door. She hands them the book to sign, offers them photo albums. This skinny teenager handles things.

Let's skip over the next two months, as the house, with no one to care about it, no one to clean, grows messier and his neat beard grows into a woolly, wild metaphor of grief. He's not to cut his beard for a month, and as the second month passes he can't bring himself to cut it. It goes with his silent howling in the night when Lisa sleeps, in talks with the rabbi that leave him depressed, visits to the psychiatrist that leave him angry, meetings with friends who seem to think they're obligated to be with him, to place hands on his shoulders and pat, as he feels he's obligated to reassure them, yes, at last I'm doing better. Better, a little better. Well, and isn't he? At least it becomes easier to fake being ordinary around Lisa.

Shira stays just behind his eyes throughout the day, through the evening, and in his sleep. He keeps to his own side of the bed; waking in the middle of the night he's careful not to disturb her sleep or imagines for an instant she's been called away for a birth. She was in a practice with four other ob-gyn's so when she was on call, it was common for him to wake and find her gone. He wakes, blinks, it hits him. Even with pills it's hard to get to sleep. He misses Shira's warm body, the hip he laid his hand on in a comradely way before sleep. Not sex; rarely does he thinks about making love with her. He takes antidepressants. Nothing to be ashamed of, the psychiatrist says, each time he alters the prescription. Is it depression or pills that account for his lack of sexual feelings? He prefers it this way. Surely, the pills don't account for his revulsion at the thought of sex.

The sweetness of his life. He knows she felt the same.

There were whole years neither of them felt this way. By the time

Lisa was born, they'd become deeply married, but after a year or so, it came apart. There were whole weeks he hated her. For what? A look. A hostile turn of phrase. And what was it? Was it something deep? As far as he knows now, it was just two people, both overworked, having to take care of a baby and each sure the other was putting work first, was doing irreparable harm to Lisa. And how did that dissolve? Like salt in water. How does salt dissolve? There was no dramatic moment when they understood one another, trusted one another. Slowly, slowly, slowly they began to soften.

The sweetness gone. But Shira is with him all the time.

She's always with Lisa, too. Many sentences between them begin: *What do you think Mom would say about . . . ?*

To take care of Lisa, he drops his consulting work; he's living on investments. Too bad, really. A regular position, though hard to handle, would give him structure. When he gets Lisa to school he goes to a coffee shop, reads the *Times* or *Wall Street Journal*. He goes to his gym and runs the treadmill or the elliptical machine, goes home and plays at commodities trading on-line, more a way of feeling connected to the world than of making a living. Secretly he feels he's a bum.

Everything he sees is filtered by a miasma of sadness. Like a translucent gray in the air. The gray is his, but he feels certain that everyone he sees—a shop clerk, a nurse at the doctor's office, the trim girl behind the counter at the gym—is inhabiting the same gray planet. So when someone he barely knows—a fellow student at his tai kwon do class, for instance, who knows nothing about Shira, comes up with something breezy, he's jarred, feels offended, is sure the guy is vulgar and superficial—when it's only that they're inhabiting different planets.

I had plans. We had plans together, they were working out. Our life down the drain, our life. We had plans. . . . Loops of thought, and at one turn of the loop, anger, murderous, at the boys, the drunken teenagers, who've never been caught. He wants to find and kill them. At other times, he imagines sitting and mourning with them for what they did without meaning to. It'll haunt their lives. He even gets twinges of anger at Shira, so stupid, as if she asked to die! To compensate, he's twice as tender to Lisa as ever. All their plans have turned to nothing. Except: here's Lisa.

Together they visit Shira's grave in the Jewish cemetery near Brandeis. No marker for a year; the ground is barely recognizable. They sit and in a whisper tell her things.

Lisa's a skinny child not grown into her bones; she walks like a funny, alien creature learning to find her footing in our gravity. She has big, dark eyes set far apart in a long face he never gets tired of looking at. But she must get tired of being looked at. Too often, he wraps up his pain in his look, looks for deliverance from pain, and she is just a child, a teen; how much of this can she take? He's supposed to be the one taking care of her; shamefully often, it's the other way around.

Taking care of Lisa this spring becomes his life. Adam isn't a businessman between positions; he's a Single Parent. He's ashamed: sipping at her life, her excitements, living through her. "What went on today?" Every parent is frustrated by a child's shrug, but Adam really needs to know, to be in class with her invisibly, his long legs mentally sticking out into the aisle. A soccer dad, he stands on the sidelines, jacket zipped up, arms folded, stands with a couple of other dads and maybe a dozen mothers; he watches her game or he shops for dinner and comes back to check out the end of a practice.

All of Lisa's life they've lived in a small house in Cambridge, not far from Harvard Square. Mornings, he does odd jobs around the house; afternoons, unless he's on-line trading, he reads. This house is a shelter at the same time that Shira is painfully present all the time. For instance, what do you do with Shira's clothes? He can't throw them out, he can't give them away. One day Lisa helps him to put all Shira's clothes into one closet and shut the closet door. But he keeps opening it to smell her smells. And the little half-empty bottles of perfume and lotions. Her jewels he puts away for Lisa. But in every room there's some piece of whimsy, some arrangement of shawls, that's her gift to the house. If there's something really pretty in a room, it was Shira who put it there.

There's not much he wants to do except watch Lisa and read Torah.

Nothing else makes sense. He reads psalms as if they were going to give him clues about how to take this in. *You return man to dust,* he reads. And *Like a hind crying for water, my soul cries for you, O God.* He reads about the four worlds, the *olamot,* a concept developed in the sixteenth century by Isaac Luria—the spiritual world, the intellectual world, the emotional world, the world of action. He reads Hasidic texts about cleaving to God. He reads Maimonides, Judah Halevi; reads Abraham Joshua Heschel. He struggles with the Zohar, struggles with commentaries on Kabbalah. Friday evening he goes with Lisa to services or, bottle of wine in hand, to the Rosenthals for Shabbos dinner. Saturday mornings he goes to services, Lisa to study trope, the musical form by which Torah text is sung, with old Gershom Samuels for her Bat Mitzvah. It was already late, postponed once—her grandmother begged for them to wait until she had her new hip; so Lisa put it off, learned a *haftarah* for this spring. And then Shira died. Now she's fourteen; all her friends have already become B'nai Mitzvah. Her ceremony has been rescheduled for a month after the next High Holidays. Her new portion will be Lech Lecha, the story of Abraham going forth. She'll be fourteen and a half. Once a week she has a lesson in chanting the new Torah and *haftarah* portions.

Here's how he formulates it: when he feels able to slacken his hands on the ropes, he can hire a housekeeper, find a position. Oh, it isn't a good time to find work, but he has so many contacts; if necessary, he can begin his own new business. He has over five hundred thousand dollars liquid enough to be used as capital or as surety for loans.

This is how they live through the spring. It seems to be the end of a story. For a story requires change; Adam gets along by pretending he's done with change. Only Lisa is permitted to change. Hope of a different life for himself would be a betrayal of Shira. God knows she wouldn't think so. Still, this is the secret paradigm under his life.

Then, how does the story begin again?

When Adam takes Lisa to Friday night services or goes to shul on Saturday mornings, does he feel the breath of the Shekhina, the sweet

Presence of God, imagined by the sixteenth-century mystics of Safed as feminine, the loving hum of the universe, suffusing his breath, touching his face? Never. It's not like that. In fact, he has a grudge against God, secret, even from himself. But he goes. Sometimes he goes to weekday morning minyan, too. He is supposed to say Kaddish, grudge or no grudge. Saturday mornings, after she meets her Bat Mitzvah tutor Gershom Samuels, Lisa walks to synagogue, sits by Adam in the sanctuary and for a little time even holds his hand. Oh—this he loves. Out of the corner of his eye seeing Lisa's hair, he also sees Shira's hair—reddish brown, wavy. When she fits her slight hand with its violin fingers into his lump of a paw, it moves him to tears. And that's not just because of Shira; it's always been like that. He loves pointing out words to her and whispering about a passage from the week's *parasha*, the section of Torah every synagogue in the world chants and studies, as part of an annual cycle. She becomes fervent. . . . This is a pleasure for him.

It's enough. His mantra, especially when he's driving in the car: *Enough, it's enough, it's* enough. . . . And he thinks, someday, maybe, when Lisa is off at college, maybe I'll meet somebody. I'll get back into something real, some work. His life, he thinks, *should* be on hold. But one morning, sitting with a cup of coffee staring into the black screen of his computer, waiting for it to magically transform into a day-trading portfolio, in the space before work begins, he feels his stomach drop, as if his desk chair were on a jet. He knows, suddenly: he's held in the hands of God.

He sucks a breath the way you do when a plane hits clear air turbulence, as if he's out in space where he doesn't have to lug himself against gravity. So he realizes how much he's been holding himself up, keeping himself from collapse, from dissolution into wisps of self. Has he always been held this way and only now he gets it? Lisa is at school. He stares at the screen as if God were going to tell him something; he breathes for the first time in three months.

And now: is it an accident his trades go so well? It's as if he's wearing the *urim* and *thummim* of the ancient priests of Israel, but he doesn't need paraphernalia of divination; he simply *knows*.

He looks at the graphs his software makes, and without consciously using any algorithms, he *knows* when the curve will break, how high the line will get. He's hardly aware what he's trading—it's not even numbers now, it's pattern, rhythm. He *knows*, the way a great outfielder knows the instant a ball is hit—knows and is already running without thought, back, back to the fence, over to the line, hardly needing to watch the arc of the ball, just knows, puts up his glove and pulls it in.

And the next day. And the next. He's riding the curve. Adam's heard about gamblers who feel sometimes they're riding a wave, dancing to rhythms that choreograph their play, black or red, odd or even, one to thirty-two. It's when the gambler tries to force the ride that he goes under. How can you tune in to the vagaries of a steel ball spinning around a wheel? But what he's done these trading sessions is more amazing. Consider the forces at play: market forces, buy-sell orders in response to institutional needs, national and international pressures. He knows so little; he presses forefinger on mouse.

He wants to tell Shira. He talks to her. Look, honey, no hands! God's hands. Look!

If he only knew more Hebrew, he wishes. . . . Because every night passages from prayers flow through his head; first, just before sleep; then, in his dreams. And maybe they're messages, maybe just the sooth-ing music of prayer. But what he knows is this: he is in the hands of God.

3

Lisa doesn't think that her father is in God's hands. As far as she's concerned, he's in *her* hands, and as a matter of incredibly dumb fact, her hands aren't nearly big enough. She's fourteen. Her whole life story now is her mother's death, but it's not the same story as her father's; it's not even the same mother, who's grown, for her father, out of a loving wife into a shining image of perfection, holy mother looking down from a heaven hardly even Jewish. Lisa knows better. She knows that if she worships that Mother, she'll lose her true mother even worse. She closes her eyes and squeezes her father's hand when he asks her to remember Mom. But she does it as an actress. It's necessary if she is to take care of him, yet hold onto the mother she remembers.

She has her own ways of keeping in touch. The pictures she paints, mostly watercolors on Bristol board, she paints for her mother. And when a painting's done, it's not just a gift, nor just a way of keeping in contact; she reads the watercolor as if it weren't hers but her mother's, a letter from her mother. When she practices violin it's to her mother. She speaks to her mother before sleep. It's not prayer; her mother isn't God or an angel. But talking keeps Mom real. It's hard to hold scraps of her real mother before they dissolve into her father's version. Which makes her mad. But she knows, more and more, it's her job to take care of him. When she hears him weeping, when she hears him talking to himself, it scares her. What might happen to him? She knows he's taking pills to feel okay. Suppose they stop working? Then what? Morning after morning she hopes he'll begin to shave again, make his beard neat again, not sloppy. But the beard fills.

There are times now when he simply blanks out and—say at the kitchen table—is hardly in the room at all, and it's her job to retrieve him. "Dad? DAD? You want to hear something absolutely great? Dad? Listen to this." Like a slow computer, his eyes come back. She invents a story about, oh, some idiot at school, until he asks, "Isn't that the girl you told me about last week?"

"Yes," she says. "We call her Fabulous, because it's her favorite word."

Stories about *Fabulous*. Lisa starts from real events but shapes them around an invented classmate so they have something to talk about. She needs to keep him in contact.

When it's time to sleep, she goes to his study. Almost every night since she was five, Adam and Lisa or Shira and Lisa have chanted "Shema Y'isra'el. . . ." Hear O Israel, the Lord our God, the Lord is One. . . . And the prayers that follow: "You shall love the Lord your God with all your heart. . . ." The music of the prayers is necessary to her, a sweetness. Now, she has to remind him. "Dad, is it time for the Bedtime Shema?"

Not that he's always spaced out. Usually, in fact, he wants to know everything about her day, about her friends, be part of everything about her life. And that's exhausting. He's more excited about her soccer games than she is. In fact, she stays on the team only because it seems to mean so much to him. She comforts him. She's his life. She knows it. She doesn't have to be smart to know; he says to her, "You, you're my life." She's supposed to nod and dip her head and look touched. But when he says this, he's *pretending* it's an exaggeration, meaning simply, *I love you*. It's not. It's exactly not. But she can't let on. Because he needs to believe that *he's* taking care of *her*.

And in a number of ways—be fair—he is. He provides their home, her clothes, drives her to Somerset School, cooks most of their meals. He's a good cook. Some nights he'll spend two hours cooking a meal, mid-week, for just the two of them. But she's the provider of life in the house. She isn't a child. The time of childhood is over; childhood has been erased. She feels older than the girls at Somerset, much older than the boys. To get along she imitates being a child. But in her class these past three months, she's quickly become the one her teachers turn to for help. And she can feel how, with her carefully chosen words, she knits her father together. She helps the way his pills help. It's her mother who's given her that strength.

It frightens her when she wakes to hear him chanting in Hebrew. "I heard you last night," she says.

"The Baal Shem Tov—" he says, "—you've heard me talk of him, the founder of Hasidism in the eighteenth century—he tells us to wake in the middle of the night and study Torah. This advice goes back to the Zohar. I'm saying I didn't make it up. Now, I don't go that far—I mean I don't wake on purpose—but when I can't sleep, I study, or I pray."

"Okay, Dad. That's great, I guess." She keeps herself from rolling her eyes; it's a habit she's trying to break.

Jerry Rosenthal calls Dad with two box seats for a Red Sox game— Talia, Mom's colleague, was given them by a patient's father. Before Mom died, he would have been ecstatic, would have changed appointments, done anything to go. She hears his end of the conversation. "No thanks, Jerry. Thanks for thinking of me, buddy. I just can't."

One evening in June he brings her to the final community sing in the school gym. She's embarrassed by his messy bush of a beard. He's beginning to look like someone from another century. Although too old to hold hands with her father, because it makes him happy she holds his hand. "Amazing Grace" has always undone him. In fact, even "Across the Wide Missouri" brings a glistening eye. But this night it's as if he's constantly crying; she can hear it in the pulse of his breath, and even "My Uncle Walter Goes Dancing with Bears" brings tears to his eyes. "Dad? Dad?"

"I'm okay. Just happy," he said. "It's not a bad crying. I can't explain the tears, honey."

They're tears of relief, not to have to hold his bones together, not have to tug the marionette strings. He feels he's handed over the strings. *Baruch Hashem*, Blessed be the Name. On walks through Harvard quad near his house, he marvels: his legs and arms carry him without work, like walking in a dream. He talks to God. Dear God, You lead, I'll follow. Lead, I'll follow. Above old specimen trees, sky folds in on itself, clouds seem to roll and bend. Pure tiny transparent circles of light dance.

And tonight, to float on the sweet voices of the children! He can't sing, or he'll weep. He grins at Lisa, whispers, "All right, I'm just a dopey dad."

It's tonight on the drive home he lays out the plans that have . . . come to him. Not that he's heard words. He simply knows. He's been told. It's end of the school year. Wednesday, he tells Lisa, the day after school's out, they'll get in the car and . . . listen for instructions.

"*Listen?* Dad? What do you mean 'listen,' Dad?"

"Let's just say, *we'll see where we go*. Grand Canyon? New York City? Jerusalem?"

Shabbat morning, as usual, he goes to synagogue. B'nai Or, children of light, is an unaffiliated synagogue in a renovated Cambridge townhouse with bay windows above one another; actually, it's a double townhouse, the adjoining wall scooped out, leaving structural supporting columns and beams and arches. The rear of the main floor has been gutted to create a sanctuary large enough to hold a hundred if no one chews garlic; below, morning services are held twice a week in a paneled, book-lined room at ground level. Rabbi Klein is leading this morning; the *chazzan* is a young woman with a beautiful, trained voice. He knows what his sister-in-law Ruthie would say: that she sounds more as if she belongs in a church than a synagogue. And in fact she is a convert and used to sing in a church choir. But Adam has gotten to love her *leining*, reading a passage from a Torah scroll.

Ma tovu ohalecha Ya'akov . . . "How good are your tents, O Jacob, your dwelling places, O Israel. . . . I love the house where You dwell and the place where Your glory resides."

They'd better love it; like a beautiful, old, wooden boat it's full of leaks and cries out for repair, and while one of the congregants is a professor of electrical engineering, they have to hire electricians; while two are physicists, they have to hire plumbers. The congregation, now almost a hundred families, began by borrowing a church on Friday nights and Saturday mornings. Then a congregant willed them a small clapboard house; they bought the house next door. It had seemed a steal ten years ago, but the mortgage and upkeep are a constant drain on the members.

Rabbi Klein, whom they can only afford to hire part-time, is a gentle, tender young man. He's deepened their liturgical life—not just in services but in making more present the turnings of the Jewish year.

This morning the *parasha* is *B'ha-a lot'kha*, verses from Numbers—8:1 to 12:12. Adam listens as if the *parasha* were trying to communicate to him, him alone. This portion of Torah tells of the lamp stand, the menorah, that God tells Moses to have built, tells how the Israelites will move on their march through the wilderness.

Suddenly, a shiver of recognition: Oh! So *this* is what I came to shul for this morning!

"Let's not wait for Monday," he says to his daughter this afternoon. "Why wait? You're out of school."

"But where are we going?" She puts down her violin. "Dad?"

He notices a fringe of light around her head. When he tries to focus on it, it disappears. When his eyes relax, he sees it. A trick of the eyes? Or is he seeing the spirit energy of his sweet girl? "But you know," he says, on second thought, "it might take us a couple of days to get ready. Close up the house. Pack. Check out the car. Stay away till you have to go to camp. What's holding us? But *where?* You ask. Okay. Fair enough. Okay. You know what a ouija board is, Lisa?"

"No."

"It's a game board, like Monopoly, but with letters to spell words and numbers and yes and no. Two people hold a piece of wood with a glass center; it slides easily. You ask the board questions." His two hands representing the hands of two different people ran an invisible disk over an invisible board and in solemn voice he asks, "Where are Lisa and I going to go on Monday?" And the invisible disk moves back and forth, back and forth. "And see, the first letter might turn out to be 'L.' And it tells you, letter by letter. See what I mean?"

"You mean the two hands figure where they're going?"

"No. That's the point—nobody figures, that's it. Nobody knows where the pointer ends up."

"They don't decide?"

"*Something* decides."

"So we're going to get a board like that?"

"No! Listen. Forget ouija boards. This morning in shul, we read how the Israelites broke camp and camped again. They followed a cloud that hovered above the *mishkan*—the tabernacle. And then comes a passage that made me shiver. The people followed God's Presence. When the cloud moved, the people moved; when it settled, the people made camp; they broke camp when the cloud moved again, camped when it settled. *Al pi Adonoy.* At a word, at a sign, at a command—literally 'by the mouth of the Lord'—the Israelites traveled. But we have no cloud like that. So we'll get in the Camry and just . . . listen. We try to put ourselves in God's hands. The car . . . is like the cloud. We let the Toyota decide. But it's not really the *car*, you understand?"

At this, Lisa just nods with great religious seriousness but she's thinking fast, frenetically, Omigod, who can I call? Family friends? Alan and Jo? The Rosenthals? What can friends do? She has her aunt and uncle, but suppose they have her father locked up and it's her fault, and she gets stuck in a Hebrew day school where everybody knows more Hebrew than she does, and she has to live with Aunt Ruthie, who's crazier than anybody, and leave her friends in Cambridge. And Dad is *Dad*—he's not really *crazy*. Or if he is crazy, even if he is, she'd rather take care of him than have him go to a smelly hospital, which would be just so horrible. Or have them pump him full of drugs and make him a zombie and leave her without a father. The process of deciding doesn't take the time it takes to read this paragraph.

"Okay, Dad. Okay. We can leave whenever you want. It'll be a fabuloso summer."

"It will."

"But what about my music lessons? And Dad, my Bat Mitzvah lessons?"

"You're signed up for chamber music camp."

"But that's a month from now. Right? Dad? Right?"

"Play now. Play the Beethoven for me. Please? I want to hear you." He sits back in the ratty leather club chair by the piano. She lifts the violin to her chin and plays for him—and secretly for her mother. She longs to play her mother's violin, but that they've taken to a violin maker who's promised to make it perfect. So she plays her own violin.

On Monday morning he hauls down suitcases, sleeping bags, a small tent; he changes the message on the answering machine, puts an automatic reply on his email. It's when he asks her help in covering the furniture with sheets that she gets scared. The house looks stranger and stranger. He draws the curtains; it grows dark. Now they pack and lug suitcases to the car, including an empty suitcase for new summer clothes. All he puts in that bag is one of Shira's pretty silk dresses, much too big for Lisa. Closing the door he takes her hand; they turn, look up at the house.

He's got the car amazingly clean, inside and out, but he's beaded with sweat. A hazy sun thickens the air. Pulling a tissue from the pack on the visor, she wipes his face. He's trimmed his beard this morning because she can't stand it when he looks grubby. He still looks grubby. But if he's kind enough to try to make himself neat just for her, how crazy can he be? At a gas station he fills up, she goes in for a slushie. He replaces the nozzle on its bracket. And sits. He just sits. "Dad?" The engine purrs.

"Daddy?"

"Shh."

"Shh? Huh?"

His ear is tilted to the heavens, like the RCA Victor dog listening for his master's voice. "I'm catching the drift."

"You're listening? You're listening? Omigod. This is too weird."

"I've listened," he says, and he smiles and leans over to kiss her forehead, behind which, he always says to her like it's this big secret, those brains of hers are doing their amazing job. He kisses her and gentles the white Camry into traffic. Up Beacon Street to Washington to 128. As he loops the turn south, she says, "I thought we were heading north. Up to Maine?" she says, her stomach beginning to churn. "You know. Like where we went last year? To Camden?"

Driving with his knees, which she absolutely hates, he shrugs and opens his palms—*I can't help it,* you *see what the Camry decided.* "Want some music?" He reaches for a CD, the first that comes to his fingers. "I know it's not *really* the car," he says, like telling a secret, to comfort her.

She picks up her giant Harry Potter book and defends herself from her dad, as if he were a sorcerer. It seems he practically is. Well, if he's a sorcerer, a wizard, he's a benign one. But suppose, suppose he's listening to the wrong voices, and they're fooling him.

No way. As Daddy always says, Itzhak Perlman and a whole orchestra have snuck into the car, and from four directions they're playing Mozart's third violin concerto. Mozart has been conjured up! Now isn't that good magic?

And last night when he put her to bed, after chanting the Shema, he stopped. "You *see?*" he said. "'Hear, O Israel. . . . Listen up, people. The Lord our God—*Adonoy elohenu*—the Lord is One, not just the One and only, but the whole ball of wax, the hum of the universe. And it's God's voice alone we're meant to hear. So honey, I'm just following instructions. I'm listening. Is that so crazy? That's not crazy. Is it crazy when we say it in synagogue?"

"That's *synagogue,*" she said. He grinned and kissed her good night.

Today they drive down Route 3 and across the bridge to the Cape. Which, she thinks, kind of makes sense. It's where they used to go with Mom a couple of weeks each summer. So it's sad but okay, remembering. Now, other side of the bridge, he opens the windows to let Cape air in, though the air's no different. They pass the giant American flag above a McDonald's, flag big as a house. The road narrows, stops at a rotary, goes on; now it really looks like the Cape to her, with boats and bay, restaurants and tourist shops. At Truro they turn down a side road towards the ocean, and she's sure she knows where they're going. They were here last summer.

"Dad? Oh! So it's Talia and Jerry! We're visiting the Rosenthals?"

"Kind of. So it seems. You know. . . . They may not be there or something."

"You mean they don't *know*? They don't *know*, Dad?"

He doesn't reply, and now she doesn't want to talk. You don't, she knows, just go barging in on people. The Camry rocks on the cracked side road, bumps down a rutted dirt road; up the long sand driveway they bounce pothole to pothole. The house is pretty in pale afternoon sun. Old. A nice little cape with gray clapboards. Jerry Rosenthal's an art historian at Harvard; Mom worked in the same practice with Talia. Two kids, boys, one older, one younger, than Lisa. It would be real nice to see them. It would be great. "Dad, they're not here. Look at the grass."

The grass is cut, but no one's watered. It's brown, weedy, sad. Storm windows are still up, no lawn furniture out. "We'll have to find a motel," she says. She says it again. Because now she's beginning to panic. "It's just June. It's chilly. There'll be lots and lots of motels."

"This is where the car stopped," he says. Those open palms of helplessness again.

"So we could camp out. The car doesn't say anything about breaking in, does it?"

"I don't get messages from the car, if that's what you think. . . . Not exactly."

"I know."

"And I'm not 'breaking in'—breaking in means like into some strange house. Our friends won't mind one bit. Lisa, you really think Talia and Jerry would mind?"

"No. Absolutely. It'll be fine. So let's call. Okay?"

He shrugs, opens his cell to call Jerry Rosenthal. But there's no cell service out here.

"We can go into town."

"I can call from inside the house. Come on."

He walks ahead of her. Now she's sorry she didn't call her aunt and uncle in Minneapolis. The door is locked, of course. But there's a storm window that he can detach easily, and the inside window, unlocked, lifts. "Go ahead," he says. "Just crawl through and open the front door for me."

"No."

"No? No?"

"No. Absolutely no. No, Dad. No."

He sighs a huge sigh and squeezes through the window himself and flops onto the couch. "Just like James Bond," he calls. She hears a loud, high-pitched whistling sound. "Dad, Dad, Dad!" she yells through the window, "that's the alarm." Now the sound breaks into beeeep, beeeep, beeeep, and now, oh!—into the most horrible, shrieking, screaming noise she's ever heard in her whole life. It makes a car alarm sound pleasant. She says, "Dad, let's just go!" And the telephone rings. She watches him hunt for it. Over the screaming he yells hello. "We're friends. We forgot the code. Of course we'll stay right here," he yells. "Tell them it's Adam Friedman and Lisa."

"Please let's go, Dad."

"Why?"

She sits on the brick steps out front, elbows on knees, head in hands. Her father comes and sits down beside her, same posture. Is he parodying her? She gives him a look. He straightens up and shakes his head to reassure her. Hand on the shoulder of his work shirt, she says, "Dad, please. Don't tell the police about God. Just say it was a big mistake. Promise?"

The alarm stops. The telephone rings. "I'll get it, okay?" Lisa says, already on her way. It's Talia Rosenthal. "Hi, Talia. Oh it's weird. I know. . . . I know. . . . Dad thought for sure you guys said you were all gonna be out here. We thought we'd surprise you. . . . Yes, I guess you were. . . . You sure? Sure you don't mind? We'll keep everything spectacularly neat. Do you want us to water anything? Sure, we'll call when we leave. How do we close up?"

|4|

Walking to the beach, just a quarter mile down the twisting sand road, he finds tears in his eyes, not entirely due to wind off the ocean. He's so proud of her, this Lisa so grown up already. "Honey, well, you did just a fantastic job."

"Well, thanks, Dad," she says, "and . . . you were great with the police. Thank you."

This *Thank you* worries him; it shows how uneasy she is. Who's the parent here? "There was a minute back there," he says, "I got to admit, I figured it was the end of our travels." He squeezes her hand, then drops it as if he needs his hand to zip up his windbreaker, but actually because he realizes he's not holding it as a father holds a child's hand but swinging it, as if he were himself a pretend child; as if they were two children, brother and sister, together.

The ocean grows louder. It's a gray morning. They climb a cleft between dunes, sea grass on both sides. Preparing for their visit, the grasses have spun elegant circles around themselves. At the top of the passage, they stop to watch the ocean, near high tide, churned up from last night's storm.

They pass the charred remains of a beach fire, step around jetsam of winter storms—Styrofoam fishing floats, sprawls of netting and splintered driftwood. "The detritus of God," he says, opening his hands to display God's bounty.

"What's that mean? *Detritus*?"

"Broken leavings," he said. "Debris. God's leavings."

"Da-ad?" She sings it in two syllables, high and low, as she always does when he's said something to irritate her.

"Uh-huh?"

She needs a few seconds, furrowing her brow, sucking on her lip, and curling her fingers as if they were wrapped around the neck of a mental violin, to get it out. "Dad? So just tell me this. Really. What's the difference if you say 'debris' or you say 'God's debris'?"

"There *is* a difference."

"So? Tell me. What?"

"Thank you for asking. Really. It's so wonderful you've grown up enough to challenge me and not let it go with a wry look, like 'How uncool.'"

"It's not uncool. It's weird. I *mean*. And frankly? So fakey. Dad? Why God's debris or whatever the word was?"

"Okay. Plain old debris is random, is ugly, is accidental; it's something to cover up. Right? It's chance, it's chaos, and worse than chance—uch—it shouldn't be there. It's garbage. *God's debris*—in my highfalutin' way I said 'detritus'—implies there's a secret plan going on, it's like God's work of art. Okay?"

"Wow. Well, so do you really think it is—is God's work of art?"

"It's hard to explain this, but the thing is, listen, it's not necessary to think of it as true or false—it's a *heuristic*—a useful way of seeing data. A *better* way. At least I prefer it—don't you? It's so much more beautiful and *just as true*. Look how simple and clear everything is. How pure. Why see it as garbage? Nobody's forcing you."

As she shrugs, a shrug muscle-by-muscle inherited from her mother, suddenly it's as if he's talking to Shira. Shira used to pin him down the same way. Years ago, he'd pick her up after her stint as an intern at Mass General, and they'd walk along the Charles. He remembers it as summer, a hazy sun going down over the Cambridge side (though often she pulled all-night shifts and came back to their place on Dartmouth Street too exhausted to speak). But the time he remembers, she walked along the river and, counting her points on her fingers, pulled apart his ideas—taking out her aggression on him but oh, in a comic way—after a day of frustration and overwork. Much smarter than he was, she loved unpacking his nonsense and demolishing it. Is it nonsense? Is it pure nonsense?

"Lisa," he says, "let me give you an analogy." He sits down on a drift-wood log and takes off his sneakers while he thinks. Lisa has already laid her sandals on the end of the same log. Out to sea just a little ways, maybe thirty yards, a big, shiny black seal breaks the surface, noses around, slides out of sight again. *Is this a holy signal?*—he wonders but returns to his analogy. "You know those cornfields where they plant a maze in the image of the Mona Lisa or Einstein?"

"No. What? You mean they plant the corn so it makes the pattern of a face?"

"Right. And if you're up on a tower or a nearby hill, you can make out the pattern of the face. I've done that. You can see people lost in the maze. But when you're walking through—that, I've never done, I'm just imagining—you can't see any pattern. It's just corn. You see rows, I guess you get lost in the maze, the maize maze, and when you get to the center, you can't see Albert Einstein. Just corn. But the pattern's really there."

"Really? Can we go to one?"

"Sure. If we're nearby. Sure. Great. But you get the point?"

Lisa just lifts her eyes to the heavens in comic disgust that he might question her understanding. She brushes sand off the hem of her jeans legs, rolls the jeans up her skinny legs, and wades the slope at the edge of the surf. "It's so cold. My ankles kill."

"I know. Walk in the sand with me."

They walk, they sit at the foot of a high dune and look out to sea. The dune, eighty feet high, flecked with grasses, gives him comfort, support. Before them, a huge swell breaks right at the shore, gets sucked back by the slope, hisses over small stones. Another, still more powerful. A steady wind off the water whips sand against them.

Clarity, he thinks. Simplicity, clarity, purity. Small stones, smoothed

"Really good, Lisa. You're right. But it's because that's what I hear when I'm listening."

She starts getting anxious again—butterflies in the stomach, Mom used to say.

They hit the Triborough Bridge just after midday, and it takes more than half an hour to get onto FDR Drive along the river. She's sure they're going to get smashed by a taxi or a truck. So little room! At 96th, he exits, heads toward Central Park; he stops at Madison Avenue, pulls over into an illegal parking spot and, leaving the engine running, closes his eyes. There are fifty people—no, more, many more—in range of, say, a Frisbee if she got out of the car and just threw. People in a clutter, each alone, crossing east and west, guys on bikes slipping between cars, people heading to this restaurant, that flower shop. The engines of how-do-they-ever-get-around-a-corner trailer trucks, trucks looking ridiculous in city streets, so loud. Noise! The word is *cacophony*, one of her vocab words from last spring. Small cars honking, sounding angry, the grinding winch of a telephone repair truck, clunking from delivery vans, the beat of rap from a car; fragments of Spanish and some language she doesn't know the sound of. All that, much more—and her father's trying to hear the voice of God?

"You want an ice cream?" he asks.

"Dad?"

"We're just a few blocks from your Great-Uncle Cal."

"You mean you want to visit this uncle?"

"Maybe. He'd be plenty surprised!" Adam giggles. "Sometime," he says, "I'll tell you stories about that son-of-a-B."

"Dad?"

"Shh." Eyes closed, he breathes; it looks as if that were his job: breathe in, breathe out. He seems to have forgotten the ice cream. He's up in his own head somewhere. Opening his eyes, he says, "Our father Abraham, you know what? He *listened*, Lisa. *Lech Lecha.* 'Go, get yourself going,' God says. Where? Does Abraham ask where? He goes. *We're going.*"

"So God hasn't told you where to go?" And when he doesn't answer, when he shuts his eyes again—because she's scared, because she's mad, she holds onto his right arm with one hand and punches away at it with the other. She grins to pretend it's a joke. And when he still doesn't seem to hear her, she says, "What about your friends? Don't you have friends here? You know—"

He nods, he opens his eyes. "The Lichts. Right. Ben and . . . Margaret. You remember, I saw Ben the night Mom died. Maybe that's why we're here. Let me think a minute." She watches him think a minute, watches him think five minutes, while she goes for her pad and pencils and sketches him thinking. It's so mixed up inside—the way she loves his face when he thinks like this, so the drawing is made with love—but made with fear, too. Oh, she's scared. What's going to happen? My God, what's going *to become of us*? It's a phrase in one of the young adult novels she used to read. What's going to become of us? He's my father? I'm his mother. I can't let on.

Tiny strokes for his eyebrows. A taxi goes crazy honking. What are we doing here? She smells pizza. Looking up, she finds the source, a small store, and inside, three people lined up to order slices. His hair, black, not like hers or her mom's. Turning her wrist she captures the curling of his beard.

She imagines she's drawing for her mother, so her mother can see what's happened to him. She's never told her dad; most of the time she pooh-poohs it herself. But she thinks of her drawing, her painting, as a kind of letter—from her mother, to her mother. For it's her mother she still looks to for protection. Doesn't her dad talk about the Shekhina? For Lisa her mother *is* the Shekhina. Why is there a difference? Drawing in the final frown line, she pauses.

She sees him open his eyes, reach for his cell, and take his address book out of his bag.

Of course. Ben Licht: I'm supposed to go back, he thinks, to that reunion night at Chase. At once remembering makes him ashamed. His victory: as if his own pride brought that stolen car weaving around the corner, pinning Shira to the door of her car, brought it just then; two seconds later, she'd have been inside; their car would have just scraped hers. Does he believe God works that way, using a car full of drunken teenagers to pay off a husband's pride? No, no! But there's guilt in his bones.

He dials Ben's number at work. The voice on voice mail's soft. It makes him feel he's right to call. "Ben'll call back." He breathes a great breath. "God enters," he says, inflating his chest and tapping it with his fingers.

"Or stinky air."

"No! Somehow in the middle of the gas fumes, honey, there's the breath of life. Yes! We can imagine breathing God in, and out again into the cosmos. *Ruach, nefesh, neshama.* You remember, those words for soul in Hebrew, they're also words for breath and for wind. So God is a part of me, in my lungs and my blood and my cells. See what I mean?"

"Oh, Dad."

"So let me ask you something. If soul, breath, enters me and fills my blood and goes to my cells and becomes me, what about the breath that comes out of me? Is that still me? Where do I end? At the cell walls? Isn't the air around me, the air in you, isn't that me, too? God surrounds all things and fills all things."

"Dad, please?"

"And water." He reaches for his backpack and, taking out a water bottle, swigs deeply. He hands the bottle to Lisa. "The water is in me," he chants. "The water is outside me. Breath is in me," he chants. "Breath is outside me. Wordsworth says, 'One soul within us and abroad.'" Adam spreads his hands out to feel his connection to everything. And nods and nods to himself.

"Oh, my God," she whispers.

He hears her; he pretends not to. He flushes hot: he hears himself, his words, as she must hear them. Right away, he wants to comfort her. What can he do? And then he thinks: *I can give her paintings. She'll love that.*

"Honey, you're going to have a great time. Can you extract your art materials from that mess in the back?"

"The museum?" she guesses.

"When's the last time you were there?"

She shrugs. "With Mom, I think, I don't know, a year ago? I'd love that."

The streets are glutted with traffic. It takes them ten minutes to move the few blocks to the underground garage at the Metropolitan Museum of Art—so close, he thinks, to his uncle's apartment. Is there a message in that? She takes her folding easel and folding stool, her watercolors and pad of Bristol board. They climb the grand marble staircase to the second floor, find the American wing and wander, stopping by paintings. It's wonderful to go with Lisa to a museum, because she *gets* it so strongly. "Look, look!" she'll say. "Unbelievable. How can anyone do that? Look at the light, omigod."

Now she starts hunting. She finds a Hudson River School landscape. "Perfect," she says.

He plants her there. He won't bother her. He goes back to the large Breugel he used to visit almost every time he came here afternoons, the painting of *The Harvesters*, peasants bringing in the grain, just finishing the morning work or eating lunch or sleeping in the sun. He enjoys the strange sadness coming over him, something stirred up from childhood. Both his parents gone. The city resonates with their life. He remembers afternoons, his mother—exhausted, hair uncombed, housedress stained—greeting him at the door when he returned from school, slurring, "I've got to get some sleep—can you manage by yourself?" Unable to sleep at night, cigarette in hand, she wandered, mumbling to herself, nodding in agreement with the bitterness with which she fed herself. Putting down his books, he told her, "I'm going to play ball in the park with—" and gave her a name, someone in his class, but went alone across Central Park to the Met. Later, when he knew Ben, they'd go together. This was his synagogue when he was in high school, his sanctuary.

His cell rings. A guard and an old lady both give him dirty looks. The guard comes up to him shaking his finger. Adam smiles and tiptoeing, puts forefinger to lips, takes the call, says, "Be with you in a minute," and strolls outside onto the great stone Fifth Avenue steps. "We happen to be in town," he says, "Lisa and I. You and Margaret have time to see us if we drop in?"

Now, giving Lisa time, he walks down the granite steps of the museum through clumps of tourists, alone up Fifth Avenue just a few blocks to the apartment building where his uncle lives. Cal has lived here as long as Adam remembers, bought his apartment as soon as the building went co-op. He remembers the awe he felt as a child—as if he were entering a great palace—to walk through this marble and glass, brass and steel lobby, to ride up in the elevator—in those days run by a man in uniform. His father would squeeze Adam's shoulder, rhythmically pat his back, a way of comforting himself on the ride up to see the Big Man. Poor Dad. My poor dad.

To the doorman in braided uniform he says, "I'd like to speak to Mr. Friedman, Cal Friedman. Is he in?"

"I'll see, sir."

"I don't want to bother him—just let me talk. He's my uncle."

"One moment, sir." He goes to the house phone.

The doorman seems damn apprehensive. *Do I look like a bum off the street?* He can't hear what the guy is saying on the phone. The doorman turns: "I'm sorry, sir. Mr. Friedman says he's too tied up to talk. He says he'll get back to you soon."

"Great," Adam says. "I'm sure he will. Thanks a lot."

The bastard. Same as always. To hell with Mr. Big-shot.

Adam walks back to the Met, goes up on the roof to be soothed by the green carpet: the treetops of the park. After a while, he goes to find Lisa. She's still at the easel; she seems to have completed something, an abstraction in watercolor. All she took from the Bierstadt landscape was his organization of volumes and spaces—his basic design. She's always drawn well, and even in watercolor paints a recognizable landscape or cityscape or still life. But this is an abstract painting in mauves and blues, and when he walks into the gallery she's staring into it.

They look at it together. His eyebrows lift and his head tilts, his way of saying, What are you doing?

As if answering in a dance of heads, her lips puff out, her shoulders lift and her head tilts the opposite way: Oh, nothing. Nothing. He knows better, doesn't he?

5

At the Apthorp, the great apartment building between 78th and 79th, they get announced by the doorman and cross the court to one of the lobbies with its twin elevators. Upstairs, Ben Licht is alone. They sit in the ponderous, high-ceilinged living room and Ben fixes ginger ale for daughter—and for father, too, because, with the antidepressant he's taking, Adam shouldn't drink alcohol. In his pudgy body, Ben looks to Adam like Elmer Fudd—but Fudd in a fine, dove-gray cashmere sweater and corduroy slacks; he's wearing the fine pale blue cotton shirt he must have worked in today, but his tie is gone. Rimless glasses sit at the end of his nose; from time to time he pushes them up into place.

Ben's not a small man; he's shorter than Adam, but only because of Adam's long legs; sitting down together in the living room, they're almost the same height. Ben's face is round and so pleasant that Adam at once feels sweet tenderness for the guy, and a kind of sadness, as if Ben is somehow to be pitied, though right away it's Ben who tells Adam again how sorry he is about Shira—sorry about your Mom, he says to Lisa, who's sitting beside her father. "I wish I'd known her." Adam can see him looking at the beard, but Ben doesn't mention it. He has this comforting voice, voice like an old tweed jacket. After a minute, Ben's face transmutes into the face of the child he was. Oh, more lines, more character, but the same face. Only the voice has changed. "I'm sad," Ben says, "we didn't see each other until that terrible night."

Adam says, "God is leading us through this. I know it."

"That's good," Ben says out of politeness. "Good. We can use the help." He sighs. In sympathy? The sigh sounds real. Before Adam can ask what help Ben needs, a key turns in a lock. "Wonderful," Ben says. "Jennifer is home. I want you to meet Jennifer," he says to Lisa.

Jennifer is sixteen. If Lisa's blossoming, Jennifer has bloomed: a beautiful girl with a thick, long tumble of black hair over her blouse. She puts her tennis racket and sports bag in a corner and comes in to say hello. "Jennifer," says her dad, standing, putting a hand on Adam's collar, patting his shoulder rhythmically, "this is my old friend, my dear friend, Adam. You know about him, about his wife and the terrible accident. And this is Lisa."

Jennifer crinkles up her face as if Adam were some alien creature to examine; then, having examined, she grins at him, shakes hands, says, "Oh. Sure. Hi," and nods to Lisa. "Sorry about your mom."

She's on stage, Adam sees. And she doesn't know what to do with herself. But he's sure she's sure of her beauty, sure that if she just smiles, she'll be all right. She's a child, but it's hard for him not to look at the sweet space between the bottom of her tee shirt and the silver belt of her jeans. Jennifer becomes vivid for him—her long hair, her intense physical presence, as if capital "L"-Life, pulsing like the Northern Lights and not knowing what to do with itself, not knowing how to handle the energy, were standing in an elegant living room.

Leaning down, Jennifer kisses her father on the forehead, messes his neatly combed hair, waves again and, wiggling her fingers in the air as she goes, retreats to her room.

Ben waits till she's out of earshot. "Since that night at Chase, things have changed a lot for me, too. Nothing so bad as for you. My wife is leaving me. Margaret, she's leaving me."

"Oh, Ben. Oh, I'm sorry. What happened? You don't have to say if you don't want."

"It's complicated." Ben glances at Lisa. "I shouldn't be saying this in front of you, but I need to. But please—it's better not to speak about this,

Lisa. I mean to Jennifer. I'm sure Jennifer has some vague idea, but probably unformulated. Unformulated for us, too. Margaret has decided to leave me. It won't affect the kids the way it would have a couple of years ago. Jen's away at school most of the time, Alan's at Dartmouth. Margaret will stay—this was her parents' apartment. She has her studio here. Margaret's an architectural designer. She'll stay, I'll leave."

"You poor guy," Adam says. And suddenly grins. He grins, delighted. He laughs, says to Lisa, "Honey, you see? You see? *That's* why we're here. I get it. Why God brought us here." He's giggling. He raps the coffee table with his knuckles. As if God has been playing games with him and now he's in on the joke. "How amazing! You see?"

"My dad," Lisa says, as if he weren't in the room, "thinks God is telling him where to go."

"You see this 'M' on my sweater? I mean this visitor's button from the Met? You know what it really stands for, this 'M'? MITZVAH MAN. Why not? All right! If this is what I'm supposed to do, I'll do it. Let's not forget what happened to Jonah!"

"Mitzvah. Like a good deed?"

"Kind of. As in '*bat mitzvah*'—which, please God, Lisa will become belatedly right after the High Holidays. *Bat*—'daughter' of the *mitzvot*—'the commandments.' A *mitzvah* isn't just a good deed—it's directions given us by God to bring us closer to God. That's basically it."

Ben looks at Lisa over his glasses. She nods. "Dad's been like this," she says.

Adam groans in mock Yiddish, "My own daughter and look how she laughs at her papa." Now Adam, looking at Ben, notices around his head, a pale, hovering, translucent fringe of energy, pale but clear against the taupe wall. He's struck silent. A sign?

"Mine laughs too," Ben says. "Lisa, honey, your dad's just got a good heart," Ben says. "It's true!—and you always have had," he tells Adam. "In the midst of those morons at Chase."

Adam remembers the morons, remembers Ben as this one spark of wit and kindness and gentleness, the only boy with whom he didn't have to be on guard. He could take long walks with Ben and think things with him. He promises himself not to let time go by again. We can be friends. But that's another story. For now he knows why he's here. He knows. "Ben, I tell you, this is why I came to New York. For you. Maybe I can help. I think I can help. Amazing!"

Ben opens his kind face to Adam. "That's good. Who knows? I can use whatever help."

Lisa really likes this Ben—right away she trusts him. She thinks if there's a capital "M" Message here, it's God bringing them to a friend who can comfort her dad. And if part of that comfort is for Dad to think he's doing the helping, that's just great.

She wants to talk to Ben. In fact, she's desperate to talk to him. *Help! Help him! Help us!* But not now. She'll get him on the phone when she can. "Is it okay," she asks, "if I wander around?" She knows it is—they need to talk without her. So she rambles through the apartment, loving its filigreed high ceilings and rosy, tapestried drapes and old-fashioned furniture. This place makes her feel safe. How Mom would love it! Lisa thinks right away of sketching it, and looks for Jennifer's room, wants to borrow pencil and paper. But of course it's not really that—she wants to see Jennifer again. Is she really that tall and that beautiful?

She finds Jennifer's room, door open, Jennifer at her computer. And oh, she is. That tall, that beautiful. Like the painting of a gypsy, with thick black hair, curling and twisting down her back. Right away Lisa determines to let her hair grow and grow forever. "Hi. Can I come in?"

Jennifer puts a finger to her lips. "Shh, close the door. Okay, Lisa, look what we can do." She hands Lisa headphones, holds a set herself. Puzzled, Lisa screws up her eyes, and that, it seems, is what Jen's been waiting for. "I've hidden a wireless mike behind the books in the living room. A *leeetle surveillance.*" She hisses the words as if this were an old spy movie.

Lisa doesn't get it. They each put on headphones, little buds that fit in the ear.

. . . So I met a woman at a conference.

Ahh, an old story, huh, Ben?

Her father and Ben! Lisa pulls the ear buds out, mugs shock with mouth and eyes, looks uncertainly at Jennifer as if for permission, puts them in again. Jennifer is grinning at her.

I know. And in point of fact, it's nothing serious. But I'm not like that. I don't do those things. Not ever. Well. Maybe it was serious that weekend. But like a magic castle, it dissolved. Then—you know—Margaret asked— I presume I was acting strange—and I'm not good at lying.

A lawyer and you can't lie?

And I know there must be other things. One weekend's stupidity can't explain it.

But she says she's leaving?

Actually, she says I'm leaving. She wants me out. I'm the one leaving. It's only fair. I told you—it's her parents' old apartment.

You see? This is exactly why I'm here. You see?

You're making a joke, right? Adam? What is it, a joke, this listening to God?

Not a joke.

Not a joke?

The girls take off the headphones. "Is that cool? My parents' friends used one of these to check on their babysitter. Not even expensive, Lisa. So now, see, I know all about their plans," Jennifer says. She stretches and struts. There's a trapeze, rolled up, hanging from her bedroom ceiling. She releases it, hangs from the bar and hooking her legs over the bar, hangs down, and keeps talking as if she were sitting in a chair. Her hair spills down to the floor. "I've had the mike there since the night I came home in June from school. I put one in their bedroom, too."

Lisa puts her hands over her eyes.

"Well, don't get all freaky about it. I've got to know, right?" She lifts her long body and sits on the trapeze. Lisa can't speak. Can't breathe normally. "It *concerns* me, doesn't it?" Jen says. "And they are so fucking polite you'd never know what's going on. It's like the way people used to be in nineteenth-century novels. Everything is cool, nothing is wrong—it is a royal pain in the ass."

Lisa soothes, "It's just that I couldn't. Like be a spy, I mean."

"Well, I can. They told me they were 'having problems.' That's all. But it's *so* boring. The problems, I mean. Like, unusual? No. Dad went to some international law conference, about estates in more than one country. And there was a woman he'd met before, they had drinks together, etcetera, etcetera. Boring, right? It really makes me mad. I mean, my own father—what a class-A idiot. But what's Mom getting so freaked about? I'm not shaking up your head too much, am I?"

Lisa shrugs, no, no, and tells her *that's* not what's upsetting her. "My mom—you know."

"Right. Your mom. She died."

"She was just coming home from a rehearsal—she plays violin, *played* violin in a trio—and some stupid drunk teenagers—the police never found them but I don't care about that—smashed into her in a stolen car, and I woke up in the morning and my Mom was dead. And now Dad—well, my dad is having a mental breakdown. I guess."

"I'm so sorry, how horrible."

"So . . . your mom is a designer? Where does she work?"

"Here at home. She works all the time. She designs spaces. Offices, apartments. . . . What's he mean, your father, about God? Is he kidding?"

Sound of the front door opening, closing. "That's my mother," Jennifer says. "Come on." Lisa follows, sniffing some interesting, tangy scent Jennifer's wearing.

Jennifer looks like her mother. Well, she had to—God knows she doesn't look like her pudgy father. Margaret's a tall woman with maybe ten pounds she's probably always fighting to lose, a soft smile, warm eyes. None of this seems to go with her clothes—she's wearing a white blouse, a honey-beige spring suit—and soon Lisa sees she's right: Margaret takes off the jacket, folds it over the back of a chair, and breathes. So she's not all that formal. But she looks so . . . clean and neat—Mom would have said *polished*—that it makes Dad look like more of a bum in his wrinkled khaki pants and stained open shirt. Lisa notices the way Margaret reads him, and she feels defensive, wanting this Margaret to see Dad the way she, Lisa, sees him. If she'd have seen him six months ago . . .

Jennifer takes packages to kitchen and bedroom while Margaret says hello. They talk about Lisa's mom, and Lisa can see her dad almost in tears, which is so strange, because he never softens that way in front of friends. Only in front of her. Usually he shrugs and changes the subject, and it drives her crazy when he does that, but now he's crumpled into the sofa, eyes full of tears, and Margaret Licht sits next to him and soothes, and all of a sudden Lisa *gets* it. What he's doing. Oh!

"We've got to go," he says. "Thanks for listening, both of you. We've got a long drive ahead of us." Now he's full-blast crying. Lisa goes over to the piano so her face won't betray her. *My God! I can't believe he's doing this! What a faker!*

"Why go? Do you have to go?" Margaret says. "Ben's spoken of you so often since the night you got together, since that terrible night."

"Oh, it's a long drive," he says, "below Philadelphia, old friend of ours—I told him we'd probably get there tonight."

"So you have no place in New York?" Ben asks. "Stay with us. We have room."

And Margaret: "Please. Think about your daughter. You've been driving all the way from the Cape. Lisa must be exhausted. She can sleep in Jennifer's room."

And Lisa, now laughing in her heart, sitting on the piano bench: "That would be so great."

And Adam says, "Then let me take you guys out to dinner."

"Don't be silly. There's plenty. Really."

And that's how he fixed it up for them to stay the night. Ben calls his garage, and Dad goes off to park. Lisa can't wait till she's alone with Jen and she can tell her, *Friend below Philadelphia*—yeah, right! What a *conniver*. That was her grandfather's word, Dad's dad. She keeps it under wraps.

After dinner, Ben moves his things back to the bedroom; Margaret fixes up Alan's room for Dad. When her father comes back, they sit around drinking tea, Dad next to Margaret on the sofa, Jen on the rug, her elbow on her father's hassock, Lisa in an upright chair in the corner, feeling like an audience. Fingering the sofa's velvet arm rest, Dad says, "We used to have lousy little fights—Shira and me. Oh—you wouldn't believe. And afterwards, we'd both of us be dying to get past it and talk to each other, and it was like both of us were in spasm—I mean like a spasm in a muscle?—and we couldn't will it to go away. And there we were, longing to touch one another, and there was this spasm. But sooner or later, we had to choose in spite of ourselves—to touch. Choose to let go. The spasm would ease up, and there'd come this unimaginable, fantastic rush of love back. Like opening a dam."

"You're talking about us," Margaret says very quietly. She exchanges a look with Ben.

"You got me. Sure, I'm talking about you, Margaret. Look, dear," he says, as if he's known her for years, his hand on hers, "we make choices, except when drunken kids take choices away from us and someone we love returns to God. So look at the beauty you can choose." Margaret's sitting beside him, and he takes her hand between his two hands. Lisa turns away: Omigod, he's so unbelievably embarrassing. "You two," he says, "you're both such beautiful souls. I'm no dummy; I feel that. And marriage, it's hard but only for the first five or six decades! I'm kidding, I'm kidding. I see by your face—you're going to say it's not my business."

"Oh, Adam," Margaret says, patting his hand, "you're very sweet, I'm sure you mean well. But you don't know, do you?—don't really know anything about us."

Margaret's voice is a little too gentle; as if, Lisa says to herself, Margaret thinks she's talking sweetly to a crazy man.

Adam says, "What seems so bad talking about it? Maybe talk can ease the spasm. Think of me as an unusual massage therapist using words. So? Would we talk better without the kids?"

Ben says, "Adam. Please. Come on, back off. Please?"

But now, maybe precisely because her husband has warned him off, Margaret says, "Of course, Adam, you're completely right about marriage."

"Margaret?" Ben pleads.

"And I love your description—the feeling of a spasm. Tension like a knot."

"Oh, Jesus, Mom," Jennifer says. *"Please!"*

"And didn't you find—you can't breathe?" she goes on, looking not at Dad but through him. "Here we are, breathing air-conditioned, purified air," Margaret says, "in an apartment most New Yorkers would give their eyeteeth to have, and we sit here barely able to breathe."

Lisa sees that Jennifer's suffering, though isn't she the one angry at their politeness, their reserve? So shouldn't she want them to open up? She wishes she could go over and put her arm around her.

Adam opens his hands: *you see?* "I guess Ben told you?—this is why we're here, Lisa and I. For *you*," he says, "we're here for *you*. I feel foolish love for you both tonight. Okay, so it's weird. So what? My girl over there must be rolling her eyes at me, but it's true. At least, I think it's true. If I'm sent to you, it must be for this; now it's your choice. How do I know if your path is together? Certainly I can't undo a heart muscle in spasm. God brought me here just to say this. You see?"

Margaret says, "Adam? Really. You don't really mean that, do you? About God?"

He raises his hand—on oath: "The God's honest truth. Margaret, Margaret, listen: you have a choice offered you. You get me? I wasn't offered a choice. Shira was taken and I had nothing to say. You see? How fortunate you are. So you need to think. Okay?"

Just suppose, Lisa thinks. She has to take a big breath, because her stomach feels as if she's on a small boat in rolling swells. Suppose it's true! Oh, she's practically sure it's just craziness. And lies. Like, wasn't it a hundred-percent total lie about Mom and Dad fighting? She would have seen it. Oh, maybe snipping about Dad wanting a certain friend over for dinner, Mom saying no. Nothing you could call a fight.

Jennifer interrupts, "Please excuse me, everybody. I'm kind of busy. Lisa? Want to hear some music?" Lisa follows her back to her bedroom. "Your dad . . . may be just a little nuts."

"And listen," Lisa says, "Jennifer, *listen*—as far as I know, we have no friend anywhere near Philadelphia. None! Still . . . isn't he amazing, trying like that?"

"Hey, babe. I'm not saying I mind he's crazy. Okay? Maybe he'll be good for them."

"See," Lisa says, "I'm glad he's here. Not for your parents. For *him*. I'm scared for him."

Jennifer says, "Maybe he'll truly be fucking good for them. So—you want to listen in?"

They put on the headphones, Jennifer at desk, Lisa cross-legged on floor. It feels like listening to a radio play. Lisa bites her cuticle, as she used to before she broke the habit. Dad says:

Ben, it's not a question of belief. Call it a heuristic, a theoretical lens to help us understand. Let's bracket off belief. We can say, let's just take as a given that God is bringing me to this place. If so—if so—what's God asking of me? What's my mission? So: A heuristic. But then I see you, Ben, Margaret, I see you and I know. It's not a heuristic—it's simply so. It all falls into place. The pattern is so perfect it stops being a what-if. I'm the messenger. And I'm willing. Actually, I'm grateful.

Voices are too quiet now for the mike to pick them up.

Lisa and Jennifer are silent.

Lisa and Jennifer remove their headphones. Jen shrugs, looks disgusted, like she's had enough.

Before going to bed, Lisa takes a shower—a fabulous luxurious shower behind a glass door, a shower that comes at you not just from above but from vertical lines of holes, so you're tickled on all sides by a pouring rain of warm water that feels so good on your skin and steams up the room. It's so great. She gets into pajamas and slips into the bed across from Jennifer's bed. This is embarrassing. Everything: coming here, her father's weirdness. She's glad Jennifer's not there—she's in the

kitchen talking on the phone—when Dad comes in to say good night.
They chant the Shema. His eyes are closed, so she's able to look and look at his face. What's going to happen to us? She closes her eyes, too, and right away sees Mom, just her eyes. When she tries to focus on her face feature by feature, it's gone. He kisses her cheek and leaves; inside her head she still hears his voice, tinny over those headphones: *Suppose God is bringing me to this place . . .*

6

Early next morning, Adam leaves a note and goes for a walk. Down Broadway he walks and across 72nd Street to the park. The sun shines. He walks through the little pocket of green with the mosaic "Imagine" for John Lennon, then up along the pond where he and Shira bumped against each other in drunken love weekends when he came to town. She was a final-year med student then. She worked like hell to carve open an occasional weekend for them. Sex, new between them, felt like discovery. *Holy* discovery, he thinks now. Mornings there'd be an awkwardness, an embarrassed innocence he didn't mind; innocence seemed a privilege they'd attained.

Holy. Oh, innocence can be denial: "We're simple, we live in our own Eden." But innocence can be a conscious stripping away of ironies, of guardedness. You look deep into her eyes, she into yours, and each of you is caught by the other and pulled under into mystery, both suffused by a holy Presence. A cheap imitation of religion? Adam doesn't think so. Simply an intimation of the holy—the best that two untrained, worldly people can do to live in God's Presence.

They'd have a cup of coffee and go back to bed; so by the time they left her apartment or, when her housemate was around, a hotel or a friend's apartment lent them for the weekend, it would be eleven in the morning, and sleepily they'd walk through the park to the little pretend castle of real rock, rocky theater behind the Shakespeare theater, climb stone steps to the terrace he's climbing now, look down at the Metropolitan and out at the massive apartment buildings along Central Park West and Fifth Avenue, one of them his uncle's, and the lawn where he played ball as a kid before the park was restored. Clean and beautiful now, it was funky, trashy, then—the fields with scattered bare patches and litter. Even so, beautiful, this castle their domain—he means his and his friends when they were children, his and Shira's later. He retraces their morning walk this morning. He won't admit it, but he's waiting for a message, maybe her voice, some indication of a direction, a secret. The castle, with its weather instruments in the tower, is a center, a receiving station.

No secrets come. But the blood is singing in his ears, his heart thumping, his whole body is humming like a great turbine. So, he thinks, he must be heading the right way. He's lightheaded but also light on his feet. He's guided by the intensity of the humming.

But suppose, he thinks, all there is, is stupid blood singing in my ears. Nothing out there. I look down from up here and maybe there is no pattern unless I create one? Just the park. Just detritus until someone makes a pattern? His heart is beating as if he only recently met Shira and she's waiting for him, an angel leading him somewhere. On the castle terrace there's only a couple of old people. But he feels he's supposed to be here. Then, all of a sudden, whoosh, he's drawn away—he has to chase the angel—and he runs two steps at a time down the stone steps, lopes through the quiet little garden, Shakespeare's Garden, south through the park. But where is he going?

Is Shira leading him somewhere? When he has to turn east or west to go around the pond, he sees a man about his own age wearing baggy trousers and a down jacket too warm for this beautiful June weather and carrying a green contractor's bag over his shoulder. The man holds out an open palm. So Adam heads his way and hands the man—or angel—a dollar. Does he want to lead him to the café on the pond? Or maybe to Alice in Wonderland and the model boats? Once they saw Woody Allen on a bench right there, near Fifth and 72nd. He keeps going as the pulse leads and the humming intensifies. He listens down under the hum of blood for her voice, which is always there, retrievable more easily than her face. In fact, he can never, behind his eyes, see her face full-on, looking at him; but if, eyes closed, he remembers her with violin lifted to the patch of silk at her neck, then he can see her. He does so now. Her eyes are half-shut; the vertical lines between her eyes could be mistaken for a scowl—but are lines of concentration. She's playing a Bach partita.

He follows the music through the park to the Plaza. So that's where he's being led! Passing the pond where he used to skate, he holds in mind's eye the gorgeous glitz of the Plaza lobby, carpeted halls with brocaded ceilings and chandeliers, elegant little shops. He can see the desk, check-outs with expensive luggage, the lobby awash in perfumes. He and Shira stayed here a couple of weekends—long after Scott and Zelda, after the hotel was refinished so that not a molecule of Scott, singer of lost love, remained. He remembers being a little nervous checking in— because he and Shira weren't married, because it was expensive and he was just beginning to make a good living.

And suppose he goes up to the desk and asks, "Did Shira Stein leave any messages for Adam Friedman?" And suppose the clerk says, "Why yes. Ms. Stein says to go right upstairs. She's in room . . ." What then? And what if he took the elevator and there she is, once again in her late twenties, knocked out from a week of study and hospital residency. And he takes her hand and looks in a full-length mirror: the two of them *both* in their late twenties, his receding hair grown back in. He'll hold her and kiss her . . . and disappear from this world. But Lisa—Lisa needs him.

Who's he kidding? He needs Lisa. To keep him in this common world.

Now, as he exits the park, just a little out of breath, he stops, stymied. Huh? It's a construction site, the Plaza. Scaffolding and signs cover the façade: the Plaza is being renovated as a mix of residences and hotel space. Residences for the super-rich. Shira's ghost evaporates.

Walking toward the architectural monstrosity at Columbus Circle put up years after he walked here with Shira, he feels adrift. Up Broadway past Lincoln Center. No angels in sight. Sometimes he feels as if

God has spread wings around him; he feels held, contained. This morning he feels like a fool having to hold his bones erect on a planet with insufficient atmosphere. At any step he could fall. He stumbles over a crack in the pavement. In his belly are pangs of fear: what do I say to Lisa? Where do we go? Back to Boston to find a job—and a different therapist? Too late to get Lisa into a good music program or sports program until camp starts.

He ought to stand at a corner and put his hand out for help.

Tables are empty at the restaurant across from Lincoln Center where, evenings, you have to battle for a table outside, a seat at the bar. That's the place where he used to eat before an opera or concert when he came to town on business. In his old life. Now, bearded and maybe grubby, he feels as if he belongs on another planet, as if, were he to see his old, suited, casually elegant self, neither would recognize the other.

Lisa, light sleeper, wakes when Ben Licht gets up at six and leaves the apartment for his morning run. She wakes again when he lets himself back in. And then she hears her father; from the way he stumbles around, she's sure it's Dad. When he tiptoes to the door and slips out, she goes over to Jennifer's bed, taps her shoulder. "Jen? Please?"

"Hmm? What?"

"Please?" Probably he's going on a walk around the neighborhood; it was once his own neighborhood. Zabar's, she knows, is right down the street. But she's worried. "If we hurry, we can catch him. My father. I just need to follow. It's my father, I'm worried. But if you don't want to, it's all right. But I thought maybe you'd come?"

For a moment, Jennifer squeezes her eyes shut and turns over, away from Lisa. But then she rouses herself, sighs, stretches; her body, in an open shirt, seems so grown up and perfect to Lisa. "I'll come. Sure. Cool." She stretches, springs to her feet. The shirt stops at the small of her back. She checks her watch. "Takes forever to get the elevator. If we run down the back stairs, we'll be close behind him. Lisa? What are you afraid about?"

"I don't know."

"Afraid he'll leave you? Or are you afraid," she asks, slipping into jeans, "he'll do something weird and get picked up and sent to Bellevue?"

Lisa shrugs. "Look. Take your cell," Lisa says, "in case we get separated. Okay?"

"Be serious. I always take my cell."

"I don't want him to know."

"Exactly," Jen says. "Stay with me. I've done this before."

Hair wild, both in jeans and tee shirts, holding the banisters and jumping four steps at a time, they run down the back stairs, swinging the landings, down the five flights to the street, out through the courtyard and archway onto Broadway, squinting in the slanting morning sun. Jen's tee shirt is loose; her midriff shows. Lisa pulls loose her tee.

Where did he go? They spot him heading south. Good spies, they stay far back. They stand in front of windows and watch his reflection walk down the street. He's wearing a gold and white yarmulke that catches the sun; it might as well be a homing beacon. He never looks back. If he stops to look through the window of a little Hungarian restaurant, they look into the window of a café. When he turns on 72nd, they cross to the opposite side of the street and stay far back. But he's so much in his own world he wouldn't see them unless they stood square in front of him.

Would he even see them then?

They pass the Dakota, cross to the park, past Strawberry Fields, follow to the castle, to the Plaza. My God, what a gigantic morning walk. As Lisa grows less anxious, this becomes a game; Lisa imagines she and Jen turning into buddies. Jennifer's older, a strong girl, but it's Lisa's dad, and that gives her authority. "He believes God tells him things. He lets the car take us places."

"The car! Meaning?"

"It took us to Cape Cod. We broke in to our friend's house and didn't tell them we were coming. He thinks the world has a secret message for us."

"How amazing!" Jen says. "You're lucky."

"Lucky?"

Staying under cover across from the Plaza, they watch him gawk at the hotel, peer in at the shut doors, walk away down Central Park South across from a line of horses and hansoms.

"My Mom and Dad—they used to stay at the Plaza. I get it. He's revisiting their past."

"Oh. Oh, the poor, poor guy. Oh, see, now that's so beautiful. Your dad . . . I mean, if someone is gonna go crazy . . . well it's such a beautiful, beautiful way. It's so wild, it's so poetic. I love it when people go out on a limb, go all the way, they don't hold back. Know what I mean?"

Easy for you to say.

It's mid morning; they're both starving. "I guess he's walking back," Jennifer says. "Home's just fifteen blocks more."

Lisa's begun to relax. She notices the way men look at Jennifer, maybe especially because Jen's so carelessly put together, no makeup, her hair a sexy jumble. Men turn and catch Lisa turning back and spotting them looking at Jen and so they grin, or they pretend to be looking, oh, anywhere else. Lisa can't imagine anyone looking back at *her* that way.

"Come on!" Jennifer darts across Broadway to the island, to the west side, and running ahead of Adam, they're already upstairs when he buzzes from downstairs, and on the intercom, Jennifer tells the doorman it's okay.

Now, from the bedroom, they hear a wave of weeping.

Silence. Jennifer switches to the mike in her parents' bedroom, but she shrugs—she can't make anything out. Now, Lisa sees, Jennifer feels self-conscious, becomes a gawky puppet. They sit on the bed and Jen can't keep her hands still. Now she jumps up, loosens the trapeze, sits on it, swinging. Then she jumps down and from a drawer takes a little package, laughs, opens it with her teeth, takes out—what—a balloon? She blows it up, ties off the end, and taps it to Lisa. They bounce it back and forth over the trapeze bar. Weird kind of balloon. And then Lisa gets it. She squeezes her eyes shut and mugs and laughs to let Jen know she knows. It's not a balloon; it's one of those rubber things men use.

A second wave of weeping—Jennifer's mom, weeping.

When they hear the elevator, Jennifer squeezes the rubber under her bed, runs to get the door. Finger to her lips, finger to her ear, she warns Adam.

There's weeping from inside, and now a man's voice—Ben's voice. And Margaret's voice. And both their voices. And silence. "Come on," Jen says. "Let's make some brunch."

"Aren't you gonna listen?" Lisa calls to Jen. But even before Jen puts a finger to her lips, Lisa realizes her mistake—the secret mike, her dad here.

Jen asks, "Adam? You hungry?"

"That's good silence," Adam says very slowly, listening. "Maybe we better keep out of their way. Want to go check out the boats down at the boat basin?"

Just then the bedroom door clicks open. Ben, dressed for business, passes by. He smiles at Adam. "Listen. Stay for dinner. Adam? You've *got* to stay. We need to talk. Please? Morning, Jen. Morning, Lisa." He's gone. Adam closes his eyes and folds his hands—in prayer? Lisa puts her hand on his shoulder. "Dad? Dad? You okay?"

Margaret comes out of the bedroom; she stands at the door to the kitchen, her skin blotched, her eyes red. She's still in a robe. Lisa stops, Jen stops, Adam looks up at her.

Margaret says, as if making him a gift but slightly begrudging it. "Well. We're talking. It's hard for us, but we're talking."

"Mom? What do you mean, *talking*?"

"I mean your father and I . . . we're talking. It's very hard."

"Omigod," Jennifer says and explodes into a laugh. She bangs her forehead. "Lisa, your dad! How amazing is this?"

"Dear, it's just a beginning, just a possibility."

Lisa stands above her father, caressing his shoulder. She doesn't say a thing. He takes her hand. Whispering to her "*Blessed be the One, blessed be His Name,*" he shakes his head and shakes and shakes his head. "You see, honey? And just when I was unsure. Just when I thought maybe I

was plain crazy. Thank God. *Thank* God. God be praised. Come on.
Shh. Come."

They pick up sandwiches at Zabar's, Adam and Lisa, stroll along the river, gawk over the railing at the boats docked at the 79th Street boathouse. He sucks in huge breaths of summer air and city dust, feels joy. You see? You see? You see?

He wraps an arm around Lisa. "When I was a kid your age, you could walk right out to the boats. Not now. You've got to be a member or friend of a member. Want to buy a boat and live here?" A warm breeze lifts river to his nose. It's a holy smell; at this moment any smell would be holy, any sound, the honking of horns from the West Side Highway like blasts of the *shofar*, holy. "See? Just when I was beginning to doubt, I mean doubt there's a plan I'm part of. I don't mean it's *my* plan."

"Dad? So whose? You mean God's? Dad? You think God is talking to you?"

"Who else?" He squeezes her shoulders, comforting, sensing what she's going through. But he can't stop talking. "You think *I* think God's a *Who*? I'm no dummy. God's not a Who. We're not talking about a big guy sitting on a throne at a cosmic computer, manipulating things. But if I'm in God's hands, and God is so beyond me I have no way of relating, I gotta personalize a little. I'll tell you how it is: I see myself as a messenger, *malach* in Hebrew. How can I speak to the One who sends me if I don't personalize? Today I'm a messenger of love. Maybe something else tomorrow. A plan—not mine. *My* plans I had to toss out three months ago."

Saying this, he finds tears welling up and oh!—they're so boring, just when he wants to come off as a normal father, that he says, "Oh, damn! I got grit in my eye." He pulls his shirt out of his pants and rubs at absolutely nothing, tucks it in again.

He's surprised when she takes his hand, holds it firmly as they walk through the park. It feels so nice, except why is it she needs to hold his hand? He knows it's not for her benefit but for his. There are old trees, and there are young trees wired to the ground; he imagines they're wired down to keep them from lifting up, floating away, tree balloons. A mother and three little kids are having a picnic on the grass. Beautiful. He'd like to sit down with them and talk, but Lisa would worry. Well, he feels a little manic. Sure. Who wouldn't? A tug races downriver. A fifty-foot yacht cruises slowly upriver. There's a haze over the tall apartment complexes in New Jersey. She says, "Dad? I *do* think you had something to do with it, with the Lichts getting back together."

"Me, too," Adam says, flushing. "But Lisa—not me. I tell you—I'm the messenger."

"You're some messenger of God."

"Why?"

"You told a kind of fib—that you and Mom, you know, had fights."

"Right. Right. We never had real fights. Not like the ones I grew up on."

"Your mother and father."

"Right."

"But Dad? I think it's absolutely very weird to talk about God this way. Very, very weird."

"Weird?" He looks at her, hair blowing in the wind, little frown lines between her eyes, her new seriousness, and he's not stupid, he knows Lisa's not upset about God—she's worried she won't have a functioning father. Well? Suppose I *am* going crazy. What would be the signs?

"Hey. I won't talk so much, honey. I promise I'll shut up."

His joy dissolves as he quiets; he remembers the signs of his mother's craziness. Not steadily crazy, often enough she fit the bill. Maybe she's given me a legacy.

In mind's eye he sees his mother in the apartment she had to put up with. All she wanted was an apartment like Ben and Margaret's, an apartment in the Apthorp or the Beresford. Instead, she lived in a run-down apartment building. They drove an old Chevy. She wanted luxury. She wanted to be defined by luxuries, as she felt defined by drab necessities. They humiliated her. He sees her standing in her stained housedress at the door to his room, rocking back and forth but saying nothing, rocking, her eyes not really seeing him. He's sitting at his desk doing homework, evading her. She rubs at her face, rubs at every part of her face. She wants to tell him about her life, but there are times she can't speak. In Yiddish she mumbles about her life, how black it is, a black life, *Schwartze leben*, and her blood, her blood is black, *You want to look at my blood?* she sings, moans in English and claws with painted nails at the skin of her arms, and blood wells up in the scratches and this she smears over her arms. She touches the tip of her finger to her blood and asks does he want to taste? *Please, Mom, please*, he says, knowing that when his father gets home, he'll bellow at her, *You crazy goddamn woman!* And then watch out! She'll come at him with her wild eyes and her nails like weapons, and he'll slap, she'll weep, and he'll carry her to bed.

She came to America from Warsaw as a little girl, soon after Hitler took power, but not because of prescience. Her father felt he could do better in America. His brother in Cleveland vouched for him. They came to New York with some English from university and with money enough to start a fabrics business. The business was never a great success, but it paid for his mother's training in fashion—Arlene, their pet, their beauty. Until she "made the mistake of her life" and married Norm, she was, according to family mythology, a "spectacular success" during the war, after the war, as a dress designer for various manufacturers.

Look at this palace, look at this ghetto. Hitler would be pleased. What? What was so terrible? An okay apartment on the upper West Side. But its walls needing paint, the building's seedy self-service elevator, obscene scratches dug into its fake wood: all evidence of her shame. "Maybe your son-of-a-bitch brother would like it if I scrubbed floors for a living. Maybe he wants us to move into a cold-water flat."

"He knows what you are," his father would say.

"Didn't you give him your money in the first place? Why don't you demand what's yours?"

Adam wondered as a child: How did they ever marry?

By the time his mother and father met, the war was over, the Depression was forgotten, everybody was buying or refurbishing houses. Starting as a carpet salesman, Cal Friedman parleyed the job into a territory, and then somebody staked him to capital for a store. He needed somebody loyal—so he called up his brother Norm in Chicago and offered him a job. Norm was loyal.

From one bare no-frills store in Queens in 1953, Cal had five by 1958, when Adam's parents married, and had ten—all over New Jersey, New York, and Connecticut by the time Adam was in high school. *CARPETS, INCORPORATED.* Customers thought that because there was no décor, none at all, just a bare linoleum floor with rolled carpets and vinyl flooring lined up on end, carpets spread open on the floor, books of carpeting hanging from bare cement columns, they were getting a good deal. Aha, but they weren't. And the money kept rolling in. The stores, with low overhead, were cash cows, each bankrolling the next.

In a sense, she told him, she fell in love with both of them, with Norm and Cal. They wooed her together, Norm the handsome, Cal, the splendid brother. Cal was married, later divorced. Cal made it a point to charm Arlene, Adam's mother—for he wanted his big brother to settle down. So they married, she and Norm. She was no "gold digger"; she was simply sure she was marrying into wealth. Dad told her he was part owner of the business. With his small savings he'd helped Cal raise the dough for the first store. But then he signed away his rights. And when she realized what she'd done, when she realized he'd signed away her rights, too, all she could do was rip at herself—or rip at Dad.

Why didn't she just keep working? Before she was married, she'd made tons of money designing dresses. But now, "To be a good Jewish wife and mother, that's my only work," she'd tell Adam. In her head, because she wasn't a well-cared-for elegant matron, she was a victim, a tragedy queen in exile. She simply couldn't stand it. Maybe it had nothing to do with the money; maybe for reasons unknown she was mad right from the start, and if Dad had been wealthy, the madness would have needed to find some other justification. Maybe she loved letting it loose, the madness.

My legacy? He walks back to the Apthorp with Lisa and lies down for a nap. He hears his father's voice. *The whole world knows what you are.* And his mother's. *The world doesn't know you exist.*

No. Like that we never fought, Shira and me.

At dinner he tries hard to sound normal. He says nothing about being a messenger, about listening to God. They're eating in the breakfast nook, everyone dressed simply, as if by design. Ben, who went out in a black pinstripe suit, is wearing a tee shirt and jeans. His belly and love handles push out a little against his shirt.

Margaret has ordered Chinese takeout; white cartons, scattered over the table, look funny against the white linen napkins and polished silverware. He's amused at Lisa: she fingered through the CDs and found Schubert sonatas for violin and piano; as if she were designing a theater piece, she put it on the stereo. Music to soothe. Then she lit candles at the table, on the counters. The Lichts don't seem to mind.

So much is not being talked about. Adam's not talking about God, Ben and Margaret are not talking about their marriage. Ben looks different tonight. There's no tension in his face. He looks more like the boy Adam knew than he did last night. At the kitchen table, Ben and Margaret share a beer. It's so sweet, the attention he pays to her. He serves her, he asks her about work with a client.

Now Ben brings up God's plan. Taking the container of rice, he asks, "Tell me, Adam. How can a smart man like you talk about a divine plan—as if you didn't know what the world is like? I know you know. What kind of God would make such a plan?"

Adam doesn't want to blab off the top of his head. He closes his eyes to listen inward. He has been thinking so much about this question since Shira got killed. What kind of Holy One would leave us in such a condition? The suffering, the suffering, such pain everywhere you turn! For a while newspapers make you groan about one suffering, then they tell you about another. And the first suffering—it disappears. But the dying go on dying. Children are trained to be soldiers, then forced to kill their own villagers or even families—or be killed themselves. Girls are tricked or sold into sexual slavery. Smart bombs and death squads finish off families. What "plan" am I talking about? AIDS and malaria and an earth half-ruined. At a table laid with white linen and polished silver, isn't it obscene to talk about a divine plan? It's put to question even by one carload of drunken kids.

Opening his eyes, he answers.

"There are three answers I can give you," he says. Picking up two of the takeout containers, he lets them symbolize the possibilities. "These seem to be contradictory, Ben, the way wave and particle theories seem contradictory. I could say to you, God's plan is complete and perfect but we can't see it—imagine we lived on a two-dimensional surface; intrusions from the third dimension might seem impossible to understand. Or the opposite. I could say to you: it's not God's plan you're seeing. Humans wreck the world. We're free to do so, it's up to us, that's part of God's plan, and just look at us—look at *us*, not at God. In fact, God is in *our* hands.

"Neither answer touches our grief." He puts the containers aside. "But they bring up other answers, deeper answers that speak to our grief. One answer is that God is not omnipotent. God has to cope with the chaos inherent in the material world. And then," he says, "there's still another answer. It's a beautiful one. The answer, according to the Zohar, is very moving, because it doesn't express a Western, rational theology with a perfect deity. It's a tragic theology. God suffers with us, God is in exile with us. And how did that come about? It depends on a very beautiful myth that seems to run counter to the perfection of creation in Genesis. In this counter-myth, in the Zohar, in order to open up space for creation God needed to contract. Otherwise all would be God. This contraction is called *tsimtsum*. Holy light filled vessels of creation. In the act of contraction and creation, the holy light was too intense for the vessels and cracked them, sending off shards, splinters, which collected in shells called *kelippot*. That's what rabbis of the Kabbalah and of

Hasidism call them. *Kelippot.* And that's the created universe. So original holy light is in fragments, broken; you could say God is broken. And it's our work in the world to retrieve the kelippot, restore the holy sparks of creation to their original unity."

"I like that," Ben says. In jeans and Yankees tee shirt, Ben looks like a graduate student. "Is this in the Bible? In Torah?"

"No, it's in the medieval text called the Zohar, 'Splendor, Radiance.' Written, scholars think now, in the thirteenth century. It's *built* on Torah. For many Jews it has the status of Torah."

"And so you're saying God's plan is ruined?"

"As we try to lift the sparks of holiness, we come closer to God and God's plan. That's how I understand it. The world is broken. *Tikkun*—repair—is up to us. The Zohar is trying to express the tragedy of our lives, our longing for God in the midst of the brokenness. And human beings can't just wait for God to act in history. We have to act. In a deep sense, that's what the *mitzvot* accomplish. They help restore the original unity. If I say I'm in the hands of God, maybe all that means is that I sense the radiance that emanates through this broken world, the unity that's promised. But this is high metaphor, Ben; it's poetry, it's not the *New York Times.* And we, with so little strength, we're supposed to lift the shards of light back to God."

He grins at them. "Thus, I speaketh . . . and at once I feeleth like a sham."

Margaret says, "Oh, it's good to talk seriously. You're not a sham. Ordinary table talk—isn't that more of a sham?"

"But Margaret, see, this highfalutin' theological fabric—that's not how it feels, not really. Me, I talk to God the way I did as a child. My head tells me God's not listening, but look at what's happened to you guys—I've begun to believe God *is* listening. I feel like I'm held in God's hand like a bird, a stunned bird in the hand of a rescuer." He buries his gaze in his soup.

Looking up over the edge of his spoon, he grins at his congregation. "As soon as I say the words, they turn false in my mouth."

"As you said, it's high poetry, Adam," Margaret says. "From you we can take it. Tonight especially—though perhaps with a grain of salt. You know, you *have* been a real friend. We owe you a lot. You may not be a Messenger, but your nudge, it got us to stop glowering at each other. It helped us."

"Please God."

"But your talk . . . the God-talk," Margaret says. "I don't mean this in a hostile way. Please. But, Adam, the term 'manic denial' comes to mind. Aren't you using God-talk to keep grief at bay?"

"At bay? Who says it's at bay?" He knows that his question doesn't answer her question.

Again, he tries to catch Lisa's eye, but she's looking at Jennifer. Is she embarrassed? For the past year, way before her mother died, she's been embarrassed. He's not cool. He can't say anything right. If he sings a Gershwin song, she's sure he's gone off key, and what's he singing for in the first place? If her friends are standing outside school, he is to drop her off across the street. She groans when he blows his nose in the supermarket or conducts a symphony as he drives. This embarrassment embarrasses him. It hurts him—what is he becoming for her? But this new embarrassment is more serious. Does she think, *My dad is pathetic.* Not just weird—really crazy?

They eat in silence. Somewhere between the egg rolls and the chicken stir fry, something stirs and blooms in his sad chest and grows bigger and bigger; embarrassment—Lisa's, his own—isn't nearly a strong enough force to keep him silent. "It dawns on me what I'm doing here. It's part of something larger; I'm looking for something. I'm tracing the lineaments of God's plan. I'm not Mitzvah Man in order to roam around and do good deeds. Nor only to perform the *mitzvot* every Jew is to perform, like daily prayer, like thanking God after dinner, like laying on *tefillin* in the morning. You know what *tefillin* are, right?" But he doesn't wait for an answer. "I think I'm groping my way in the dark, spelunking from clue to clue looking for shards of light, so I can put the pattern together. And I haven't got a clue where to start. To enact God's plan? That's pretty pretentious, when what do I mean but stumble in search of my life."

Margaret says, "But there's Lisa," she says, as if the word is enough. "Adam, I hardly know you, but I can imagine what you're going through—"

"You're so sure it's just grief? I don't blame you. That's what I'd have thought. I bet that's what his friends said to Hosea. To Jeremiah."

"So. My friend the prophet!" Ben says gently. "What a heroic enterprise."

Adam shrugs. "You think prophecy is gone from the earth? The rabbis thought so two thousand years ago. They still say so. I'm not sure." He sighs, chants—quietly, expeditiously—a brief form of the blessing after the meal. Lisa murmurs along.

Ben asks, "Is this search going to happen here? In New York?"

Adam shrugs. "I don't know yet. Maybe we'll go back to Cambridge."

"How do you know," Ben asks, "that you're not in serious emotional trouble?"

"I *am* in 'serious emotional trouble.' I'm grieving, I'll always be grieving. But you mean, am I nuts?"

"Look, Adam. If you have to go off somewhere, maybe it would be good—I don't want to intrude," Ben says, "but think about leaving Lisa with us until you know what's happening. Have you any relatives in the city?"

"Just an uncle Lisa's never seen. Uncle Cal, the son of a bitch. He won't accept my letters. I couldn't even tell him about Shira. My mom, my dad—you remember them—they're both gone."

"You need time to yourself," Ben says. "You want to leave Lisa with us for a few days? While you sort things out? It might be better for Lisa. We'll take wonderful care of her."

"I know you would. Well. I never considered that. Maybe it's a good idea."

"Take some time off," Ben says.

"It's up to Lisa. Honey? What do you think?"

"If you want, Dad. I like being here if that's what you mean. I mean temporarily." Lisa smiles into his eyes. "Overnight. A day or two. Dad? Is that what you mean?"

Lisa is uneasy letting him out of her sight. In her mind's eye she sees him wandering Broadway, getting lost, getting picked up by a cop or getting into a fight. He's a fighter. He could hurt someone, he could be hurt by a gang. At the same time she sits on the bed across from Jennifer's, smiling at Jennifer, taking in the posters of rap stars diagonal over walls and onto ceiling, crazy-quilt. She wants to see this as adventure.

"I've got a fantastic place to show you," Jennifer says in a breathy voice. "I promise. You're gonna love it. You know what we're doing? We're going dancing. We're gonna party till we drop. And we're not gonna drop."

"Dancing? I haven't got anything to wear."

"You can borrow—earrings or a bracelet or a blouse. But babe, jeans are fine. It's outdoors at Lincoln Center. They teach dancing, then everybody dances. I think it's salsa tonight. Too late to take a lesson, but we can dance. There's a zillion people. It's awesome. You'll love it."

Lisa doesn't say anything to her father. It's so strange. He's actually going to leave. Just like that. He gets his things together. She kisses him goodbye. "I'll call in the morning," he says.

"I'll ride down in the elevator with you, Dad. All right?"

So under the eye of a security camera, they ride down in the sweet paneled little room, mirrors enlarging the space and giving them multiple images of each other. She runs her fingers along the molding around a mirror. "You'll come back soon?"

He holds her cheek between his hands. "As soon as I know what I'm doing. A day, two days."

Lisa rides back up alone; in Jen's room she wraps herself in a silk shawl of her mother's, mostly mauve, paisley, and ties another, gold, around her waist. She and Jen walk a few blocks down Broadway. They can't hear the music until they turn into the grand open space in front of

Lincoln Center. So many dancers, so many watchers. "Really, zillions!" Lisa says. The lit-up dance platform is loaded with dancers, and dancers surround the stage. You can hardly walk. On a raised stage a salsa band, six musicians, are pumping their shoulders and bobbing their heads. In the dark area around the dance space, people grin, couples dance, kids dance with parents; a beautiful black man in his twenties dances with a fifty-year-old white woman dressed as if she came straight from an office. His moves are so slinky and gorgeous, but she knows a lot too, she's got style. She looks as if she's in a business meeting, no pleasure in her face, but she's able to stay with him.

"I love it," Lisa says. "I love this place. Thank you. Omigod."

"Dance with me."

"I don't know how to dance salsa."

"Just do this basic step. Like this. And then, whatever."

Lisa follows. "Like this?"

"Great." Jennifer takes off her blouse and ties it around her hips. Beneath she's wearing a frilly, sheer, mauve camisole that shows just everything—breasts and belly button. As she turns, Lisa sees a tattoo, some creature, a gazelle?—on the back of her shoulder. Do her parents know?

Dancing, Lisa glows: soon she picks up the beat. She watches the couples around her, and lets herself go, and it feels great—Jen doesn't seem to care how sloppy Lisa is.

After the second number Jen holds up her hands. "Lisa? I'll be right back. I just spotted somebody. Why don't you dance with that guy over there? He's been eyeing you. Just smile and you've got yourself a cool partner."

"That's all right. I'll wait, Jen. Okay?"

Jen's gone, gone from sight. In the midst of so many people Lisa begins to feel alone, scared in the belly, like the time she got lost at the beach. She was seven, eight, and they'd rented a house in Wellfleet in the summer, and Mom wasn't watching, Dad wasn't watching, she wandered left instead of right, remembering the lifeguard chair, but it was the wrong chair. And finally she had to go to a lifeguard, and he made her laugh, took her up on his chair, and blew his whistle, actually held her up high like a lost camera, and Mom came running. It's like that now. She's ashamed to be so spooked.

After a while Jen's back. She seems weird, won't meet Lisa's look, Lisa imagines a story of romance. But she doesn't ask, and soon, they're dancing again, and Lisa trills a cry, and Jen trills back. They dance until Jen's blouse and Lisa's tee shirt are soaked, and they walk home buzzed. But Lisa can tell—Jen's got secrets, Jen's spaced out, talking strange. Still, it's great. She wonders: where's Dad?

| 7 |

Dad—Adam—is temporarily on his own. On his own except for maybe the hand of God guiding him. And Shira—is she in on this? It's just her kind of playful enterprise. Remember the birthday he met her for dinner at a downtown restaurant in Boston?—tired after a hard day, and then she wasn't there. His birthday. Grumpy, he ordered a drink. Then the waiter came up to him and said there was a call, follow him. Okay, she's been held up at the hospital. Walking into a private room, Adam is splashed with music! Her string trio, playing Mozart; ten friends cheering; Lisa not with babysitter as he supposed but applauding and hollering, the table set with silver and crystal.

Where is the private room where Shira plays for him now? He's convinced there are other worlds. According to the rabbis, we live in four of them at once, four *olamot*—so while Shira may have died in the world of action, the physical world, *assiyah*, how can she die in worlds not subject to death, the worlds of "formation," of "creation," of "emanation" (the world closest to God)? He's always imagined a spirit melting into the radiance, not remaining separate like a kind of spiritual ghost, not poking into this world like a busybody. But Shira, present in spirit, wouldn't she want to intervene in his life? It would be just like her. To have her say. Why should physical death change that?

Leaving the Lichts, he kissed everyone—family, even Margaret. Looking into Lisa's sleepy eyes, he promised, "I'll be back soon." "Be careful," Mama Lisa said. And he left, purportedly to drive home to Boston, to spend a few days thinking, resting, and to return for Lisa.

But he knows he's not through with New York. There's something he's supposed to do. By cell he books a room at the Westbury and, leaving his car parked at Ben's garage, takes a cab to the hotel. It's his favorite little hotel in New York—his favorite when he used to come on business.

He goes to bed early; next morning, he wanders midtown, pokes through a bookstore feeling for messages—perhaps a book he's supposed to buy? But he gets no messages, buys nothing. It unnerves him: suppose he misses it, whatever *it* is. The message. And here's what unnerves him even more: suppose he already knows where he'll be "sent." Suppose "sent" is pure self-deception and all this prophetic activity just cover for an agenda he's squirreled away from consciousness in a camouflaged pocket of his mind.

For doesn't he already know the first place God or his sad heart is leading him? He knows. Back to the faux castle in the park. A jumble of weather instruments sits atop the tower, instruments actually in use, and maybe he imagines the castle as a receiving set linking him to the other worlds. *Maybe he imagines:* now what the hell can *that* mean? Does he or does he not imagine God will speak to him through the whirling black balls and sensors? He does not. Absolutely not. *But . . .* aha! It crosses his mind and makes him wonder: is that what I secretly think?

It's a beautiful day to walk through the park. He's opened the top buttons of a fine white cotton shirt left over from his workdays as elegant businessman. As happens almost every day, from time to time, unannounced, a wave of sorrow swamps him, and he has to stop to sit on a park bench and lift his head above water. It's as if the grief floods in at the chest and crushes him down, down. It's become a palpable reservoir of pain at the bottom of his belly.

Now he's okay again. He smiles, breathes deep, spreads his arms, and tilts back his head as if trying to catch the sun with his chest. He's off to the terrace of the castle, from which he can look at the park and the buildings surrounding the park. And at once, scanning the line of buildings along Central Park West and Fifth Avenue, he understands where he's supposed to go. *Oh, there!*

But what has this to do with God?

For in one of those buildings along Fifth Avenue lives his Uncle Cal, his big-shot uncle who refused to talk to him on the house phone. What a fool he was for not knowing, without all this rigmarole, what he was intending to do.

Not *why*. *Why* is beyond him. But at least the unease of not-knowing where he's headed lifts. *So I'm going to see my* uncle. My son-of-a-bitch bastard of an uncle!

Don't ever let yourself get into that man's clutches, his mother used to say from time to time. He ruined your father and destroyed my life. I don't want to see him get his hands on you.

And yet when Uncle Cal dropped by a couple of times a year and took them out to dinner, wasn't she charming to him? Oh, she flattered and cajoled him, and he ate it up, Cal. There was always a tinge of sarcasm in it Cal didn't let himself catch: "Well, aren't you a handsome rancher in that grand Stetson. Two-gun Cal. No one, my dear, would know you came from the streets of Chicago." Meaning, *You're as phony as a three-dollar bill. I hate to tell you this, Cal dear, but you're no goyishe rancher—you're a poor Jewish boy who made money buying and selling. Your poor mother worked like a slave to raise you. During the Depression she took in boarders. In them days, Mister America, your name was plain Charlie. Chollie.*

Cal must have found great pleasure in overturning, like fated siblings in Genesis, the birth order. And Adam's father let him. "How can you let him treat you like such a shlepper!" his mother nagged his father, over and over. "How can you? What kind of a man would permit his little brother to treat him like a slavey?"

Answering for his father now, as he passes the Egyptian obelisk and skirts the south end of the Met toward Fifth Avenue, he whispers an answer: "The same kind of man, Mom, who lets his wife yell at him night after night, and night after night call him *fool, coward, putz.*"

So his father, the elder by four years, was bullied by his younger brother and by his wife. His only defense was to grin and flatter the Big Man or hide inside the cave of himself or push his wife away with a heavy paw. Bullied! Adam has never thought of it that way—*bullied*; he and his father, bullied at the same time! Cal would send Dad from "headquarters" to one of the branches with a package. Then he'd snap at him, growl at him, yell at him for not getting back soon enough. He'd send him over to the precinct house with a carpet for the captain's office. He'd make him open up "headquarters" at seven, make him stay until the place closed, then send him to get cold cuts for one of Cal's parties—to which he and Arlene weren't invited.

Walking up Fifth past the Met and the Guggenheim and the Jewish Museum, Adam turns in at Uncle Cal's green canopy and gives a fat smile to the doorman, a different doorman than last time. "I'm here to see Cal Friedman," he tells him in the outer lobby. "Do you know if Mr. Friedman is in?"

"I believe so. I'll see, sir."

"Tell him it's his beloved nephew. Adam Friedman."

The doorman picks up the receiver and buzzes, his back to Adam. He hunches over the phone to speak privately. The conversation goes on and on. From time to time, Adam hears, "I see. Yes, sir. Yes, sir. I'll tell him." Now he puts down the receiver. "Mr. Friedman says he regrets he's too busy to see you." He can read wariness on the doorman's face.

"Almost eighty years old—the old man must be terribly busy. Coded messages arriving from London about high international finances. Listen! Can I just talk to him myself?"

"I'm afraid that's *my* job, sir."

"Let me have the damned phone." Adam makes a lunge.

The doorman plants his body in front. "You want me to call Mr. Friedman back?"

"I want you to give me the phone." And when the doorman turns away, Adam says, "Yes, all right, call him back. You tell him I'll sit down here in the lobby until he's got a few free minutes to see me. Tell him I've got all day. I'll let all his neighbors know."

"I'm afraid that's impossible. You're going to have to leave, sir."

"He told you to get rid of me."

"There must be some conflict between you and Mr. Friedman?" The doorman, a beefy, florid-faced man, puts his palm to his chest. "Please. I'm sorry. You'll have to leave."

"Or what? You're going to call the police? Mr. Friedman would love it if the police came and the neighbors all knew"—Adam says, raising his voice, almost singing now—"that Mr. Friedman sent his own beloved nephew to jail rather than see him."

"Just a moment, sir." The doorman picks up the receiver and presses a buzzer.

Waiting, Adam stares at the bubbling fountain in the inner lobby. He feels the power of his own craziness. He feels real sympathy for this doorman, that he has to cope with a nutcase. Yet he also wants to push past him and make a dash for the elevator. The doorman's busy talking; over the doorman's shoulder Adam yells, "ARE YOU AFRAID TO SEE ME, UNCLE CAL?" He knows Uncle Cal hears nothing but the anger.

"Mr. Friedman says he's coming downstairs. If you'll just sit on this bench, sir . . ."

Adam feels like a boy at school. He feels like the child he was when they'd dress up to visit the Big Man. What am I doing in this place? This is the wrath of ego, not the rage of a prophet! He's swallowed his mother's bitterness and his father's shame.

It's as if he's separate from the Angry Man, watches him enact his wrath, as if this were a tableau in a school play. Get it? He gets it.

Maybe he's seen what he's supposed to see! And having seen it, does he need to meet his uncle? Except for his father's funeral, it's been twenty-five, thirty years. When his mother died, his uncle sent a note:

Please excuse my absence. I'm sorry for your loss. I never take a chance on germs in crowds. Also, for many years your mother and I didn't get along. I'm sure you'll understand.

Germs didn't keep him away from Dad's funeral four years later—

just three years ago. But Cal stood apart. He hired a private limo and was driven alone to the cemetery. He didn't hug Adam, didn't shake his hand or speak, but he nodded grimly at him across the grave.

Dear God, what am I doing here in this lobby?

He sits on the leather bench and fingers the brass medallions at the corners.

He's gone from being parent to being child. It's thirty years ago. Back at the big blowup: Gunfight at the Aegean Grotto. Walking up to the maître d' and holding his sleeve between thumb and forefinger, Cal puts his lips close to the man's ear. The maître d' looks at his list and leads them to a table. "Nah. Not this goddamn table," Uncle Cal says. "What do you take us for? Furriners?"

"Nice," Adam's mother says. "Refined. What culture!" This is just loud enough for Cal to hear, not so loud he has to take notice. *Très, très élégant*, she whispers. "Arlene!" His father hisses. Cal leads the way to the table he wants. The maître d' scurries behind. Cal, shaking hands with the maître d', slips him a ten spot. Smiles, smiles. Everyone sits. The waiter, a tall, elderly black man, comes over with menus. Cal plucks a twenty from his wallet, tears the bill in half and hands the waiter the smaller half. Waving the larger, he says, "George, ya look like a professional to me. This is gonna be yours when ya give us the service we know we can expect from you."

George, after George Pullman, inventor of the Pullman sleeping car, the name white men gave to black conductors. It was like calling this man "boy."

This is too much for Arlene Friedman. She asks calmly in her best almost-upper-class British accent, "What kind of gross animal are you, m'dear?", as if she were asking him about business. And isn't this exactly why he went through the vulgar charade with the waiter, to get this woman's goat? But her goat has turned into a mountain lion. "You can lead my poor husband around by the nose, but don't expect me to find your racist vulgarity cute or charming. Your wife left you for a reason. We both know it, mister. Phony big-shot charm but no heart, m'dear. I'm too much of a lady to tell you what else she says was missing. Adam and I are leaving now. It's been a pleasure."

And she led Adam right out of the restaurant. His father went after them, "Arlene! Arlene!" Then back to the table. Then back to his wife, back again to his brother, and finally, with a shrug—*You see how it is, Cal*—he ran after Adam and Arlene. Adam was walking backwards, keeping one eye on his father, his poor, overweight father. There were times he despised him. Not that night.

When Adam had a family of his own, he tried to make contact. He wrote and called. Cal's number had changed, and the new number was unlisted. He wrote again—*We're past that family bitterness, aren't we, Uncle Cal? You're my only older relative. I'd like to come to know you as an adult.* Cal never wrote back. That was ten years ago. He let him know when his mother died, when his father died. When Shira died, he wrote, but the letter was returned unopened, refused.

Now, looking like a million dollars, dressed as if he were about to play golf at the swankiest course on Long Island, in open white linen shirt and beige linen slacks, white cap tilted on his bald crown, Uncle Cal comes from the elevator. Long, white hair falls below the edges of the cap, as if he's old enough and rich enough not to need to be perfectly groomed. He's lean with a little belly—probably sucking in what would be a bigger belly. He looks great for almost eighty. Before he reaches the bench he begins to holler, "What the hell you bother an old man for? You think I owe you something? I don't owe you a goddamn thing. When I die, my money goes to Sloan-Kettering!"

"Fine! I don't expect a goddamned thing," Adam says, raising his hands, palms forward—see, no weapons. Now he turns his hands palms upward as if to present a gift—of what? *Rachmones.* Compassion. Empty hands. Who knows what he's doing here? Suddenly, he does know!

"Uncle Cal," he says, "I think I'm here to ask you a question and give you a blessing."

The question goes back to something his mother always hinted at;

two months before she died she did more than hint. They'd rented a hospital bed, and the bed was cranked up. It was her last throne. That's the impression she gave, in spite of the pain. A queen. And he was her audience.

I could tell you something that would surprise you, my darling.

Yes, Mom?

Nothing . . . it's about your uncle.

What about my uncle?

Do you think someone as smart as you could come from someone like your father?

What are you telling me?

You're smart enough to figure it out.

Well, Mom was always crazy. And maybe it was too little oxygen to her brain—or too much—that encouraged her delusions. Later that afternoon, she sighed.

The man always loved me. Always.

Uncle Cal? I thought he couldn't stand you, Mom.

Naturellement, she smiled—shutting her eyes to contemplate her secrets. He never spoke to his father about her fantasies.

"May I ask you one question, and then I'll never bother you again in this world?"

"You've always been a peculiar person," his uncle says. "Like your mother. Look at that phony beard! What are you supposed to be—a rabbi or a professor? Or a bum? You've got one minute to get out of this lobby or I'm having Frank here call the NYPD. Get me?"

Now an old lady leads a lap dog on a silver chain across the lobby to the elevator. At the last moment the dog takes a detour around Uncle Cal, and the chain catches his legs. "Goddamnit!" He extricates himself and turns all his scowling energy on this woman. "They shouldn't be allowed in the building!" he yells. "Dogs! Who needs the pissy little things?" He turns away. "And you—"

"One question?"

"For crap's sake."

"Lisa? Come in, come in. Can I get you something?"

"I don't want to bother you—" She enters a beautiful room, beautiful because the walls are lined with hardcover books in bookcases of dark wood, the same wood as the desk under a window ledge where Margaret Licht sits at her computer. One wall has engravings and a print from a Corot show. Margaret does interior design, works out of this apartment. Her work table is really two tables, L-shaped, with a cleared space for sketching, piles of work on both ends. Margaret's dark hair is pulled back with a barrette. She's wearing an open silk shirt, mauve, *really womanly* Lisa says to herself, seeing the shadowed cleft between her breasts and her full skirt, and Lisa thinks, *When I'm old I want to wear just that kind of blouse and just that kind of skirt.*

"You don't bother anybody. Please. Sit down, dear. You play so beautifully."

"Thanks. I'm just letting you know—I'm going for a walk."

"By yourself?"

"Jennifer's gone out. Just to the park."

"The park by the river?"

"*Central* Park. Mrs. Licht? So will somebody be here later on to let me in?"

"Absolutely. Till two. Then I'm going out a while. And the doorman can let you in. But please, please do be careful. You don't know the city. Do you have a cell?"

Carrying her violin in its fiberglass case, Lisa walks past the Museum of Natural History and enters the park at 81st by the Diana Ross Playground. It's a school day for the public schools, so only little kids are in the playground. The day's clouding over, it's muggy, and suppose it rains? She worries what the damp will do to the violin and finds, when she climbs the steps to the castle, that it's already slipped horribly out of tune. So to an audience of birds and a mother with a little boy, she tunes the violin and begins the Mendelssohn again. She's imagining, oh, knowing—*knowing*—it's make-believe, that the melody can reach them both, her mother, her father, and draw them both to this place.

Two boys, she notices, have stopped to listen. They go above her onto a high rock, and she feels uneasy, not because she has an audience—an audience always makes her play better—but because their eyes are narrowed, and they're smirking. The boys are maybe fifteen. Now she stops playing, and, keeping her eyes off them, puts bow and instrument away in her case, and, looking up, kills the boys with a look. But they don't die, don't turn away embarrassed, don't grin at her. The fat, homely one says, "Come here, chickie, chickie, chickie."

She hears the Spanish in his voice. She turns away, her heart beating, and not looking at them, carries the violin down from the castle terrace towards the great lawn and lots of people walking through the park.

"Hey, ba-by," the tall kid calls, "show us that little violin, ba-by."

She reaches the path, and swinging around, puts hands on hips: "*¡Vete!* Go away."

"Hey, she speaks Spanish. Hey, baby, you know this Spanish? *¿Cariña, quieres besarme?*" He puts a hand to his chest in mock politeness.

"That's revolting. Uch! *¡Eres asqueroso! ¡Déjame en paz!* Leave me alone!"

"Aieee! You hear this little one?"

"We could take that violin so easy. You want a violin, Manuel?"

Reaching the path that skirts the Great Lawn, she starts to walk fast, almost run. They're after her. She's fast—the fastest runner on her soccer team, and she thinks she can beat them—especially the fat one—to Central Park West, where she's sure to come upon somebody to help, even a policeman. But she stops, faces them, takes her cell phone from her pocket as if it were a weapon, and waves it at the boys, who are still maybe half a soccer field away. "*¡Alto!, ¡Alto!*"

They stop. They're laughing. The tall one cups his hands around his mouth. "Hey, *no hay problema.* Okay. We're cool. Okay? I swear to God. Hey! Where you get that Spanish?"

"At school," Lisa yells. "*Really* no problem?"

"Really. Hey, no problem. It's cool. We just giving you a hard time. Old're you?"

She holds onto her cell, punches in 911 but doesn't hit SEND. "Fourteen." The boys are coming close. She holds her finger on the SEND button.

"Your Spanish, it sound a little funny. You know? It *sound* like school."

"Well? So? That's what I told you—"

"Yeah, yeah. Okay we come over there? We sit down together? You play for us a little?"

She has to decide this second whether to trust these kids. Something in the tall one's voice, something in the way he holds himself, decides her. She sits down on a bench and, before they sit beside her, she's taken the violin from its case and, partly out of nervousness, she's tuning again. What to play? Something tells her: not Mendelssohn. She knows some Klezmer, and plays a slow, sad, bluesy Jewish tune that becomes the basis for a melancholy improvisation.

The fat boy says, "Wow. That's nice, real nice. How long you play?"

"Oh, forever. Since I was four. I'm Lisa." To herself, she seems cool, grown up. Oh, it's a fake, she knows it, hopes they don't know—a fake because she's still wary, and inside feels alone and scared but she can tell they like something about her, so she plays nice for them. After a couple of minutes a lady pushing a child in a stroller stops to listen, rocking the stroller, then a little girl with her mom and someone who looks like this homeless guy in the soup kitchen where she works sometimes in Cambridge. Someone says, "You know any Beatles?" And she begins "Yesterday."

It becomes a listening circle. She's never played for pure strangers. Lisa imagines an invisible camera above and to her right that's taking pictures. It's her mother watching. There's a second lady with stroller, a couple of ten-year-old girls. Lisa focuses on the violin in order not to be distracted, and so her father, puffing hard, is almost at the bench before she glances up and sees him.

He's been running; he grins, stops, heaves breath. Lisa opens her mouth, mugging the surprise she actually feels, and flashes a huge smile at him, but she doesn't let on. Keeps playing. Now the tall kid takes off his baseball cap and works the little crowd. Amazing! Some change, a few bills, a five from her dad, and the kid bows to her, as she finishes "Yesterday," and presents her with the money. "We'll split it, okay?" she says. "You take all that. I'll just take the five-dollar bill. This," she says, putting her violin and bow in their case, "is my dad. And you? You are—"

The tall one is Manuel, the fat one José. Like men, they shake hands with Dad. Now they walk with them past the Diana Ross Playground and out of the park.

"How did you find me?" she asks. "And what are you doing here? I thought you went to Boston? I can't believe this was an accident."

"Accident? That I quit jogging and left the reservoir track just then? I wouldn't call it an accident."

"You been running in those nice shoes?" José asks.

"Dumb, huh?" He tells Lisa, "I saw my Uncle Cal. He wouldn't see me but I made a fuss. I was a little nuts."

"Omigod, you're just real lucky nobody called the police."

"Who'd put me in jail for wanting to see my uncle?"

"But Dad? They might put you in the hospital."

"You guys want an ice cream?" he asks, pointing to a white pushcart at the corner opposite the Beresford. Sure they want. They go over to the man selling ice cream and there's a long discussion of what he's got and what they want.

Lisa's not interested. "Dad? Dad? Can't we just go home? Can't you take me home, Dad? And maybe. . . . Dad! Maybe you should get a job? Wouldn't that be good?"

"You out of work, huh?" Manuel asks, licking the chocolate coating of his ice cream on a stick. They walk past the planetarium toward Columbus.

"Kind of out of work," he says. "I intend to get a job."

"Good luck," Manuel says. "The kind of job I bet you look for, not so easy."

"And, Dad, Dad! Let me get back to work on my Bat Mitzvah? And my music lessons?"

"Your daughter plays real good, man," Manuel says. Then, to Lisa— "You play real good. You take my cell number? I give you my cell number, you talk to me, huh? You IM?"

"No accident," Dad says. "I'm telling you, honey. I'm being led."

The boys look at him. "Who's leading you?" Manuel asks.

Lisa says, "He thinks maybe God."

"Wow," José says.

"Give me your number, too," Lisa says, writing her number on a scrap of paper. "I liked playing for you." She turns from them. "But Dad? Can you please ask God to please, please lead us home?"

Hearing the upset in her voice, being unable to block it out or sweet talk her into going along with him, what else can he do but take her home again? He's been noticing the way she sits with elbow on a table or the arm of a chair, her knuckles pressed against her mouth. He reads it as worry, secret sadness, and concern beyond even her longing for her mother. And maybe, he thinks, maybe her sadness, too, is the voice of God. So they say goodbye to the boys; he walks her back to the Lichts, and they say goodbye to Margaret over a cup of tea. Jennifer comes in and gives Lisa a hug and they promise to get together soon, goodbye, goodbye, drive safely. . . . Maneuvering the transverse through the park on his way to pick up his bags at the Westbury, he calls Ben.

"You don't know how grateful I am," Ben says, "that you came to visit us. Messenger or no messenger. Thank you. My friend. I swear, you'll always be my friend. You can even be Mitzvah Man if you want. Margaret and I, we're bruised, but it seems we're together."

"You know," Adam says to Lisa, folding the cell away, "we could stay at the Westbury a couple of days, visit MOMA, take in a show. Would you like that, honey?"

She doesn't answer; she shakes her head and stares out the window.

"Okay, home it is. Home, you bet. But we'll barely get there in time for Shabbos."

It hardly feels like home. It's as if their house, a narrow, white clapboard house at the end of a private court near the Harvard quad, isn't ready for them. He takes this as a bad sign: has he left something undone? Was there someone else to bless? Someone else's life to change? The phony ebullience of the car ride—he coaxed Lisa into singing numbers from *Guys and Dolls, Showboat, South Pacific*—fizzles. Seltzer with the bubbles gone. Lisa goes room to room, taking the sheets off furniture and folding them away, pulling back curtains to last sunlight, opening windows, playing a Haydn quartet on the big stereo in the living room. In every way, he sees, she is conjuring light, order, calm. Adam goes along—of course goes along—but he's weary, flaccid. He sees stains on the carpets, marks on walls from where Lisa used to play ball as a little kid. He makes a list in his mind, jobs around the house. It's a small, Edwardian house, small rooms, cramped for a family, but it feels too big now. Everywhere he turns, another job.

What this morning, in his manic condition, didn't matter at all now weighs him down and down. He sits at the kitchen table, half-hearing Haydn nudge him toward calm with harmonies that not only don't fit the modern world but didn't fit Haydn's own. Who said the eighteenth century was an age of peace? Papa Haydn would smile: Isn't that what music is *for*?

He sits at the table and writes a list of people to call, jobs to take care of. What about his karate buddies? His *sensei* called. It's time to return to the dojo. Adam's been practicing his forms, his strikes. It washes his heart every time he works out for an hour. Sensei's right—he should come back. And Lisa—what to do with her the rest of the month till camp?

Has he been manic? Now it seems to be Lisa's turn to get into a frenzy. She makes call after call to friends, and, laughing, laughing, sets up dates to hang out. She keeps one eye on him, he's sure, fixes him herbal tea, cooks up a packaged soup mix for dinner, sits at the kitchen table with him and reads *Pride and Prejudice*. "Listen to this," she says, and reads him a passage about the foolish Mr. Collins. He feels even lousier that she has to keep up her spirits this way.

The sun has set; late, they light the candles for Shabbos and share a glass of wine. Father and daughter hold hands over the table. There's no *challah* tonight, so they make do saying the blessing over crackers. She pours soup into their bowls and crumbles in the crackers. He recites the blessing a father gives a child on Shabbos, hand on her bowed head. He's getting teary again; he doesn't want to let go of her head.

Next day he doesn't go to synagogue for Shabbat service. He doesn't know why. He sits in his study facing east—facing the painting of Jerusalem that hangs in the middle of the eastern wall—and prays the morning service from the Sidur, the prayer book. He feels some shame in this, for Judaism is a communal religion. Even the great Jewish mystics of Safed, though they may have contemplated the letters of God's name until the letters became black fire on white fire, also prayed in a community of friends, a community that supported their solitary exertions. But this is not exertion. The letters seem to lift from the page of the Sidur, float, buckle the way he saw the sky. Weeks ago, the first time he saw the letters float, it scared him a little. Now he feels honored. It would be better, he knows, if he could translate more of the Hebrew. What's a sign when you can't make out the words?

After prayer, he works through his list of odd jobs, fixing door handles, changing light bulbs, fixing a leaking faucet. As he does, his spirits sink and sink. He leaves a residue of screws, tools, sheets of newspaper with glue. Lisa's off somewhere with a friend. Without Lisa there to be damaged, he's free to regress to the condition he was in three months ago; he turns from his laptop, from his phone calls, and weeps as if weeping were the crucial work he'd left off the list. It's Shabbat. He's supposed to be joyful on Shabbat. The weeping three months ago was in response to shock; now it seems to be a permanent condition. Everything is lost, the beauty of the world lost. If he didn't have Lisa to think about, he'd think about joining Shira.

He remembers a conversation they once had—what happens after you die. Shira believed you were absorbed back into the pool of light that is the energy of creation. Your individual being would rejoice at being able to dissolve into this light. He said, But what about the other worlds in which we exist? Maybe it's just our bodies that dissolve, physical perception, cognition, but in the other worlds in which we have our being, we are as alive as ever. And maybe we can be aware, somehow, of the world we've left. She felt it was a sin to think too much about the world-to-come.

Now, he quiets his weeping and contemplates other worlds. It's the Shekhina that's accessible to us, the Shekhina mediating the Godhead. The *sefirot*, the map of the Being of God in Kabbalah, seen as tree, as a human form, is always operative in our lives. *As above, so below.* And in our actions in this world, we help to lift energy to the *sefirot*. We restore holiness. *As below, so above.* Shekhina is the link. Retreating to his study, Adam sits in his *tallis*, skullcap on his head, and tries to imagine himself suffused by the Shekhina, who is also seen as the Sabbath Queen, the spirit of Shabbat, a spirit—remember—that he's been desecrating today with phone calls and jobs. Now he goes inside, to a quiet cave of light. His breathing changes. His breathing is a prayer.

But emerging from the cave, he blinks, and the cave disappears. What cave of light? What Shekhina? This is all false. Phony, everything phony. The blessing he dared to give his uncle, false. Phony-baloney. He's no Mitzvah Man. He's a guy who closes his eyes against sadness.

The front door opens, closes; Lisa is back.

"Dad? . . . Oh, sorry," she says.

She tiptoes away. Eyes shut, he listens to her shoes squeaking on the wood floor.

Seeing him sitting in skullcap, Lisa stands at the open door to her father's study, stymied. It's been an hour since she came back to the house after a make-up lesson with Sonia, her violin teacher, and lunch in the Square with Annie Morrel. He hasn't moved; she doesn't know what to do. It's not unusual for him to meditate in that straight-backed chair. But over an hour?—it's getting weird. In fact, since they came back, he's hardly said a word to her. He cries and tries to hide it. She asked him to please call the Rosenthals. *We could take them out to dinner—thanks for letting us use their house?* He doesn't say yes, he doesn't say no.

The house won't speak to her. It's a dead place. It just sits. It's not home.

Twice she's dialed her Aunt Ruthie's number and twice hung up without leaving a message. Of course, Ruthie would never answer the phone on Shabbos. Uncle Max in Minneapolis—if he lived nearby, she'd definitely call him and Aunt Evie. And her grandmother. But Grandma Nina is not clearheaded anymore. And Aunt Ruthie, that's a mistake. Although Ruthie's absolutely polite and all that, she really can't stand Dad. She'd just love the opportunity to meddle. Once during the week she and Dad sat shiva, Ruthie said, right in front of Lisa, "Well, Adam, at least you'll have plenty of money left you by my sister to help with bringing up Lisa. That's one thing, *Baruch Hashem.*" And Dad answered, "We don't talk about such things during this week," embarrassing Aunt Ruthie. She'd be glad to stick her nose in, find Adam a doctor, take Lisa into her family. Which is the very last thing in the world Lisa wants. But she's scared, because suppose he really needs a doctor, suppose the longer he's allowed to zone out, the harder it will be to pull him back.

It's the first big decision she's ever had to make on her own. She's always had her parents to help her make decisions. And if she's wrong, anything could happen, maybe he'll go absolutely crazy, maybe even kill himself. It happens. But she could go wrong by asking for help, too. If she lets him alone and just takes care of him, maybe he'll come out of it.

Just after the funeral, being driven back from the cemetery in the black car, Dad said to her, kind of confessed to her, *Your mother was my strength, honey. You know that? I was never a strong person before I met her.* God, to her he's always been such a strong man! And funny and goofy, because he's not afraid to be, and that's stronger than a tough, silent guy, the type she absolutely can't stand. Now she thinks of what he said as a warning: *You'll have to be the strong one.*

And this excites her, like winning the lead in a play. And she's ashamed of the excitement, ashamed of liking the role. But the longer she sits with it and ponders choices and consequences—the less exciting it seems. And the more scary.

And the more draining. And the more exhausting. And the more infuriating: it's not fair—he gets to be the sad, crazy one; I've got to be calm.

Except maybe for her friend Annie, there's no one to share her troubles with. She wants to tell Mom. Her friends—she calls and laughs with them on the phone, they meet for tea in Harvard Square, they tell her the secrets that bond them. Sherry's mother and father are getting a divorce; Allison's brother got caught smoking pot; things she'd tell her mother, not her dad. She sits with them.

Annie Morrel she can talk to a little. Walking along the Charles today, Lisa got teary, said, "Oh, SHIT! Just SHIT!" Annie held her, she was able to cry. At home she doesn't dare to cry.

Home, she finds him sitting where she left him. Oh, God! She goes outside, sits on the porch in late afternoon sun. In the house directly across them in the little cul-de-sac, the new baby is crying, crying. The baby's mother has asked her to sit for them when the baby is older, and that would be great, because she likes little kids, and this one's so close to home. But today the crying just gets to her. She puts a finger in one ear and calls Jennifer. Not there; she'd have to leave a message. She doesn't. Because really—is Jennifer a friend or just someone she kind of looks up to, goofed with, danced with? What is there to say to her? She shuts her phone.

And it's after this that she kicks him. It's supposed to be a wake-up kick. Because when she comes inside, he's still sitting and won't say a thing, so she goes away and practices and calls Sonia to set up a lesson, and fixes dinner—a nice stir fry. She sets the table with linen the way her

Mom did, lights candles in spite of the June early evening light seeping through Mom's kitchen curtains, puts a Mozart violin concerto on the stereo, and returns to get him.

"Dad?" He nods his head. "Dad?" Now, not even a head shake. Pathetic! So WHAM! She kicks him really hard on the shin—not in front, on the shinbone, but on the muscle. Parent abuse. He opens his eyes. "Dinner's ready," she says, sweetly as she can. He rubs his shin. "*Now*," she says. So he shakes himself off and rubs the kicked place and stands up.

"I'm recharging my batteries," he says to her. "Thanks for making dinner. Tomorrow I'll cook. Suppose I make us a nice roast chicken. Would you like that?"

"Oh, *please*! Where do you *go*, Dad?"

"Go? Oh. Well, I'm listening." He cocks his head and holds a hand behind his ear.

"Omigod, Dad. Listening. Omigod. I'm getting really, really, really worried."

"I know. Sorry. I'm being self-indulgent as hell. See . . . it's not like God is sending me messages. Specifically not. I'm listening and hearing nothing. See? God says *Shema—hear*. Hey, God, I'm listening. Hello? Come in, God. . . . Or maybe, what's to hear? I've been fooling myself maybe. Maybe nothing. Oh, Lisa, hey, you fixed everything so nice. What a kid. What a kid." She sees his eyes are wet. He blows his nose into a cloth napkin. How disgusting.

"Dad? We have to live without Mom. We just have to. You think we can do that?"

He bows his head; she doesn't know if this is prayer or an expression of defeat.

She serves them. He mumbles a blessing but barely eats, and she has to say, "Dad? You eat!" Her heart is going a mile a minute. It's absolutely freaky. She says "eat"; he listens to her—he eats.

She listens to Mozart. "Here comes a beautiful part, Dad. The slow movement."

He begins to cry and right away apologizes, "I'm sorry, I'm sorry, but right now it's not Mom, it's *you*. I'm crying from gratitude and pride, honey. You're some blessing."

"Dad? You didn't even go to synagogue today."

"No."

"Aren't you supposed to say Kaddish for Mom?"

"I promise. I'll go whenever there's a minyan. I was a dummy today. I worked on Shabbat, and the more I worked the worse I felt. So I needed to spend time in being quiet. That's all."

"You're supposed to be Mitzvah Man. Right, Dad?" He doesn't much look like any superhero. He's in a tee shirt that says Marlboro Music Festival. M.M. Like Mitzvah Man? But he's wearing baggy khaki pants and scuffed tennis sneakers. She says, "Dad, do you know that someone can increase their score on the SATs—like ten points or something—anyway, increase their score by putting on nice clothes, shirt and tie for a boy, skirt and blouse for a girl, like that?"

"Interesting. So? You want me to get dressed up in a shirt and tie?"

"Dad? Are you taking those pills you're supposed to take?"

"Yes, honey. Kind of. They don't do that much good. . . . You think it's depression."

"I don't think anything."

"It's *sadness*; why label it 'depression'? Shouldn't we be sad? And maybe it's my soul moving to a different place."

His soul? Well, maybe. But looking at him, she just sees *grubby*. He hasn't trimmed his beard; he can't pretend it's for mourning, not if he worked and didn't go to services. It blurs together—sadness at losing Mom, sadness seeing his sadness. She wants to kick him again, wants to kiss his bristly cheek. "Okay. . . . Why don't we go out after dinner. Want to go to a movie?"

"Well, we could."

"Or a concert?"

"I'd rather. What's playing?"

"I'll look." Going on-line to check, she finds a pianist playing Bach at Tsai Performance Center. She asks him to put on a real shirt and fresh

pants—for *her*—the way Mom asked when, in her words, he'd "let himself go." "Do it for me?" Mom would say. Now Lisa says, "Do it for me?"

She calls; but there are no tickets left. That does it; the pangs in her belly do it; the simple fact that every time she takes a breath, she can't get enough air. That does it. She looks up the Rosenthals' number in Mom's address book.

"Hi. Talia? It's me. Uh-huh. We wondered if you happened to be home. We're back from our trip. Uh-huh. Dad wants to know, would it be okay if we drop in after dinner? Great. Great."

So that's what they do. She's the one who thinks to stop for flowers; he pays. They walk through Harvard Square, glowing in late sunshine, past punks, summer students, a street guitarist, and up Brattle past stores and theater to a row of old mansions and finally to her favorite house, little one among giants, the Rosenthals' mid-nineteenth-century house near Longfellow House. She loves the way it's set way back from Brattle all by itself, with its slate roof, and, inside, clarity, simplicity, with small many-paned windows overlooking the gardens, Talia Rosenthal's gardens. As she rings the bell she has the notion that this house and the calm inside might change her Dad, give him a chance to breathe.

It's not the first time they've seen each other since the week of the funeral, since she and Dad sat shiva. Still, Jerry wraps bear-arms around Dad—two big men hugging; Jerry makes throaty sounds of sadness and thumps Dad's back. Already Lisa's glad they came. Lisa remembers the Sunday mornings a million years ago before Mom died, when Dad and Jerry would go off to the Mt. Auburn Tennis Club and play a set. That was their friendship—tennis at the club, a Monday night at home watching football. That was their friendship.

And she realizes: Dad has hardly any real friends, the way Mom had friends. His one close friend was Mom.

Talia takes the flowers, smells them though in fact they have no smell, holds Lisa, holds her, and when they separate, both of them have tears in their eyes. Talia's absolutely the most beautiful older woman Lisa knows. Mom always envied Talia's beauty in a comical way. "The woman's incredibly queenly," Mom used to say. "Oh, those high cheekbones and long neck and long legs and the way she walks! What I wouldn't give." And Lisa would say, "You're just as beautiful, Mom." But Talia is most definitely regal. And soft, too. Lisa loves her softness. That's the cool thing, that mix. Talia wears the most romantic clothes. Her mom made fun of them but in a nice way. Lisa has always wondered— does she dress more . . . professionally at work? She must. Now she's wearing a loose, maroon silk blouse with a scoop neck; her hair is long, real long, halfway down her back, and at home she doesn't bundle it up and pin it, she leaves it loose. Jerry's just a big slob, but Talia doesn't seem to mind.

Now comes the dance of drinks and cookies and the sitting around a coffee table meant to create a center for communion. *The rite of the coffee table*, Mom used to say. This table is Chinese, of dark polished wood, rimmed like a picture frame, sitting on heavy legs and carved feet. If you asked her to describe a nice coffee table, this is the one she'd pick. You get lost in the grain of the wood. It's not painted, but there are landscapes in the mahogany. She remembers, as if it were years and years ago, how she'd come here with her parents and they'd talk; and, unless the Rosenthals' kids were home and they could hang out, she'd go inside the pictures the table made.

But now, with the Rosenthal boys both away on the Appalachian Trail, she's treated as an adult, one of the four, as if she's replaced her mother. But they talk about Shira. Remember the weekend we went sailing and Shira . . . and they laugh about the fabulous surprise party Shira threw for Adam's fortieth. Wasn't that one great party?

"She lived a damn good life," Jerry says. "We should all live such a good life."

And that does it. WHAM! As if you opened a faucet, Dad's weeping and can't stop.

Talia sits next to him on the sofa and rubs his back. Lisa has seen too much of this. She walks over to a set of French doors leading to a beautiful little garden and an undulating brick wall. The big houses on Brattle block the very last of the sun, but its light still suffuses the garden; the brick paths and mulched borders glow. She walks outside and tall white flowers float alongside. She remembers the white garden at Sissinghurst that Vita Sackville-West designed. It was just last summer that they visited. Omigod. Less than a year ago!

From the garden she can hear him. Worried about what might happen, she goes back inside. He's poured a second glass of bourbon. He's not really supposed to drink when he takes those pills of his—he's told her that. What would he do if *she* started acting weird and drinking bourbon?

But she doesn't. She doesn't want the Rosenthals to think they're stuck with a whole nutty menagerie. She curls up, a cat, in a big leather armchair and, changing the subject, says, "We loved being at your house kind of off-season. The beach was so empty. Like completely. We saw seals."

"I'm glad you felt comfortable driving down and . . . dropping in," Jerry says. "That's great."

She notices his eyes open wide and the silly smile on his face, an imitation of a smile to indicate that it's okay to break into our house. She decides to drop it.

"I did a lot of drawing," Lisa says.

"I'd love to see your work," Talia says, smiling. That's a smile! It's like her mother's smile, and right away tears come to her own eyes. "Your mom used to tell me about your talent. A violinist and a painter both! Will you come and show us? Adam, really, we'd love to see her work."

Adam nods. He asks how the medical practice is going. Talia says, "We think we've found someone, but she's not experienced like Shira. She's just out of residency at Albert Einstein. She's from Sri Lanka. . . ." Lisa hears Talia's energy trailing off. Talia's listening to herself say it. Lisa feels for her.

"Good, good. We're all replaceable," Dad says, and nonsensically, he rubs his hands together. "Nothing wrong with that."

So if there's nothing wrong, Lisa thinks, why say it? "Replaceable" is cruel. They've got patients. The practice has patients. Shouldn't they hire another doctor if Mom's gone? She can't look at her father's goony face. For the first time in her life she thinks, *Just five more years and I'll be in college. Can we make it for five years?* She's like a wife planning a divorce long in advance.

"I love your garden," Lisa says—says to Talia, because it's mostly Talia who works on the gardens. "It makes me think of planting a garden at our house. Like, what's that flower with the floppy, white petals?"

"We have a garden," Adam grumbles. "Next year we'll have a garden again."

"*More* of a garden," Lisa sighs. "Okay?" She turns away to avoid seeing the shrug of his shoulders, pout of his lip.

"Show me," Talia says. She leads Lisa out onto the garden paths. Measuring herself against Talia, Lisa realizes she's grown taller—even since Mom died. She's as tall as Talia Rosenthal now. The sun has set. In the dusk the two of them seem to float among the white flowers, two shadowy ladies the same height. "There."

"Oh, yes. Japanese iris. It's abundant. I can divide some for you if you'd like."

"Great! You will? Thanks!"

"Stop by tomorrow—we'll be home and I'm not on call. If you promise to bring over some drawings, I'll dig up some bulbs and put them in a bag for you. Aren't they lovely?"

"Lovely." Lisa understands: this is an invitation to talk privately about her father.

Stopping at the French doors that lead from the terrace to the living room, Lisa and Talia stare at Adam. His eyes are closed, he's rocking.

"Dad?" He's rocking. "DA-A-AD?" she calls in descending fifths, as if it's a kind of joke.

Jerry, arms folded across his chest, head cocked to the side, examines her father as if he were some sort of strange art installation.

"I listen down and down into myself but I'm scared I've lost contact," Adam says, sitting still. "Definitely. Hello, anybody home? Like sonar; but nothing comes back. I think sadness gets in the way." His eyes are open; is he seeing anything? It seems to Lisa her father's strange, fast-talking craziness is back. Just a minute ago, there was only sadness; now, frantic speech.

Without discussion, they sit down around the communion table. "Contact," Jerry Rosenthal prompts. "You were saying about contact. . . ."

Jerry Rosenthal, she can tell, means contact with people.

Dad doesn't. He looks up. "See. The way it goes is, suppose I'm not held in God's hands anymore. If I bless someone, suppose it's just *me* doing the blessing."

"And before? You felt you were in God's hands?" Talia says. As she says this, carefully, sympathetic physician, she leans over from her chair and presses her hand over Dad's hand.

"So . . . like with my uncle," her father says, as if Talia hadn't spoken, "I blessed him, my bastard of an uncle, but you know, it was slightly phony, the blessing. I mean I meant it but I didn't mean it, and maybe that was when God gave up and left me to my own devices. Which makes me sick. You know what it feels like? Now I have to hold my bones upright. Back bone connected to the hip bone?" He stands up and holds himself upright; he's on a high wire trying to maintain balance. "I almost have to decide to breathe. Not really. In point of fact my body is doing my breathing for me. Thank God. But I've lost the power just to flow, to flow in a holy current. Like swimming. Now, if I act, it's on my own. If I bless, I have to give myself the authority. It scares me. See, when I was with God, I was connected to Shira. Now—now I'm not. 'Hip bone connected to the thigh bone,'" he sings. "I mean, there's a pattern beyond us, but I've lost touch. I'll bet you think I'm sounding strange. Peculiar." He looks up and grins at Lisa, at Talia, at Jerry. "Hey. If I can't admit to old friends I'm broken up and glued together, well who then? . . . And I'll tell you a funny story about this bastard of an uncle. It appears, ta-dah, it's quite possible, now I'm not certain, folks, but get this: it may be *I'm* the bastard. Me. Yours truly. Literally. Am I blabbing? I'm blabbing, aren't I? You want to hear a weird story? I guess you're old enough, Lisa."

Lisa winces in advance. She can do without hearing everything. She waits for a gap in his talk so she can take him home.

"Are you *sure* you want to talk about it, Adam?" Talia says. "Maybe we'd better have dessert—I've baked a tart."

"Here's the story. My mother, she used to hint from time to time my father wasn't my father. Now, if that's true, it'd be jake with me—you know that expression? Nobody uses it anymore. 'Jake'—cool. Anyway, she used to hint that my uncle was my real father. Yes, Lisa, I *know* this is incredible. At the end, well, she more than hinted. So I cornered the guy when we were in New York, and the thing is, he didn't say yes, but!—he didn't say no. Now, that's interesting."

"Family stories," Talia says, "family stories." She goes to their iPod, docked in the stereo, and in a moment Miles Davis is playing a sad love song. "So—who wants dessert?"

"Now, wait just a minute," Dad says. "Just maybe this is more than a story. Aha!"

"Then *maybe*, Adam," Jerry says, "this isn't the time to tell your daughter? *Look* at her."

And Jerry's right, all right. Lisa is feeling strange. Lisa wants, as a matter of fact, to throw up. But she smiles, she shakes her head. "Dad," she says, "is upset a real lot. He *does* things. Like just going to your house at the Cape. Because, I have to say, he didn't really think you were there."

"We wondered about it," Jerry says. "You know it's all right with us. Of course it's all right. But Adam, why didn't you call first?"

And Adam says, "She's right, she's right—I *do* things." He laughs with just his breath, pumping breath, so you can see his belly bulge out and shrink and bulge out and shrink. Lisa is slightly disgusted. "See, I couldn't call, Jerry, because *I had no idea where the hell we were going.*"

"And God told you to go to our house?" Lisa watches Jerry's head come forward as if Dad were a child and you needed to get into the child's space.

"I do *not* want to talk about God. Please. I'll just get phony again."

"No. Really. I'd really like to hear," Jerry says.

He sighs. "It's complicated, Jerry. It's not crazy to know God is flow-
ing through all things and I can ride the flow—hey, that's metaphor, not
religious boogie-boogie—like I'm some holy surfer, right? God can use
me. But suppose—suppose I start using God. Then it becomes phony,
and God—whoosh—departs. You get me?" It looks as though he's pondering what he's said. "Or seems to," he adds, "because in fact God's
even present in my phoniness. I mean. I mean. Can God really depart?"
Her father laughs. "Where's there to depart to—where is God absent? I
mean what's God do with his frequent-flyer miles? But right now God
feels absent. Get me?"

Jerry nods. "Sure. You mean you get to feel false when you sound
like you're personally acquainted with God. Sure. And sometimes it all
goes flat. Sure. Isn't that normal? I present a paper on nineteenth-
century painting and I really believe what I'm saying, then halfway
through the paper I feel I'm handing out a bucket of bullshit, making it
up. That it? That what you mean?"

"Exactly!" Dad says.

9

You'd imagine, he thinks on their walk home from the Rosenthals—more than a bit buzzed, he has to admit, on the bourbon à la antidepressant, trying hard not to stumble at curbs and find himself LOOKED at by Lisa with that worried look of hers—you'd think Talia's tenderness and Jerry's grin and his daughter's love would ground him sufficiently. But Harvard Square feels like a movie set, the facades hollow. He gawks up at the Church of the Inaccurate Construction—that's what Shira used to call it—the church on the corner of Church Street that leans, slightly crooked, into the wind. There *is* a wind, by the way—harbinger of rain? Maybe a metaphor. Yes. That's how he decides to read it. Message of change: *Teshuvah*, turning, turning back to God. Yes. He'll listen. From now on, no-frills prayer and study, sans sudden thumps of holiness in the gut. Dear One, teach me to love You simply. Oh, yes—and teach me to get by.

And if those two prayers contradict one another?

Shira stands, of course, in every shop door, every gate to the Harvard Quad. It's not a visual hallucination—just memories that connect his heart to her this place and that—music rushing out of this place and that. He wants to address Shira and has to nudge himself to talk with Lisa in an ordinary way. An open Porsche convertible cruises by. "Look, honey," he points. "Think I should get one of those? Or keep our name on the list for a Maserati?"

"Oh, Dad." She rolls her eyes, or on the dim street

he imagines her rolling her eyes, but she's relieved, he knows, when he kids around the way he used to.

"Remember, you said I should get a job? Well, I should. When you're right you're right."

"Dad? How could you tell the Rosenthals that awful lie? Ych!"

"What lie?"

She shrugs. She shrugs harder.

"The story upset you? I should have had more sense. Just fantasy. My mother's fantasy. I don't want to upset you. Tell you what. This week, I'm gonna start looking for a job. A position."

"Good! Good!"

"But it may take some time."

"Oh, please! Who wouldn't want you?"

He wraps her in a comfort arm. "Thanks, honey. That's what I need. A cheerleader, not a Porsche."

They live in a cul-de-sac near the William James Hall off Kirkland Ave. So they always look up when a car comes down their little street. As he stands on their porch, keys out, headlights shine their way. Adam puts his hand over his eyes. The lights turn off; the engine shuts down. A big American minivan. Who do they know drives a fat, nine-person American minivan?

Ruthie and Leo, his Orthodox in-laws. Of course. For them, with all those kids, it makes sense. With six kids they practically need a bus. Ruthie's first out of the car. "Leo, Ruthie, how nice. How did you know we'd be home?"

Ruthie says, "Let's talk inside."

Le bourbon plus pill is giving him a little trouble keeping things together. And this is one time he wants to be very clear and very, very calm. A few inhibitions wouldn't do him any harm right now. He imagines himself liable to go wild, boot Ruthie off the porch, toe to sanctimonious buttock, and since an Orthodox woman can't touch a man who's not her husband, this might cause problems with her rabbi. Now, Leo's a good guy, a fat, smiling man Adam likes a lot, partly because Leo reminds him of Zero Mostel. Adam's always felt for Leo, married to a force of un-nature like Ruthie.

"It's late, Ruthie."

"We drove over as soon as Shabbos ended and we'd made Havdalah. As a Jew, I know you must know about Havdalah—the ritual that ends the Sabbath? Of course you know. You didn't answer your phone. We knew you'd be home. Where else, when you have a child? Look at the way your beard has grown! Maybe you'll turn into a real Jew yet. So. Aren't you going to invite us in?" She brushes past him, onto the porch, into the house. Leo is carrying a bouquet of flowers. When Ruth can't see, he winks at Adam, puffs out his lips and shuts his eyes: code for *Nothing serious, you know my wife*. . . . Lisa takes the flowers and puts them in water. Nobody regards the flowers.

"Come in," Adam says. "Can I get you some wine?"

"Adam, you know perfectly well," Ruthie sighs, exasperated, "we can't drink from your glasses or eat from your plates."

"I forgot. That's because you shouldn't cook a kid in its mother's milk. Makes sense."

"Adam, I know you and I have issues—"

"Please, Ruthie," Leo begs. This big man, paunchy, sits himself in the soft peach-colored armchair and plays with the fringes of his *tallis katan* that hang over his belt. The armchair is a fat, bourgeois chair Adam grew up with and would never allow Shira to replace. Too bad, he thinks, as Leo half-lifts himself from the chair, then sits back—because if Leo could extricate himself easily from the damn chair, he'd maybe go over to sweeten Ruthie, but it's too much work. "*Shalom bayit*, peace at home," Leo says with a sigh. "All right, Ruthie, dear?"

"Issues? No issues," Adam says to his sister-in-law. "We just don't feel so hot, you and I, when we're in the same room."

"Clever. Clever. But your daughter called. *She* called *us*, my dear. We found your number on our call-answering screen after Shabbos." Triumph—and to cover it, she refolds and rearranges the shawls that draped the sofa: Shira's shawls.

"I was just saying hello," Lisa says. "'Cause we were away. That's all I was calling for."

Ruthie ignores the lie. "Adam?" she says, thumping her sternum hard enough to make her sound like a drum, "can you understand just a little bit how Shira's sister might be feeling?"

"You mean *you*, don't you, Ruth? Why speak of yourself in third person?"

Her eyes narrow and aim at Adam. She's got a good answer, he can tell. "I mean myself *as Shira's sister*—and as Lisa's aunt—not just as me personally. Me, personally, you think I'd be here? I wouldn't be here. Leo, do I tell people what to do? Each Jew must decide for himself."

"As Shira's sister, then—what might Shira's sister be feeling, Ruth?"

"About the loss to her people of my own sister's child." Ruth holds onto the corner of a silk shawl, strokes it as if it were a *tallis*, and look—she has real tears in her eyes.

"Oh, my God! You really think that? Unbe-fucking-lievable!" So here they sit in the living room, a room in which the pale golden draperies, the photographs on the mantel, and every piece of art glass were chosen by Shira. Shira stripped the paneling to bare wood; she replaced narrow, sensible, boring windows in living room and dining room with new multi-paned, light-bearing windows. To be in this room is to take on Shira's vision. They sit, Adam mistrusting Ruthie's separatism, Ruthie despising Adam's secularism. Secularism? What does Adam want more than to draw close to God? *Devekut.* They've had this talk so often over the years. She considers his Judaism peculiar, sentimental, neurotic, even a little crazy; he's influenced by Hasidic texts for their passion, but he's unwilling to live the disciplined life of any Hasidic path.

"I can't help worrying. Why isn't she going to a Jewish camp? Why isn't she going to a Jewish school? Do you really think she'll stay a Jew swimming in the sea of American culture?" Ruthie can't look at him. She gets up and looks from photograph to photograph on the mantel, then she turns and stares at Adam, and her look is full of grief.

Adam wants to soothe. "Ruthie, about a lot of American culture we're in perfect agreement."

"Of course you are," Leo says. "We're all good Jews at heart. Lay off, will you, Ruthie? Was it any different when Shira was here? You had the same things to say." Poor Leo has always hated fighting. He likes talking about things they agree on—AIDS in Africa, the ugly values of hip-hop, the meretricious nature of popular culture. But Ruthie, in her sexless brown, straight dress, won't take yes for an answer. *Your mother, Nina,* Adam wants to say to Ruth, *was a funny, generous, loving person. She still is—just that she's old and hasn't all her faculties. As was your beautiful father. So this has nothing to do with Judaism. Where did you go wrong?* Of course she'd snap back, *Wrong? Because I know I'm a Jew? Because I don't try to hide it? Sins of the fathers,* she'd say. *Unto the third or fourth generation.*

This argument they don't have.

Leo turns to Adam. "Maybe you could give a little, too, Adam. Stay with us next Shabbos so you don't have to drive. Walk to shul with us."

"Leo, he's not going to stay with us. He thinks he can be a Jew by himself. He's read a few books, he chants *nigunim* composed by lesbian rabbis ten years ago, he calls that Judaism, he wants to be a mystic. Some mystic. You know what you are, Adam? I'll tell you. You think you're big enough to invent a new Judaism on your own. You can invent all you want, but it's not Judaism."

"We can't come because as a matter of fact Lisa's got Hebrew school."

"Some Hebrew school," Ruthie sighs. No grief now, just hostility. Lisa, Adam sees, keeps looking back and forth, at Adam, at Ruthie, but catching no one's eye.

Ruthie's wig—the *sheitel* an Orthodox woman wears over her own shorn hair—looks like a brown helmet. Is it just his mind making it look like that? Adam knows she must have paid a bundle, knows it's the best Leo's money could buy. But it makes her look like a soldier. As does her face—and this is disconcerting, because he can see hints of Shira's gentle face in Ruthie's tough one, and it absorbs him, he stares into her militant eyes for living signs of Shira. Leo sits back in the easy chair and smiles, smiles to take the pressure off: *You know how Ruthie gets . . .*

Even as a teenager Adam was an observant Jew. He was active in Hillel at Brandeis. But right from the beginning, the first time Shira brought him to her older sister's, almost twenty years ago, Leo was a mensch, Ruthie was a bitch. Nothing personal. Adam was the wrong kind of observant. Yes, Shira hadn't brought them a Hindu, *Baruch Hashem*, Blessed be G-d, but marriage to a man like this "Mr. Assimilation" as she called him to his face, would be the beginning of a slippery slope. They'd sit, men and women together, in the nice *goyishe* service called Conservative Judaism; their children would turn to Reform; in another generation they'd be Episcopalians.

At Ruthie and Leo's, he wears a yarmulke; otherwise he wears one only in shul or Torah study. The Hochberg boy, then boys, then more boys, wore them as toddlers, as well as the *tallis katan*, a "fringed garment," beneath their shirts, the fringes showing over the belt. Adam respected—respects—the fullness of their religious lives. In some ways he wishes he could live the way they live—the liturgical year structuring their lives. He's impressed that the older boys lead services and the girls talk about Torah. But—admit it—it pains him to see little kids in uniform—black pants, white shirts. He's charmed, envious, that they study Talmud together as a family—this Leo is no dope. But Adam hates it that there isn't a book in the house except holy books. Ruth's afraid Lisa will be only an American; he's afraid the Hochberg kids will be *only* Jews, not prepared to thrive in America, to live culturally complex lives in America. Their school has a curriculum that includes science, includes other literatures. But at home there's no interest, none.

Lisa puts out on the coffee table some peanuts still in their can so Ruthie and Leo won't be tainted by their plates, which have been washed in a dishwasher that's cleaned both dairy and meat dishes. Opening a cold bottle of seltzer, she serves it in plastic cups. Lisa hasn't said a word.

"I see a *chumash* on the coffee table," Ruth says. "I'm surprised. So—

you read Torah, Adam? Or is it just a coffee-table book? Now—Lisa, dear," Ruthie says, turning from him, "of course, your father has the final say, but you have an important choice to make. You're a smart girl. You'd have to catch up in Hebrew, but you can do it. You can come live with your cousins. Gershom's in college; Nathan's at yeshiva. We have the room. You'd live in a big family with lots of joy and clear order, and you'd know what it is to live a Jewish life and pass on a Jewish life. Does that appeal to you?"

Okay, that does it! He almost lets go, grabs his sister-in-law by the scruff of her wig, and boots her out the door. But the way he's acted recently doesn't allow him this delicious freedom. No need to give her ammunition. He stands up, says in a quiet, firm voice, "Ruth Hochberg, you're no longer welcome in my house. Leo, I have nothing against you. But your wife is impossible."

"Ruthie, dear, apologize," Leo says. "He's right. You can't take a man's child away, dear. That's not up to you, and it's not really up to Lisa. Adam is right. I know your heart's in the right place, you want the best, you have holy intent, but you can't, you just can't—"

Ruthie binds herself together. It looks to Adam as if she's squeezed all of herself into a brown stick. "That's plenty, Leo. We're going."

They go, thank God they go. It's this easy? He wishes he'd known years ago. The engine revs up. Lisa calls, "Goodbye, Aunt Ruth, Uncle Leo. Don't worry about me, okay?" And standing on the porch next to the woodpile from last winter, with moths and flies spinning around the golden lamp, she turns to Dad. "I'm sorry I called them. It was *so stupid*. I changed my mind, but I did call." She puts a hand on his shoulder.

"Why, honey?"

She shrugs.

"Honey?"

"Uh-huh?" She's not looking at him. She's not really breathing. She's a statue.

"Was it the story? It really freaked you out—the story that my uncle . . ."

"I called before I heard the story—remember?"

"It's the way I've been, you mean? You changing your mind about your aunt's offer?"

"Oh, Dad, of course not. Oh, but really, you can be such a jerk." Under the porch light she lets go his shoulders and hugs him hard, thumping him on the back with one fist.

The *New York Times* comes to their door as it does every Sunday; Lisa takes it in, lays it on the kitchen table as she's done just forever. Her father has made coffee and has pancakes going. The coffee makes the house smell good, smell happy; the pancakes relieve her: he's not so sad this morning. So at once she finds herself down—and gets it: when she's afraid for him, afraid he might do something like you know, or just get someplace she can't reach him, then she has to pump up her own energy to keep things going. As soon as he's kind of okay, she can let go a little and feel what she feels. She can remember other Sundays. Anybody would remember times with a mother. But she got along so great with Mom. Mom was so funny, especially on the Sundays she wasn't on call and could bake with her, though she wasn't a great baker, or go for a run along the Charles, though she wasn't all that great a runner. And they had a good time making fun of Dad when he got peculiar. They'd go out for tea in the Square and gossip: friends' secrets, but it was okay telling Mom.

After breakfast, she goes into her room and calls Talia, and tells Dad, "I'm going to take a walk."

"Honey? How are you getting along? You don't really tell me anything. With your friends? What's happening?"

"Oh, Dad," she groans, shrugging, fluttering her fingers. "You know. Good, I guess."

He sighs one of his sighs.

Lisa promises herself not to be stupid and cry or complain about Dad, not make Talia into a mother. She will be one lady visiting another. And she dresses the part, in a pale peach linen skirt her Mom picked out, and a cream-colored blouse she used to love to see her mom wear. She puts on her mother's string of pearls, and for a minute before she leaves the house, she stands at her dresser mirror and looks at herself. Skinny. Toothy.

She decides to leave her plastic retainer at home. Into the mirror she mouths a smile.

Lugging her black art portfolio, she hurries through back streets and across Mass Ave to Brattle Street, walks around the side of the house and, tapping at the garden gate, walks right in, and sure enough, finds Talia in slacks and a big floppy straw hat on the brick terrace at the garden's edge, doing the *Times* crossword, and on the wrought iron table a paper bag Lisa is sure contains the Japanese iris bulbs. "How lovely you're here," Talia says, laughing. "Well, don't you look nice!"

She hugs Talia, and Talia kisses her cheek hard, very hard, not the polite kiss of your parents' friend but a super love kiss, a kiss of support and tenderness, an I-understand-what-you're-going-through kiss that asks, please, for honesty, openness, an open heart, but Lisa pretends to read it as *Hello, dear*, and grinning at Talia, breaks away and pokes into the paper bag: a white bulb with roots, the green cut off diagonally. "It's so great to be here this morning," Lisa says, looking up and spreading out her arms as if she's basking in the garden's glow. Oh, she knows she's being *corny*, her dad's word, being *theatrical*, her mom would say. *Fake*, she'd put it. But it *is* nice here, it's such a relief to be in this sweet city garden among the flowers and the totally sane—kind people not twisted by sadness. Not that she'd want to stay or anything. But really nice.

"You look so beautiful, dear. The strength of the young! How's your dad this morning?"

"Good. Really. Pretty good. He made us pancakes. Did Dan and Rob get back?"

"Late this afternoon. I do want to get you together. So, did you bring me any drawings?"

Lisa is embarrassed—not because she didn't bring her work, but because she did, yet she can hear in the question that Talia hadn't quite expected it until she saw the big, black leather portfolio. And now she unzips it and putting the bag of bulbs on the brick, she opens it up for Talia. On top is one of Lisa's favorites, nothing special, flowers in a blue glass vase in pastel, soft, pastel petals over delicate black lines of stem. She's proud of the transparency of the glass.

Talia's in-breath relieves her, makes it okay.

"Really lovely. Really lovely."

"It's my favorite. Corny, I know, but—"

"Beauty is never corny. Go on."

So Lisa goes on, moving from flowers to clumps of houses to a beach scene she did at the Cape. "This is yours if you want it for letting us use your house like that, so weird, I mean, without calling." And Talia says, "Thank you. Thanks so much. Wonderful. I'll frame it and put it up in the little room where we keep our Cape things."

Now pencil sketches, portraits, her friends, her mom from a few months ago, *Please hold still, Mom*, and then her mom from memory and photos. And last, her dad; lots of her dad. Her bushy dad in profile sitting in the car off Madison Avenue, her thinking father. Her father sunk in his chair at home, but somewhere else, in some other world. Her dad sitting by the ocean, the dunes, striated sand and clay rising up fifty feet, as background. Dad grieving.

"Oh, Lisa dear. Oh, Lisa dear."

Talia pulls her black, wrought-iron chair closer and wraps an arm around Lisa, and this time Lisa stops fighting her, stops holding back, sinks against her, but she doesn't cry, well, not a lot, though her eyes are sour with near-crying.

Talia tosses her big hat down on the table so she can draw Lisa closer. "It must be so tough. How are you handling things? How are you able? You seemed amazingly strong last night."

"Oh. You know. Dad's so sweet and wonderful, just a little crazy. I've thought about it. Here's what I think. I think it's kind of a gift. It's making me feel older."

"I know what you mean. I see that in your sketches. You know, you shouldn't need to get older so fast, dear."

"Otherwise, I'd be a mess. I'd be a complete utter mess. But I can't be. See?"

"I'm afraid that later on you'll pay for it."

"I guess I will. Talia? Thank you. I mean for thinking about me. But here's a kind of secret." Lisa tilts her chair onto its front legs and leans so close to Talia she can take comfort in the smell of her soap. "I still have Mom."

Talia nods and doesn't say anything. She busies herself with the portfolio.

10

He told Lisa he'd try to find a job, but the notion of working in a corporation or even of starting a new company: dreary, slogging rocks from pile to pile. Why, except to put food on the table? And, food is already on the table. Food and, praised be the One, the table itself, and what about the room in which the table sits, not to mention the house in which the room sits, and, it goes without saying, money to pay taxes on the house and taxes on the money itself, and Lisa's education. He's grateful not having to worry much about the means of living this extraordinary, ordinary life. You need a computer? You buy it. Bills come in? You pay them. Not a fancy life, no Porsche in his future, but enormous freedom of not having to worry how to pay for ordinary things. Of course *ordinary* includes fresh organic food, an iPod, books, films, concerts, plays. Includes membership in B'nai Or. For that life to continue, he has what he needs. Clothes to last him for years. He can be a book junky and not go bankrupt. So what will he do with his life? If this sadness continues, if he spirals down into day after day of God having no special purpose for him and he has to invent his life on his own, what should he do? Go back to consulting?

While pondering, he wanders from room to room. Lisa off with a friend, he pokes his head into the doorway to her room. He doesn't go in. Lisa's room is hard for him to enter. A row of photos on the bookcase seem scattered but Adam knows they're not—they're carefully arranged—knows because she told him. On the bed are relics of Lisa's childhood, but when he asked about the stuffed animals, the torn scrap of baby blanket, she said, "I know it looks stupid and childish, but it's for Mom. So if her spirit comes here, it'll feel good. I don't believe in it. It's so dumb. But it's like a gift to her." No, it's a beautiful idea, he told her. But he stays out.

He reads a page of Talmud, which, in the absence of a teacher, doesn't speak to him. He's also begun to read secular books again—he's plunged into *Middlemarch*. Tuesdays he goes to the rabbi's lunchtime text study in the downtown office of one of the congregants, a therapist. After one session, Rabbi Klein asks him to take a walk. They stroll through Harvard Square. It's like a summer fair, full of young people, full of the colorful clothing of young people. So why does he feel sadness, like an odor, coming from so many? Is he drawn to grief? Is he projecting it? Is he sensitized to it? Three possibilities. Look at that young man, a student, jeans and a tee shirt advertising B.U.M.—God knows why! Look at the slouch of his shoulders so that he seems to hide, crumpling in on himself to take up less space. Look at the way the poor s.o.b. masks his eyes so no one will see. Adam sees. Or thinks he sees. Sighing, he turns away to listen to Rabbi Klein.

Rabbi Klein, Joe Klein, has a sweet tenor voice; he's one of the mainstays of a Boston choral society, and you can hear the clarity and warmth in his speaking voice. Adam guesses the rabbi wants to check in with him—how are you doing now? Can I help? You want to talk? But no. Rabbi Klein says, "I've got two things to talk about. The first, it's about your beard, Adam."

"Something's wrong with my beard?"

"Of course not. Wrong? A Jew with a beard? Not so long ago, if you were a Jewish man, of course you had a beard. But now there's grown up a tradition that after the first month of mourning, you cut the beard when it's noticed and suggested. So I'm noticing and suggesting. Maybe it's time. It's up to you. Maybe you want to grow a full beard. I'm saying it's not necessary."

"Lisa wants me to cut it."

"Well?"

"I think I will."

"Good. You'll look better. I think you'll feel better."

"And the second thing?"

Rabbi Klein is smaller but stronger than Adam—a marathon runner. Adam has taken to the rabbi's family, a wife who teaches literature at Tufts, two little kids. He wants the congregation to grow big enough for them to hire this man full-time.

"The second thing," says the rabbi, "is a family who just joined." He's speaking now in the up and down singsong with which they study Talmud. Not his ordinary speech, which is American Midwestern, but the special singsong, maybe unconsciously meant to designate what he says a religious matter. "This family, the Eisens, have no money. Of course, we're happy to take them in as members. But they also have no money to live. They're from Johannesburg. Uri's working as a computer programmer, but Judith has to stay home, take care of their boy. Their boy has medical problems, cancer; she has to nurse him through the chemo. And their medical insurance is dismal."

"Sure I'll help. Send him to me. Or give me the number. Of course. I'm honored to be able to do the *mitzvah*."

So that night he calls Uri Eisen. He hears the sweet South African vowels. "No, no," he says, "you should know better. It's not 'charity.' It's a requirement, right? It's halachically required I find *mitzvot* to do. So it's your gift to me. I'm grateful. Also, if I can ever help with your boy? I mean relieve your wife sometimes so she can do other things?"

And Uri Eisen thanks him again. "Please. Come see us."

"I will. Next few days. I certainly will."

He attends services on Shabbat and says Kaddish. After Hebrew school, Lisa goes off to the Museum of Fine Arts with a friend. Adam loses himself in a book; suddenly, mid-afternoon, he feels the emptiness of the house, puts down the book, listens, listens, says aloud, Dear God, I'm listening. Tell me, what am I to do? How do I draw close to you? What does it mean to love you?

Towards dinnertime, Lisa comes back with a white paper bag. "Dad? I got you something."

He lifts a tee shirt from the bag. On the front, in the middle of a design of Hebrew letters, letters as they look on a Torah scroll, red, blue, black, is a logo:

MITZVAH MAN

"You like it okay? Dad? Now don't cry, please, Dad. Just go put it on."

"You did the design? It's so beautiful."

"It was easy. I drew the design and the copy place printed it on a tee shirt. Come on."

"How great! How damn great, Lisa. Okay, I'll shut up and put it on." He goes to the bedroom, takes off his WGBH (Boston PBS) tee shirt and puts on Mitzvah Man. She follows him and watches as he looks at it in the mirror on the back of the closet door. "Looks pretty good," she says.

"Looks fab. I am now officially a superhero." Holding his arms out, he demonstrates small superhero muscles. He's afraid he won't be able to sustain the humor, afraid he'll sink into sadness again. But for now, he doesn't.

"You *are* a superhero. You're Mitzvah Man."

"Ta-dah!"

"Mom would approve."

"Oh, I think so. Maybe I should put ritual fringes on the shirt."

"You mean like on a *tallis*, the knots and fringes represent the *mitzvot*?"

"Right. But for now," he says, "what's my first *mitzvah*, coach?"

"Well, you've done it. It's a *mitzvah* just putting it on, Dad, because it's a kindness to me, and kindness, that's like *chesed*, a really, really big *mitzvah*."

"That was easy. Whew. Just 612 to go. You know about the 613 *mitzvot*, right?"

"Sure, but some are impossible. Like having to do with the Temple and sacrifice."

"Right. So that lops off a lot of *mitzvot*. And like not muzzling a
beast to keep him from eating the crops. I mean who has a beast? Who
has crops?"

"Does a dog count?"

"Do dogs eat crops? And no, we're not getting a dog. Didn't God
sayeth, 'Thou shalt have no dogs'?"

"No way-eth."

"And there are tons of negative commandments I fulfill just by not
bowing down to an idol. Like to a Porsche. Does a Porsche count? I
don't bow down to no damn Porsches. And I'm definitely not marrying
my aunt or eating of things that creepeth upon the earth. And then I've
got some positive *mitzvot* under my belt. I wear a *tallis*, I strap on *tefillin*
mornings when I pray."

"Not to mention you *do* pray."

"I do. And I say the Shema twice a day."

"I'll play you your superhero Mitzvah Man theme song. Okay? You
ready?" She goes for her violin and comes back, violin already tucked
under her chin. In the few moments she was out of the bedroom sadness swept in, and he lost most of the superhero spirit. But he smiles at
her and listens to her *Hallelujah*, Psalm 150, played in one of the
melodies she knows from services.

"You're so damn good to me, honey."

"Argh! No more tears, Dad! Enough!"

"Nah. I'm a superhero."

"Right." She leads him out of the bedroom to the kitchen. "It'd be
another *mitzvah* if you fixed the string beans, Dad. But please wear an
apron."

It's a game, he says to himself, a mutual kindness, a talisman against
an excess of sadness. And why do I need to justify? He snips the ends off
the string beans and praises God for this girl.

It's the next morning, Sunday. He's off from cul-de-sac to Mass Ave to
morning minyan and bagels in the smaller sanctuary in his synagogue,
just a little room downstairs, carrying a bag with *tallis* and *tefillin*, to say

Kaddish for Shira. When you come down to it, he says to himself, crossing a nearly empty Sunday morning street, the majority of the 613 *mitzvot*, the commandments, positive and negative, have nothing to do with him. They refer to lives lived in the holy land or lived when the temple was standing. And he's unlikely to glean the corner of a field since he has no field. Except as metaphor. And what are we talking about but metaphor? *Don't be greedy with your substance.* Anyway, stupid, it's not yours, it's on loan, like all energy, passing through worlds, so open your heart and let energy flow in, flow out. More metaphor.

A Ford Lotus cruises by! Black, low, sleek, powerful. He gawks after it.

And, he continues, I'm unlikely to curse mother or father. . . .

Then, laughing, he realizes—maybe I *have* been cursing my father! If Uncle Cal is my father, that's exactly what I've been doing! Cursing and blessing. Put that in your pipe and smoke it!

But for the most part, obeying the *mitzvot* means what?—living a life of conscious kindness, charity in the big sense: *You shall love your neighbor as yourself.* Love of God and love of others, all created in the divine image. Like helping the Eisens, for instance.

There's no end to the possibilities. He recites to himself the passage from Deuteronomy. Moses tells the people, "Surely the teaching I'm giving you is not beyond reach. . . . No, the thing is very close to you, in your mouth and in your heart."

Adam remembers sitting in the kitchen with Shira—when?— must've been just before the High Holidays, when Deuteronomy is read. He stood at the counter cutting the ends off green beans or slicing onions, something to help Shira cook. And, looking up, he said to her, "Shira, you get it? It's right here, right in this kitchen. *Close to you.* And remember Jacob's words—*God was in this place and I, I didn't know it.* In this kitchen!"

And Shira laughed at him. He loved it when she laughed at him. "Are your eyes tearing up because of the onions or because of God?"

Under his shirt he wears not a *tallis katan* like the Orthodox but his Mitzvah Man tee shirt—the way Superman hid his more elaborate costume under Clark Kent's nerdy shirt and tie. He feels different wearing the shirt. Maybe he'll hear whisperings. He wonders: really—is it kosher to tie ritual fringes to a painted tee shirt? No. The garment needs four corners.

He hopes that somewhere in the Square he'll find the usual homeless guy with the shoe box for donations. He'll donate. But that usual guy, with the big sheet of cardboard publishing his sad story in Magic Marker, isn't there. Instead, in an unused side doorway of a building owned, he thinks, by Harvard Law, is another poor soul, a young man dressed in old jeans and sneakers, somebody's cast-off shirt, stained, faded. Thank God, he looks healthy anyway.

Which is peculiar. Adam thinks, Who knows? This homeless guy on an empty street on a Sunday morning, his rusty supermarket cart holding a green contractor's bag of his worldly goods, maybe it's the angel Elijah, who is said to disguise himself as a pauper. Maybe this is a land of continual miracles I'm walking through, and I just need to learn to see the miracles.

Not that he thinks it's really the angel Elijah. No, no. But maybe if you see rightly, it's always Elijah. So Adam goes up to him. The man's about thirty, strong, his face smudged, Red Sox cap pulled down over his eyes. But as Adam stands there trying to think what to say, feeling that just to hand the guy a couple of dollars is too easy, the man looks up. "Listen. I'm not what you think I am. You better move on."

Adam moves on, looks back, wondering, will the man disappear? *I'm not what you think I am.* Is he a cop on stakeout? A spy? Or truly Elijah—holy dressed up as homeless? But if so, would he tell him to move on? Adam walks on to the synagogue, and inside, past the sanctuary, to a tiny room with a portable wooden ark, fronted by blue curtains, on a table covered at one side in a blue gold cloth with gold trim. A few chairs face the ark. It doesn't take fifteen people to make this room feel crowded. And that's perfect, for even when there are only seven or eight, not enough to comprise a minyan so they can say Kaddish, the room feels full, a container, a blessing.

He's feeling a little lightheaded. Is this from last night, wine plus pills? He wraps himself in *tallis* and lays on *tefillin*, centering one black leather box on his forehead—at the hairline, between his eyes—and wrapping the straps of the other box tightly around arm and hand; and as he does so, he murmurs the blessings. Then the blessing for study of Torah, the morning blessings, and in the middle of these, swaying to the rhythm of the Hebrew, he finds he has to sit down and behind his closed eyes a spiral dissolves into a point of light . . .

. . . And he's out in the street talking to Elijah, who's wearing the same dirty sneakers, the same faded shirt, and Elijah says, *I'm working under cover,* and gestures behind him, and the dreamer understands perfectly and goes in through a crack in the wall to a cafeteria line. He slides his tray along the aluminum rods and hands the plate to the server as he used to at Chase School. Shira, in white lab coat, is server. *Shira, Shira, what are you doing there? Talk to me.* Shira smiles, the cafeteria disappears as if it's been Shira's joke, and here she is, she takes his hand, he needs no food, he's been fed. *That's the point,* the dream analyst says even in mid-dream. And here she is, they're walking through their house but in a foreign place, rented, a strange city. Lisa comes in and hugs her mother. But the tonality of this dream, which the dreamer knows to be a dream, is so sad—because the dreamer knows he's making up Shira.

"Adam? Adam? Adam? Are you back with us?"

Dr. Greenberg is touching his throat to feel his pulse. Adam opens his eyes to see old Sam Greenberg, in bad breath and big black-and-white tallis, stand above him. Arthur Koenig, leading services today, has turned from the ark. Adam feels guilty. "Please, I'm okay, go on, go on."

"What day is today?" Sam Greenberg asks. Adam answers. "Who's the President?" Adam laughs. "Has this happened before?"

"It's probably the pills," Adam says. Sam pats him on the shoulder. "Sure, sure. But you come out to the car for a minute. I've got my medical bag."

At his mobile office, a Volvo, this lovely, warm sunny morning, Dr. Greenberg listens with stethoscope to Adam's heart. It seems he's all right. Just stress, Greenberg says. "You poor guy. No wonder. But let's keep a watch on it."

And saying that satisfies Dr. Greenberg. He pats Adam's back. They walk inside and catch the end of the morning service; Adam gets to say Mourner's Kaddish. Adam is dying to get away to be alone with his dream, his vision. To think: what does Shira want of him? Where is she leading him? He's almost sure it's a dream meant to tell him something. Almost sure she's still nurturing him, taking care of him. Rabbinical texts disagree: while according to Torah "interpretations belong to God," in Talmud a dream is said to "follow the interpreter's mouth." His mouth can interpret nothing, is simply open with wonder at the dream's mystery and authority. He saw Shira's lovely face and now still sees her face more strongly as it was in the dream than as he remembers from their life together.

It's said that if a dream is repeated, that's evidence of its being prophetic. That night the dream is not merely repeated, it continues. In the next episode Elijah is again a homeless man in sneakers, again the wall, the crack in the wall, the cafeteria; again Shira is leading him. Now she's wearing diaphanous white. A lab coat? A chef's coat? He isn't even surprised as he follows her into the kitchen; this time no dream analyst stands back as he dreams. And this time he's the one expected to do the cooking. Dream pots hang from dream hooks; he busies himself making food. There are lines of hungry folks waiting, and feeling their suffering, he's cooking fast as he can, and everyone in the kitchen is working together. It's more than hunger. Everyone has lost something. They have a hole in the middle of them but you can't see the hole—their hands cover it. He cooks, he cooks. And he wakes at four, head hurting from the work; he prays in a whisper.

Through the shakes, light from the street lamp seems so bright. He gets up to pee and pull the drapes.

Asleep again at last, he's back in the dream kitchen feeding, feeding, and Shira, whom he can see only from the back as a shimmering presence, is serving, and the line becomes faces, strong faces, maybe images from movies? Or people he's seen on the street?

His Uncle Cal, wearing a big, felt Stetson, stands beside him; together, they're serving up soup from a great steel pot.

Waking, still half asleep, he finds he's swimming in an idea. It's barely tangible. *Mitzvah. Mitzvah.* At breakfast, he says to Lisa, "Something has come to me." Then he stops. He notices that Lisa has covered the wooden kitchen table with a white tablecloth and set their places with silverware and napkins. "Thanks," he says, pointing to the table. "I mean!"

"Oh, sure. Looks a lot nicer, doesn't it?"

"Something," he repeats, "has come to me."

"Uh-oh!"

"Don't be a clown." And saying that, he realizes she looks a little clown-like with her big eyes like Giulietta Masina in *La Strada* and her tee shirt with the head of Ganesh, the elephant god of the Hindus, printed on it. "Really, Lisa. Something jelled as I was waking up. What can Mitzvah Man do? I can make money for people. I have the skills. I can do that. Why not? I think it was a prophetic dream."

"Well good for you. What about that beard, Dad?"

"Come to the bathroom with me. Bring Mom's sewing scissors. My dear, you can have the honors."

"Really? No! Really?"

In a giddy mood they process to the bathroom, where he strips to the waist, lays overlapping sheets of newspaper on the floor and sits down on a chair from the bedroom. She cuts without mercy. A couple of minutes and—"Oh, awful!"—he looks even worse, and there's black hair, gray hair, all over the sheet. "Now it's up to me," he says, and goes to work with his electric trimmer, then an electric razor. She sits on the edge of the bathtub, elbows on thighs, an audience. "Omigod," she says. "It's really my father. You look a little weird, but it's my dad. Why didn't you go back to the old, elegant little pointed beard?"

"I don't know. I guess I wanted a clean sweep, a new life. Can you imagine Superman with a goatee? And don't worry. The weirdness will go away when I get out into the sun. Now, let me tell you my dream."

It *was* a prophetic dream! For that very day, who calls but his uncle! Adam's out with Lisa buying sheet music for camp. When he gets back, the message is on their machine. Curt. *It's Cal. I've been thinking. Call back.* His telephone number, which he never gave before. "Lisa! You'll never believe who called!" Adam calls back; in the middle of Adam's message, Cal picks up.

"You can never tell what kind of bastard might be calling. Political calls and charities. You wouldn't believe how many, 'spite I got an unlisted phone. So. Anyway. I've been thinking."

"Uh-huh."

"I've been thinking. How would you like your old uncle to come for a visit?"

The quaver in Cal's voice. A put-on. Parody by an old guy of an old guy.

"You're saying you want to *visit* us? You're going to come up to Cambridge?"

"What's the matter? You think I'm too goddamn old to get up there? I take a cab to Penn Station, pick up the noon Acela high-speed train, get some lunch and a drink and take a snooze, and I'm at Back Bay. What the hell."

"Sounds good. Well, I'm delighted. Now you're talking." He looks over at Lisa and bugs his eyes in amazement. "*When* are we talking, Cal? What's a good day?"

"This goddamn afternoon we're talking. Back Bay Station, 3:40. I used to come into Boston selling carpets for old man Schultz back when. I ever tell you about that? Sure. Today. Hey. And you take a cab. Don't drive. *Take a cab.* I got my reasons. I don't kid around, mister. Okay, I want to see my granddaughter before I drop dead. Not that I'm kicking any buckets right away.

"You said you want to see your granddaughter? Your *granddaughter*?"

"We got a few things to talk about, sonny boy. I been thinking. You got a right to know."

11

Lisa hears her dad take the stairs two at a time to her room, knock, and open. Her mom was always so quiet you'd turn around and—magic—there she was. Not Dad. He clumps around. Now, standing in the doorway, he strips off his outer shirt to show her the Mitzvah Man tee.

She laughs, admiring the artwork on his chest.

He lifts his hands in heroic gesture and says, "Didn't I say? Here I dream about Cal last night, and this morning he calls! My uncle—or is it my father?— he's coming up to pay us a visit."

"You serious, Dad? Your father? I have a new grandfather?"

He puffs out his lips.

"And you think it's prophecy?"

"What else? Yes. Maybe. Don't get cynical. Yes. I think so."

"Dad? My handsome, beardless dad? You ever think this might just be traumatic for a kid?"

"*Traumatic!* Where'd you get that word? *Traumatic?*"

"*Trauma, traumatic, traumatized....* Oh, please! No big deal. It was one of our vocabulary words last term."

"Sure. Of course, traumatic. Changing grand-fathers in midstream?"

Because Cal is coming, she takes a new look around the house. It all looks different from the way it looked to her five minutes ago. Uch! Such a mess. All this time, she's tried to make sure it's pretty, happy-looking, with flowers and tablecloths. She hasn't thought about dirt. It's as if she's been asleep for a century and the house has gotten omigod dirtier and dirtier. No Celia to come in and clean twice a week. She has to put her foot down. "Dad? I'm sorry. I can't stand anyone coming to this house and the house looking so awful."

"Does it look awful?"

In answer, embarrassed to seem *autocratic* (another word from vocab), she points to the cracker crumbs on the living room floor. She waves at him to follow her and stands, arms folded, in the doorway to the kitchen, and she points to the floor, to the counters.

"Okay," he says. "Now?"

"Please, please! Yes, now. I'll work with you, okay? We'll blitz the house."

"That's your mother's word, *blitz*."

"So? Let's make a list," she says, "and check it off." From the back pocket of her jeans, she takes a pad and pencil, puts "To Do" at the top and looks up at him.

The activity helps a lot. Still, her belly churns. It's not just traumatic, this weirdness about Cal—it's like freaky. Her grandfather! At least maybe. She remembers the stories—what a bully this man was to his brother, her Dad's real dad, the dad who brought him up. Stories about what a show-off he is. That funny story of the restaurant where they walked out on him. Her father almost getting himself arrested in his uncle's lobby. She's definitely *traumatized*. And *freaked*. But with the house vacuumed, the floors cleaned, the piles of books returned to the bookcases, she takes a shower and dresses up in school clothes—white blouse, brown skirt.

They get to the station early; the Acela pulls in right on time. So sleek, so pretty! She'll insist they ride the Acela next time they go to New York. People get off, people get off. As the very last man steps down, her father laughs and starts forward, taking her with him by the elbow, waves. "Look at that guy!" The man doesn't walk hunched over like some old people. In a pale beige linen suit he struts from the train and up the platform as if he were a (retired) Marine general. Long strides and a suede jacket with padded shoulders that make him look like a big man—which he's not. He carries a light overnight case. Look at that big cowboy hat, look at those corny old brown and white shoes. Lisa has seen shoes like those only in movies—in *Seabiscuit*, for instance. Spotting Lisa and Adam, Cal touches brim with thumb and forefinger; Lisa kind of expects him to say, *And how're y'all, li'l lady?* in Western drawl. But he stops ten feet off, puts down the leather case, stands hands on his hips, says, "Well, come *on*. Ain't somebody going to carry this damn suitcase of mine? So—you're the daughter."

She goes up to Cal to give him a hug. He is, after all, *some* kind of relative. But he pulls back, offers a hand. "No offense—what's your name— Lisa? Lisa, no offense, but I haven't had a cold for three years, and I ain't gonna start now. Kids are notorious germ carriers. But I'm very glad to meet you."

"I'll take that bag, Cal," her father says, and does.

"I'm just staying one night," Cal says. "Just so you don't worry." His voice! Lisa wants to giggle. It's as if he has a bass speaker inside his chest. His voice is full of vibrato, and it's so obvious he loves the sound.

Her father says, not smiling, "Stay, don't stay. I won't kick you out, Uncle Cal, the way you tried to kick me out."

"Tried? Listen—if I really tried, you'd be out on the pavement on your ever-lovin'. I see you shaved your old-man beard. Now you look like something." He pats his own cheeks.

A limo—a black Lincoln, not a stretch limo—is waiting just outside the station, the driver holding up a sign in Magic Marker: *Mr. Friedman.* "That's me," he says. "Pile in, kids." *Kids?*

Dad tells the driver how to go.

They drive slowly through Copley Square traffic and cross the Charles on the Mass Avenue Bridge. "Look at those sailboats down there. This is one of the only cities made something of their goddamn river." Her Dad at one window, Lisa in the middle, then Cal. Now he doesn't mind sitting close to her, though when he turns to her, he leans back to avoid getting breathed on. Now he pats her shoulder, pat-pat-

pat, as if she were six years old. A dumb pet! She doesn't like this atten-tion at all. As a matter of fact it makes her mad. How weird this guy is! "Some girl you got," Cal sings to Dad. "What a kid. Some kid. Huh? You're really something," he says. "Gonna be one hell of a knockout in a couple of years."

At this, Lisa rolls her eyes at her Dad, then shuts them and slumps way down in the leather seat, and the two men blab past her all the way home.

"Well how do you like that? Real nice place," Cal says, as the limo turns into the cul-de-sac. "Like a country house right in the goddamn city. Smart!"

They sit in the living room. Cal is still wearing the Stetson. Tilting it back on his head, he stretches out his hands along the wooden rim of the couch back. You know what he's like? Lisa thinks. A silly five-foot-nine John Wayne wannabe.

"Got some things to talk about, Adam."

She takes the hint. "Can I make you some tea?" Lisa says with her best school manners.

"You bet. Real black tea, kid, none of this faggoty herb stuff."

"You bet," she says. "Black, absolutely." She's grinning all the way to the kitchen.

Adam waits till Lisa's out of earshot. He knows Cal's delighting in the suspense, and Adam, not wanting to give him the gift of eagerness, keeps his voice as low-key as he can make it. "All right, Uncle Cal. So . . . you've got something to tell me?" Cal's leaning back, so Adam leans back in his easy chair.

"No, no, goddamnit, I'm gonna tell you *my* way. Okay?" He clears his throat and what he's got to say, he kind of chants. "Okay, Adam. You remember how your Mom used to slip you five-dollar bills, ten-dollar bills—'Don't tell your Dad'? Am I right? Sure. And you, out of loyalty to your Dad, you'd refuse. Right? Well? Where you think she got that extra moolah?"

"From you? You're saying you gave her money?"

Cal holds up a hand for silence. "Your mother, God, she had such a mouth on her, that woman. I tried to sweeten her up, sugar her up with a little dough now and then. A hundred here, a hundred there."

"But what did she mouth *about*? Wasn't it that you wouldn't give my Dad a raise? So why not give it to *him*?"

"A raise is for performance, kiddo. Okay, so let's go back a few more years. Your Dad was in Palm Springs out in California, taking care of our Pop. He was a good soul, your Dad. I'd never say different. He got the *nice* genes, I got the *smarts*. So anyway, one day your mother gets all dressed up and comes down to see me. This is when we had the place on West 54th. She won't take no for an answer—just like you as a matter of fact—and I say, 'Arlene, what do you want from me?' and she says, 'It's time you brought my husband home, don't you think, Cal?' and I say, 'Hey. The guy's not my slave. I don't own him. Maybe he's got his reasons.' I meant reasons for staying away from her—a little dig, but I didn't get explicit. I tried to sweeten her up, see? She was some beautiful woman, your mother, even if she was too damn argumentative. For a woman, I mean. So I wanted to be nice, I said, 'You're lonely, that's your problem. Let me take you out to dinner.'"

"And so you took her out to dinner."

"Right. I took her out to a swanky place, I can't remember. We have a great dinner, and we're laughing, I get Arlene laughing, and I promise her I'll tell my brother to get on a train and come home. Your Dad hated to fly—you know that, right? So I take her home, and I stop in for a drink, and we get to talking, and . . . we have another drink, and we talk some more, and we look at each other, and we run out of words, and next thing we know, m'boy, it's the following morning, I got to go to work, and right away I call her up, I tell her, 'Christ, I'm sorry, Arlene, oh Christ, this is crazy, he's my big brother.' See, I introduced them. At the time I was still married. But when this happened, I wasn't married anymore. So I said, 'That was one night, let's put it out of our minds.'"

"And that's it?"

"Not . . . exactly. No. We decided we ought to talk about that night we had. Just talk, you understand? And we got together, and, well, you can figure out the rest. And so on."

"So on?"

"So on and so on. And then your Dad comes home, I feel like shit, I say nothing. He never knew a thing. Your Dad and I go up to Saratoga to the races the way we did every year. We pal around. A couple of sports, all dressed up the way we used to. I give him a raise. Couple of months go by, we find out your Mom's gonna have a baby—that's you. So I don't know."

"You don't know," Adam says.

"Well, maybe I do. I looked at the dates, and I guess I know. All right? Now, your true Dad—no question—" Cal says, hand raised as if he were giving holy or legal testimony "—that's the guy who brought you up. My big brother, Norm. But biology is another story. Now, in 2005, we could do a DNA test and maybe figure it out, but I ain't about to, and you're not gonna after I'm dead, cause I'm gonna have myself cremated and the damn ashes dumped in the ocean."

"And my Dad never knew."

"I hope to Christ not. Your Dad was a decent guy. People say I'm a selfish bastard. Well, they're right. That's me in a nutshell. I hope you don't have my selfish genes. You don't seem to. I can't believe it—" Cal starts laughing, can't stop, takes out a big, white handkerchief and wipes his face, the laughter building, tears in his eyes from laughter.

"What?"

"You! *You* coming to bless *me*. Blessing me—what a goddamn joke!"

Lisa is standing at the door to the kitchen, big wooden tray in her hands, looking un-amused. "Tell him, Dad. It's no joke. You tell him you're Mitzvah Man."

"What's that?"

"Partly," Adam says, "it's blessing a relative even if he tries to get rid of you." But he's surprised at Lisa's seriousness. "Look." Adam unbuttons his shirt and points to the tee. "Lisa made this for me. See? *Mitzvah Man.*"

"You drew that picture? Pretty damn good. So—'Mitzvah'—like a good deed? Right?"

"Thanks," Lisa says.

"Well, it's translated that way. It also means a commandment. Both. A good deed and a commandment from God are kind of the same thing. But strapping on *tefillin*, say, that's a *mitzvah*, but it's not a 'good deed.'"

"So what's the joke—Mitzvah Man?"

"Well, it's half a joke. Like a holy Superman? But also, Lisa's right—it's no joke. So, for instance, one thing I do well is make money. That's my gift—"

"You?" Cal laughs. "What the hell kind of money can you make?"

"You see? You don't know a thing about me, Cal. I built and sold three companies in the nineties. It's something I can do."

"Well, hell, the nineties. A guy took his hat off and held it upside down, money plopped in. I was retired by then. Too bad. So you do okay in business? See? My genes, all right."

It comes through Adam's mouth without thought: "I can make a foundation. A *mitzvah* foundation. *The* Mitzvah Foundation."

"It's got a ring to it. What the hell does it mean?"

"I don't know. The words just came this second. A foundation to help—help whom? I don't know. People in pain, people who've got a need. I hear their cries. You can't walk out on the street and not see it in their faces. Oh, they cover it up, but you can see right through the masks. I don't want to raise big money for huge issues—like Bill Gates taking on malaria—just help on a personal level, in a small way. Lisa knows, she's been to one family, the Eisens. A good family, the boy recovering from leukemia. Their insurance won't cover their expense. The medications. I haven't thought this out, Cal. But that's what I want to do. Small loans. Small gifts. Through a diversified investment portfolio, so the money is replenished."

Cal shrugs. "It's a peculiar idea. But I get it. I can see how it could work out. Now, Mitzvah Man, how about Chez Robert for dinner? My treat. I already made the reservations."

Lisa sets down the tray: banana bread, a pot of tea. Adam says, "Lisa baked this herself."

"Say! What a fabulous wife she's gonna make," Cal says. Then— "Sorry, yeah, yeah, you're not supposed to say that anymore. I'm an old unreconstructed macho s.o.b., Lisa darling." He takes hold of Adam's tee shirt. "You made this, you make the drawing? Fabulous. So—where you gonna put me, Adam? I've got to get a real nap in or I won't be worth a damn thing tonight when we go out on the town."

For the first time this afternoon, Adam looks past the pizzazz, the display of vitality, to see the dark sacs under Cal's eyes, the sallow skin. The Stetson hides it. Old. Cal's getting old.

In the gracious, quiet dining room at Chez Robert, while they wait for appetizers, Lisa feels like being just a little wicked. She interrupts Cal's chatter. "So, Mr. Friedman, do I call you *Grandpa*?" She's playing a game. If she tosses him this hot potato, what's he going to do about it? But truly even more it's for her dad. To shock him as payback for his shocking her.

Her grandfather—or whatever this man is to her—wears a navy blazer and white silk shirt tonight, with a beautiful pale cream tie. Très expensive. The way he looks to her is he believes he's being photographed for a movie magazine. At her question, he gets ruffled, puts down an olive and wipes his hands on his napkin to give himself time before he speaks. "So, your dad told you the whole story, huh? These days guys can't keep their trap shut."

"Dad tells me everything. He does. Absolutely everything. Right, Dad?" She makes intense circles with her forefinger on the white tablecloth to deal with her unease.

"First off, I'm too young to be 'grandpa.' I'm just seventy-nine. Practically a teenager myself. And 'grandpa' ain't got no couth, you get me? I may be toothless but I ain't couthless. You can call me 'Grandfather.' I'd like that."

"*Grandfather*. Grandfather," she says, "please pass the rolls."

"That's it. Now *that* I like the sound of. S'okay, Adam m'boy?"

"It's okay with me."

"And you, mister, I don't expect you to call me 'Dad.' When it says, 'Honor thy father and thy mother,' it's not talking about some guy who plain had too much to drink a couple of times."

"Sounds like more than a couple of times, Cal."

"See? First you bless me, now you stick in a dig." Cal puts a hand on Lisa's hand. "I tell you how sorry I am about your Mom? My own Mom, your great grandmother, died when I was sixteen. So don't think I don't know what you're going through. Well, I'm off to the little boys' room." He slaps down his napkin and excuses himself.

"Weird," Lisa whispers as they watch him go. "Really, really weird."

"When I was a kid your age," Adam says, "he was such a big deal in our lives. You can't imagine. When my mother wasn't despising my father, she was hating Cal."

"Why did she hate him so much?"

"Well, because he kept my father a *shnorrer*, a beggar, poor. He kept him on a short leash."

And here comes Cal, trying, as he negotiates a path between the tables, to appear smooth like an old dancer or athlete, but she sees by the mechanical way his shoulders roll that he's stiff and creaking under the grin.

"So," she says, "you think he's really your father? I mean like genetically? Do you want him to be? I mean, he's such a fake, such a big-shot phony. I don't think I like the idea."

Cal comes to the table at Lisa's *I don't think I like the idea.* "What idea, sweetheart?"

"Well. The idea of you all of a sudden being my grandfather."

"Well, hell," Cal says. "You just give me a chance. I'll bet I grow on you." He tilts his chair toward her, gingerly wraps an arm around her shoulder and pats with the tips of his fingers.

Lisa eases away and giggles. "Oh, Grandfather, you just love this, don't you?"

"I didn't start all this, Lisa, my dear. Did your dad tell you how he put on a one-man show in my lobby? And what about you, Adam, m'boy?"

"You mean, do I want you to be my father? I'm not sure. Some genes to have, if you don't mind my saying so! I don't know, Cal. Does it matter what I want? We're who we are."

"Hell," Cal says. "Now you tell me. What we have to do t'get food around here? They shooting the damn cow back in the kitchen? You call this *service*?"

This, Lisa thinks, rubbing the poked shoulder, is supposed to be charming. *Quel* phony.

12

It's one thing to wear a Mitzvah Man tee shirt and write a check to Uri Eisen, another to build a foundation. What is it he's building? He hears cries for help, but aren't those cries in his own head? Whom will he help? How will he help them? And why? Is he trying to blur away his own suffering by changing its terms, coping instead with the pain of others?

Would that be a bad thing?

But isn't it true that when he shops at Whole Foods or the farmers' market, when he walks through Harvard Square or runs along the river, he feels the pain of others like a song he hears faintly? Listen up, he's told. He's listening. Even at the dojo. Some of the men and women in training are completely there. But others are straining; you can imagine the original pain that's led them here, as he knows the humiliation and rage that led him into training more than twenty years ago.

Whom will he help? He can imagine a guy who's got a dead-end job at McDonald's or a Wal-Mart, someone with a family to support, and maybe he can help the guy get a G.E.D. and pay his tuition at a community college or at UMass-Boston.

Now that he thinks it through, he's going to need a lot of money, much, much more than he can take from his own pocket. In fact, if he wants to make a real foundation, he'll need to develop serious capital. A couple of calls to his lawyer, Arthur Fischberg, and the paperwork gets set up. Getting non-profit tax status from the IRS and the Commonwealth, he knows, will take some time.

Then, when the foundation grows—*if* the foundation grows—he'll require a board to oversee it and someone to attend to funds coming in, funds going out. But for now what Adam requires is money. He remembers the strange (admit it) exciting roll he was on the last time. Days of success, playing the lines on a graph, knowing he was in God's hands. Then that feeling seemed to evaporate. And now? Is he in God's hands now?

Lisa goes off to play for the morning in the trio her teacher helped her find six months ago, all early teens, a boy on viola, girl as cellist. Then, after practice, the violist's mother has agreed to drive them up to Plum Island. Lisa carries a swimsuit. He knows she's a little embarrassed showing her gawky, skinny beauty in a bathing suit. She's embarrassed at how little her breasts still are, how narrow her hips. But this morning at breakfast she didn't once hold her knuckles against her mouth. She went off grinning, the bathing suit in a backpack. So Adam's relieved about her, happy she's okay. He's alone for the day; he sits down in his study with a cup of coffee and goes on-line.

Shira used to hate to see him day-trade, though she never said so. He understood; he understands. While what you do reflects real production and sale, to stare at numbers on a screen, the dance of a graph, seems disconnected from anything in the real world—rice, corn, cotton, tin, men in a field, in a mine. Yet he says, *If it be Your will that I make a foundation to perform the* mitzvot *of* tzedek *(justice, righteousness) and* chesed *(loving kindness), guide me today.* He logs on.

For an hour, he just watches. He feels clumsy, self-conscious. At one moment he thinks he'll make a move, then holds back. He watches until he's nothing but eyes; whatever's happening is outside his ken. He finds his breathing deepen and slow, becomes aware of the blood humming in his ears. There's no dropping away of his stomach this time as if he were in a plane hitting clear-air turbulence. It feels gentler this time, as if he's hovering, sitting still in his chair but hovering just above himself. Now he buys. Buys again. Jots down notes on the legal tablet, though the trading program keeps a record for him. When he was a serious tennis player, there were days when from the first warm-up volleys his racket's rhythm met the ball's rhythm, ball met sweet spot at the golden moment. He didn't try. He didn't have to remind himself, Drop the shoulder, follow through fluidly. So it goes today. Nothing mystical happens. It's simply as if the perfect buy, the perfect sell, have already happened, and, remembering what they were, he buys, he sells accordingly.

He knows for sure: this is no way to make money in the market; neither in futures nor stocks. God won't help a gambler for very long. He secretly believes—secretly in the sense that he avoids acknowledging it to himself—God has shown him that he is held. But in the long run God will run with the guy who makes solid long-term investments, builds a diversified portfolio. Today is warm-up, volleying, stretching exercises. By the end of the day, not having bet the house, he's made two thousand dollars; with one thousand of it he'll help the Eisens.

He calls Judith Eisen, makes an appointment for tonight. Giving thanks, he puts on an apron to prepare brisket and onions.

Lisa comes into the kitchen, bubbling, scuffing her flip-flops along the quarry tile floor. "Sonia wants us to perform this Sunday at a wedding. Okay, Dad? Like, we actually get paid." She runs her hand like a separate creature along the countertop. "I think she's been planning this a while, and that's why she's given us short pieces, baroque, Renaissance, dumb, pretty little pieces, to practice. We complained, but I bet this is why." She stops. "You okay, by the way?"

"Oh, I'm great. Lisa? After dinner I want to take you to meet the Eisens."

"That family? With the sick kid? I guess. How come?"

"First because it isn't right to relate to them impersonally. Then— I've got an idea."

"Uh-oh."

"Wise guy."

"Girl. Wise *girl* in case you haven't noticed." She pulls her hair back with one hand while she lifts the top of the casserole with the other. She dips her face. "Mmm. Smells so good."

"Brisket."

"Omigod, I love brisket. . . . It's not a lot of money, but it's a professional gig. Wow."

"Lisa!" He suddenly notices. Well, no, actually he noticed right away but didn't have the courage to interrupt. "Have you been wearing those all day?"

"What do you mean *those*?"

"*You* know. Flip-flops."

"I've been wearing flip-flops every single day and it never bothered you."

"And those mini jean shorts you're wearing so low on your hips with that awful, garish silver belt. There are a good three inches of the middle of you showing. And don't say 'Oh, Dad.'"

"Oh, Dad! Please."

"Just because Jennifer does? Jennifer Licht? I've seen the way they let her dress."

"Please!"

"And don't tell me all the girls dress like that. I'm serious. What would your mother say?"

"We'll never know, will we?" Lisa says. She becomes solemn, dour, he wishes he hadn't brought it up. He can't reply. Her thin girl-legs—he looks—and feels a little embarrassed looking. Same legs she walks around the house with; it's her consciousness of her budding teenage prettiness that makes the difference. "Lisa? So I made some money today. Money to give away."

"To the Eisens."

"Right. You'll change that outfit. Okay? For me?"

She doesn't answer.

But her outfit has changed by the time they drive to Somerville. Now she's wearing her mother's pearls, though they don't belong with the pretty, cotton tee she's wearing, a tee with a neck scooped low enough to reveal her little cleavage. He decides not to complain. "Nice to see you in those pearls. I got them for your mom."

She knows.

The Eisens live in a third-floor apartment in an old wood-frame house, a floor of big rooms, refinished wooden floors, high wainscoting, heavily varnished. Uri Eisen stands at the top of the stairs smiling down. "Mr. Friedman, welcome, welcome." Adam sees he's dressed up. The white shirt is fresh, pressed, has definitely not been through a day at work. It's the first time he's met the Eisens. From the voice he'd somehow imagined a man about his own age, but Uri is young, oh, thirty at most and could pass for twenty, a delicate man with a long, thin, handsome face. "Come on up, Mr. Friedman." Before they're even at the top, he asks, "What can I get you?"

"A Coke," Lisa says.

"Definitely *not* a Coke," Adam says. "Some iced tea for both of us, okay, honey?" It interests him she'd make a Coke-move like that. *And* the shorts worn at her hips. He doesn't mind; in fact, he's glad. It means she's letting down her hair a little, means she doesn't feel she has to be so perfect.

He likes the simplicity of the apartment. And he knows Lisa is pretty comfortable here, knows by her big, easy movements as she pokes around. When he was a student he'd lived with housemates in an apartment very like this one. His was a lot less neat. Maybe the Eisens have straightened for him. But at least it means their troubles haven't sucked them under. Books and wood, assorted furniture probably picked up at tag sales, nothing matching anything else but all of a piece. There's a large covered porch outside the living room; it's hard to see the view—just of other tall houses—through the laundry that hangs on two lines outside.

Adam is never comfortable at first meeting a man; it's women he's good with. Uri's wife, Judith, is big-boned, big-hipped, calm; she doesn't look haggard as Adam had expected. With a warm smile on a broad face, she wears a soft, youthful beauty that, at least he imagines, doesn't bother examining itself. Adam is comfortable right away. Come on. More than comfortable. So comfortable with her that he becomes uncomfortable. And the boy, David, whom he expected to find drooping in a hospital bed, is up and around, baldness covered by a Red Sox cap, and in spite of the cap, he's soulful, deep-eyed, smiling. Except for hair loss, he looks like an ordinary kid, a bright-eyed kid. He's maybe eight; his sister Marjorie is about a year younger than Lisa but further along toward looking womanly.

Judith, he's learned over the phone, was marketing manager for a clothing catalogue. She was working nights on an MBA when the leukemia hit David. "Our boy had the most beautiful head of hair," she says when David and his sister go off to watch TV. Lisa goes with them.

"He will again. I'm sure."

"Please God," she says. "There's every indication he's getting stronger. The bone marrow transplant from his sister worked. She was able to be the donor, and since then, he's become more special to her. She hopes he'll have her hair, and he might. Now he's in remission; it's just being steady, being patient, being careful with his food, with his medicine, and keeping up his spirits."

"I look at you five minutes I know you'll do that. I guess you've heard—Lisa and I know a lot about having to keep up spirits."

"Yes, Mr. Friedman. The rabbi told us. Rabbi Klein. I'm so sorry."

Uri tells him about the Jewish community in Johannesburg, dwindling, yet cohesive, since the end of apartheid. They felt at home there but came to the States because he was offered a great job—and Judith could study here at Boston University. Adam shakes his head—seeing that suddenly their upwardly mobile lives were turned upside down. He likes the unpretentiousness of this man; and he sympathizes. But Judith, well Judith is something else. Adam glows in her intensely female presence. Can he work with her, knowing this? Of course. He'll never act on it.

He knows about Judith's background from Uri and from the rabbi. And before he came he had a hunch about her, the idea he mentioned to Lisa. "Here's the scoop. I'm starting a foundation. A 'Mitzvah Foundation.'" And he explains. "It's just beginning. Just getting off the ground.

Well, look. For me it's a gift to be permitted to give you a gift. But I know how you feel. You don't want gifts. So Judith, if you want to help out, only a little at first, well, I could use the help. You think? Working on organizational details, money details? From your home, of course—that's the point." He lays it out for her.

Uri slaps his hands together, laughs from pleasure and breaks out a bottle of port. "Adam, I can also offer some help if you wish. I can help you put up a simple website. So you can refer people to the site and money can come in. Contributors can pay with a credit card on-line. Easy!" Adam knows Uri's trading on his youth, his ingenuousness. Youth is his shtick; there's a falsity about it. But that doesn't change anything. The fact that it's so visibly a shtick makes him seem all the more an innocent. Adam wants to take him on, take him in; love for this family opens in his chest.

"How great. Yes, absolutely. Thank you." Glancing around the pale yellow kitchen, white-painted tongue-and-groove wainscoting, pots hung up from hooks, Adam nods. Oh yes, yes, Judith's gone out of her way to make everything so neat and clean. The way, he says to himself, his mother did when Cal came to the house.

Saying good night, he pumps Uri's hand, Judith's he shakes more delicately, kisses the top of David's cap—and all the way home feels stupid having done so. He handed Uri the check along with research from the web into the kind of help he can get from the state and federal governments for medical bills not covered by Uri's insurance. On the way down the stairs he takes Lisa's hand.

"That's a real nice family," she says on the way home. Aach, he thinks, that's the kind of comment Shira used to make, and make with the same intonations. He nods. "She'll be a help, Judith will. She can handle administrative details. Once this gets going, she'll be necessary."

"Pretty, isn't she?" Lisa says. He raises his eyebrows at her. "I saw you noticed, Dad."

"Lisa, my honey, I always notice."

"Not always. . . . Dad? You don't seem so weird anymore. I'm noticing that, which is great."

Next day, next week, he calls in favors, plays unconscionably on consciences of good men.

He gets on the phone with Ben at work in New York and tells him about the Mitzvah Foundation. At this point, no, he can't take a tax-deductible check; the foundation needs to be processed as a non-profit. He wants pledges. He's not looking for small, get-off-my-back pledges. We're talking serious gifts. He calls in favors, men and women he worked with over the years, people for whom he wrote lavish praise that helped get them good positions. People who simply liked him, respected him—residue of a career-full of mostly good relationships.

He keeps the thought of Uncle/Father Cal on the back burner. Why not try? He might very well come through. But he lets it simmer.

Next he goes after the membership list of his synagogue. Academics, lawyers, hi-tech folks, only one or two families really wealthy, but all with enough to make him feel fair bothering them. From these folks he expects smaller pledges. He tells them, via email and over the phone, that this foundation is in honor of Shira. Who could refuse? Everyone in the congregation loved Shira. She was a member of the *chesed* committee. She'd helped organize, busy as she was, the last two Chanukah parties. And what about the folks from the community orchestra, and what about her trio? Few of these are rich people, but a hundred here, fifty there, add up. And her colleagues, the circle of medical professionals she knew. He's merciless. He calls the parents of Lisa's peers at Somerset. Nobody seems to get upset. Everyone likes the idea—not a big, impersonal charity, but small help person-to-person. Small loans, small gifts. In Shira's honor.

And it *is* for Shira. This is *tikkun*, the repair of the world. It doesn't make up for Shira's death, but it's a way of making something holy out of it. He doesn't say this to Lisa.

By the end of the week, by the time he drives Lisa up to music camp in Maine, he's raised pledges of almost a quarter of a million dollars—some of that, his own money. And that's enough to invest, enough to get started. Most of the drive to camp, he lays out plans, offers alternatives, asks her what she thinks, spins out ideas he knows are cockeyed.

Lisa's eased by his work on the foundation, relieved that he's deep in it. He doesn't seem so crazy to her now, no crazier than he ever did. He talks about God's plan, but he doesn't get that Look in his eyes. Mom used to call him Mr. Hyper. On the drive up to camp, Lisa takes off her shoes, puts her feet up on the dash, and out of a case of CDs, plays disc jockey for him. "Dad? Listen to this."

She's brought her mom's violin with her to camp, repaired so beautifully that she has to get six inches away to find where the wood had cracked. On the ride up she's afraid to take it out of its case, but when they stop at a rocky beach on the side of the road in Camden and finish sandwiches and drinks, alone there at the table she caresses the violin like a cat. It's damp here by the ocean; she absolutely should *not* take the violin from its case. But it soothes her, makes her happy. "Play for me," he says. Without sheet music, she plays the first part of a piece by Dvorak that Sonia gave her last week, and he listens, his eyes dimming, shutting. She likes it when he nods like that, as if he's saying *yes* about the music. *We can have a pretty nice life together,* she thinks, *kind of sad but nice. We'll remember Mom for each other.* Half of her stays with her fingering and bowing, half with the moment between them—or among them: she, her father, her mother's violin.

She gets to the big house her dad calls Victorian and to the big lawn going down to the sea, where you crush thyme as you walk and the smell mixes with the smell of ocean. There's kids everywhere and music everywhere, music in the house, music from the studio out back and the stage of the covered amphitheater, and it comes back to her how she loves this place. It's her fourth year here; she goes looking for kids she's stayed in touch with and kids she hasn't. Meeting, laughing, and hugging, she finds that everyone knows about her mom. She doesn't have to say. She gets serious kisses. Her dad carries her enormous duffel to her room, room smelling of pine that composes the beds and walls, where she bunks with three other girls. Then she takes him out to the car. "Call me, honey. If you get lonely or anything, call me, email me. I love you." *Goodbye, Dad, goodbye, I'll email when I can get computer access, I'll call. Love you too.*

At the beginning, camp goes the way it always goes. Busy. So much so that there are whole hours, or anyway half-hours, when she doesn't think once about her mother. But when she goes into a practice room by herself, she talks to her. "Hello, Mom. I'm having trouble with the bow here." "Hello, Mom. My teacher told me the strangest thing: 'in practicing finger exercises watch your bow; in practicing bow exercises watch the left hand.' It seems true! How cool is that!" She imagines she's visiting places along a complicated path that her mother once walked. So her mother is present at this problem of bowing, at this exercise to gain finger independence, at this tender moment in the music, Mom's music. Much of the music she's brought belonged to her mother. This summer she wants to catch up to her mother on the path; she knows she can't, but she can get closer.

Girls with instruments run, march, back and forth across the camp, often arms locked, a trio.

The food, though they complain, is really pretty good.

How can she be lonely?

There's a shortage of pianists to accompany the string players. She's found one boy who's very good, a great sight reader, and she makes up to him, trying to keep him close. She even takes his turn washing dishes one night. She finds it easy to practice. Not thinking about the time, she finds that between chamber work and work with the orchestra plus individual practice, she's playing or studying theory five, six hours a day. The camp website makes a big deal out of their pond and sports, and sure, they get in a swim everyday, sometimes down at the beach, but good luck finding time for anything else. She emails Dad; Dad emails back. She emails Jennifer; Jen says hi back but not much else. She text messages Annie. After dinner sometimes she calls Talia.

After breakfast in the "barn," the wood-beamed dining hall with sliders cut into the walls offering a view of the bay on one side, the grand house and hills behind on the other, the campers collect at one of three duplicate bulletin boards which tell them when their lesson will be and with whom, tell each rehearsal group when and where to practice, each level of student when to go for theory. There's a wonderful busyness about the camp; everyone scurries off in opposite directions; a boy from her main chamber group scoops her up to walk together to practice. She's so busy she's almost happy.

Then, with no warning except maybe evening sadness, everything stops. On the fourth morning she finds she simply can't play. The violin weighs fifty pounds. She tells a counselor she's not feeling well and walks out of rehearsal, knowing that the eyes of the others are following her; the teacher takes her place in the trio. In the room alone, other girls at practice, she holds the violin and cries. Maybe she should use her own violin? Is that the problem? But it remains in her case under the bed. She strokes her mother's violin, she curls around it. *How weird*, she thinks, as if it were someone else's weirdness. Through lunch she stays in bed. When somebody comes in she says she's having a particularly bad period. She can't get up, she has a serious crying jag. She thinks no one notices, and while she wants to be left alone, she also wants someone to come. Mid-afternoon the camp director comes and sits with her, just sits, strokes her temple, kisses her cheek. Lisa doesn't know Miss Cole well enough for that. It's embarrassing. But she doesn't really mind. "I promise I'll positively be all right tomorrow."

"Of course you will. I know that."

That night her dad, notified by Miss Cole, calls. "Honey, here's what I think is going on. Maybe you think you're taking your mother's place? You think? You know she'd want you to play her violin, she'd be so happy. You know she'd want you to have a great summer."

"Dad! Stop!" she says, fuming. "Oh! I hate it when you do that. Psychologize. Like you know what I'm thinking better than I do. And anyway, anyway, you think I don't know that?" Next day, she's up again, hungry as she's ever been in her life, and certain bumps in her playing are smoothed out, as if she's practiced through them the day before. As if her mother had come in the night and helped her practice in a dream.

And the violin—something strange has been happening as she

plays. When she was a little girl, just a couple of years along in violin, her mother stuck strips of tape under the strings, the tape labeled with the notes—A, E, B, F, and so on. After awhile, she took off the tape. But now, as she plays, Lisa sees the points at which she places her fingers down as if they were those taped notes. And then, as she continues to practice, that changes, and it's not those pieces of tape but the notes as they appear on a sheet of music. She kind of sees the notes as if on a stave.

Towards the end of the second week, Miss Cole asks her to come to the office.

"Lisa, you need to get some things together. You're going home for a couple of days. Your father got hurt. Oh, he's perfectly all right. But we know you'll want to be with him. A friend—" Miss Cole looks at the slip of paper—"Talia Rosenthal?—is driving up right now to get you."

"What's wrong with Dad?"

"He's going to be fine. But he has a couple of broken ribs. And a mild concussion."

"What? He has a *what*?" She's at the edge of tears.

"Apparently, he did something *exceptional*. Your friend will explain. Oh, I'm sorry, Lisa. You've been through enough. But your dad's all right. He's at home and they say he's completely comfortable."

13

Adam's been waking up early, no need to adjust his schedule to anyone else's. He wakes before dawn, exercises, and *davens*, alone or at the synagogue, then goes to the dojo for practice or a private lesson with his *sensei*. Some mornings he jogs the paved walk along the Charles, watching the single sculls and crews skimming the quiet water. Today he's earlier than usual, just past 5:00, and he's jogging along the path, the river still and empty of boats. Mist rises from the water. He breathes in cool air before the city heats up.

He becomes aware of some noise by the river, behind the bushes—some animal, he thinks. Big. Too big for a raccoon. Are there bears in Boston? Then he sees a clump of men, three young guys bent over, and he hears a scream, a howl, and sees a woman on the grass. Adam stops to catch his breath. "Hey!" he calls, absurdly. "HEY!"

One of the men stands up and says something, bends down again. He sees him for two seconds at most, but the man's sway and the stumbling, clumsy stance of the others, it's enough to let him understand that they've been out drinking, and the woman—was she drinking with them? Did they stumble upon her here, was she sleeping off a drunk, is she homeless? Whatever, they're trying to get into her, he's sure of that, and yells, "You guys stand up and get out of here. Right now."

He can't see what's going on, but he sees her pants have been ripped half-off. He expects her to be a middle-aged lush, but no, she looks young, maybe twenty, who can tell?—a mess, lipstick smeared, dark hair a jumble. "Mister, you get *yourself* the fuck out of here," one of the men calls, and hunching, comes toward Adam, who backs away down the bank toward the river so he can't get jumped from behind. Three drunks without weapons. They're younger, stronger, but he stays calm. Of course they're not the same punks who slammed Shira into the car door, but at this moment it's as if they are, as if he can do them damage. It's more than helping the woman. He wants to punish them.

He takes a defensive stance, foot forward, foot behind, hands open and ready to block, body turned. The youngest man, early twenties, a messy head of blond hair falling over his face, guffaws. "Hey, will you look at that, man. Guy's scaring the shit out of me."

"Oh, yeah. Old prick's definitely taken a karate lesson."

"Should we give him another?"

The woman staggers to her feet and one of the men punches her twice and pulls her down, though by now they must know they're not going to gangbang her. In fact, Adam thinks, they're doing that for my benefit. That guy holds onto her, so he's facing only two of them. They're young and tough, white guys—accent sounds like Charlestown or South Boston. One guy, hunched down, comes at Adam slow, looking for an opening, and now he yells "FUCK!" and charges, and when he charges, it's easy, it's a move he's practiced for years. Adam simply steps aside and as the guy tumbles forward, slams the back of his head, tumbling him hard face-first into the mud at the edge of the river. Adam keeps track of him in the fight map in his head, and he turns back to the others. Now another man, beer-fat, his belly hanging over his belt, his shirt open and flapping back like a cape, dives at him to make a football tackle, and the first, behind him, is getting to his feet, so Adam, not to be caught between them, backs away from the tackle, and the guy stumbles and turns. When he swings, Adam blocks the drunken swing and clips him in the throat. He comes again; Adam gets under the punch swing, pulls the guy off balance, slams him hard on the side of the neck, and, grabbing arm and elbow, uses his hip as fulcrum to throw him hard into the first man. He hears a bone crack—arm snapping at the elbow. Thank God they're drunk; he sees the third guy let go of the girl; he's got a knife in his hand, and he's higher on the bank; Adam runs up the bank, keeping his distance, yells to the woman, "Get out of there, run! Go! Go!"—and backing off, takes his cell from his pocket and just has time to call 9-1-1 before a rock catches his temple.

For a moment he's stunned. A lone car stops on Memorial Drive. The driver steps out. Adam yells, "The cops, the cops, call the cops!" Yells—but the road is so far off he doesn't know if the driver heard. Now they swarm him; two of the men slam him from behind. He's down. No chance to use what he's learned in practicing Brazilian jiujitsu. Fool! Fool—looking down at a cell phone in the middle of a fight! Before he can make a move he's kicked in the side, kicked again, kicked in the head, and that's all he knows.

He wakes on a gurney, two EMT guys and a cop are carrying him to an ambulance. The cop pats his shoulder, "You did real good. We heard from the woman. You did a good thing. It's cool. You gonna be okay."

"I lost focus," he says, as if to his sensei, before he's out again. When he wakes again, it's in the ER at Mt. Auburn Hospital, just up the road. Black doctor in white coat looks at an x-ray, grins at him. "You're awake? Good man. Good man. Lie still, okay? You've got a concussion. Not so bad. No swelling, no fluid. It's gonna hurt, my friend. You've got a couple of broken ribs. They'll hurt worse. But don't worry—we'll take care of you. We're gonna spoil you rotten, right?" he says to a male nurse.

"Seems you're a hero, Mr. Friedman," the nurse says in a booming bass voice. "So the officer tells us."

Adam tries to laugh; the pain stops him. *Big Mitzvah Man—Lisa will laugh. Big damn kung fu superhero!* By afternoon they're ready to release him. It's Jerry Rosenthal who comes for him, drives him to their house and sets him up in the guest room. It's a pleasant room looking out on the garden and undulating brick wall. Next to the bed Jerry sits reading. "I love this goddamn Innes," Jerry says, turning the book so Adam can see the pastoral landscape, a train curving behind the hill leaving a trail of smoke.

"Right, you're working on George Innes," Adam mumbles, and gets a long answer but it falls through the floor of his mind. "Be a while before we play tennis again," Adam says.

"I'm looking forward to it, man."

The Rosenthal boys are back; they knock and say Hi, hi. They've known him forever, but seem a little awkward, shy. Danny, in a Dartmouth tee shirt—his father's alma mater; he's only in eighth grade—touches his hand gingerly. "Man," he says. "All this time we know you and here you were Jet Li and we didn't even know it." And Rob, just a year older than Lisa, a smart guy Adam has fantasized as a candidate for Lisa's hand maybe a decade from now, says, "It's on local news. We just heard it on WBUR." Adam grins, is happy to see them, but in five minutes he's exhausted and closes his eyes, pulls the flowered sheets over his head, and they tiptoe out.

He wants to get home. He wants to talk to Lisa, he tells Jerry.

"We figured you would. Talia's driving up to camp this afternoon," Jerry says. "We wanted to make sure that's what you'd want." Adam's about to mumble he doesn't want to bother Talia, but Jerry waves this away like a bad smell before it's said. "Adam. Please don't be an asshole. It's really important she sees you're okay. It's obvious. Not for you—for her. Some impressive girl you've got there," Jerry says. "Her sketches are beautiful. You know, I do have some expertise. So they tell me. I'd enjoy working with her. We ought to spend some time together, Adam, the families. Out at the Cape. Anyway, Talia's driving up. She loves Lisa. It's no problem. She'll listen to a book on the way up. You'd do the same. You would, wouldn't you, you bastard?"

"Yeah, maybe."

"Anyway, heroes deserve special favors. What's this Talia tells me about 'Mitzvah Man'?"

"It's nothing. A joke between Lisa and me. They didn't catch those guys, did they?"

"No, they got away. Sorry. The drunken shits."

"After all the training I've had. What was I thinking, losing focus, using a cell phone in the middle of a fight? What happened to that girl? The girl they were trying to rape?"

Jerry doesn't know. "She stayed around, talked to the cops. The girl—her name . . ." he consults a scrap of paper—"is Terri McEvoy—didn't know them. She knows a few details, probably not enough to find them. She met them at a bar. That's what the cop said. That's all I know. I do know what *didn't* happen, thank God. You did great, man. Just great. You want to call it being in God's hands, it's okay with me."

|14| He and Lisa spend a quiet weekend together. A reporter for *The Globe*, a reporter for *The Herald*, call. The NBC affiliate picks it up, wants to bring in a reporter, a cameraman. "Sorry. Not on Shabbos," he says. "How's Sunday?" They stop by Sunday morning. Later Rabbi Klein visits, bringing bagels. Lisa talks him into letting her stay home and nurse him for a few days. Then he'll drive her back to camp. She makes him lunch, she makes him dinner, she sits by the bed and reads *Pride and Prejudice* to him. Not to lose momentum from camp, she practices. And murmuring the Hebrew, she listens over and over to the cassette of her teacher chanting the *haftarah* from Isaiah for Lech Lecha. "Dad?" she says, sitting with him over tea, "you could have been killed. Suppose one of them had a knife. Or a gun."

One of them, he remembers, *did* have a knife. But he laughs, "I'd catch the bullet between my teeth. That's what we superheroes do."

"When you couldn't catch a rock? And then where would I be?"

"Not with Aunt Ruthie. Don't worry. I've written a codicil to my will."

"You better not die, Dad. I mean it. I'll be furious."

He smiles at her to make it a joke; looking up, he sees it's no joke. "Sorry, honey. Really—I think I was meant to help that young woman," he says.

"I hope God doesn't mean for me to be a total orphan."

When the flurry of calls by reporters is done, it's like they're on an island together in the middle of a world. They have to create a way to get through the day while he heals; they have to hammer in the posts of a life. "It reminds me," he tells her, "of a time your mom and I went to Bermuda too early in the season, and it rained and was cold, and we made the best of it reading or playing cards. Of course, I've got the foundation. There are emails and calls to make. And it's not just busywork."

"It's absolutely not. It's wonderful, Dad."

Judith Eisen stops by; she brings her son David, who hangs out with Lisa while Adam confers with Judith about the foundation.

It's painful. The second day, a headache. Then that dissipates, but every move hurts. His sensei comes by, a young Korean many-degree black belt, and they go over the fight and laugh. Laughing hurts.

The next day he takes painkillers and drives her back to camp. Just before they're leaving the house, a call from Cal. "You're a hero here in the concrete canyons," he says. "I heard it on the radio. We got a human interest story on our hands. They did an interview with that young woman and her mother. The kid's a student, a good student. You'd be embarrassed how grateful they are."

"You heard about it in New York? Really?"

"But this call isn't about your heroics. I been thinking. You got a good project going. This Mitzvah Foundation. I'll put some dough in. Okay? How does a hundred thou strike you?"

It gives Adam and Lisa something to talk about on the way back to camp. "Three hundred and fifty thousand dollars to invest," he says. "That's already serious money. But I need a couple of million to make it really work. To build an endowment, give it continuity. Beyond personal connections, how do we publicize the foundation and raise money? It's a big job."

This turns out not to be a problem.

Adam expects the story to blow over in a couple of days. But it builds. He gets a call from Ben and Margaret. They've read about him in *The Week*. In Boston there's an editorial in *The Herald*. Cameras snoop through the house. The story makes a couple of news shows. He's called "The Mitzvah Man," and they translate this into "our favorite Boston superhero, the Mitzvah Man, Mr. Do-Good." Larry Adler, the producer of a radio talk show, asks him to come on the air, get some free publicity for his foundation. "I've really got nothing to talk about," Adam tells him. But for the good of the foundation, he goes downtown to studios of an FM station he's never listened to.

They sit at a small round wooden table behind a glass wall, an engineer in the adjoining booth; it's a plain-deal table, underneath, high-tech black equipment. The studio is bare except for scattered travel posters, celebrity posters, posters of Boston, shelves with thousands of CDs, alphabetized. They talk, he responds to call-ins. He's called "Mister Mitzvah, the Good-Deed Man."

Larry Adler, late thirties but wearing an old-fogey, clip-on bow tie, has a potbelly beginning to bulge, but there's force in his eyes and in his voice. He asks how it feels to become a superhero.

"I'm no superhero. That's my daughter's joke. I've started a foundation to give help to people on a personal basis, one-on-one, that's all. We're calling it The Mitzvah Foundation." He sees that Larry Adler is barely listening, is making hand signals to the engineer. Adam gives the web address. Then he thinks for a moment and makes a serious mistake: "Look. I'm not deciding to do good. I'm trying to perform *mitzvot*, to follow God's commandments. I'm trying to listen, to do what God tells me. It's the exact opposite of a superhero. A Batman or Superman, they're full of themselves. I'm trying to be filled by God."

Now Adler is with him; he takes this up. "That's what it said in *The Globe*, Adam. *What God tells you?* So would you say you're a kind of contemporary prophet? You see yourself as a prophet, Adam?"

"That's a foolish question, Larry. Now, look. 'You don't need a weatherman to know which way the wind blows.' I don't need to be a prophet to feel violence approaching. To feel cataclysm approaching. Violence of nations, a rending of the planet, an agony of the earth, wild storms, an earth out of balance. Don't *you* feel it?" He quotes Moses: "Would that all God's people were prophets."

"You think you found yourself at that spot on the river because God wanted you there?"

"I'm not sure," Adam says. Then—". . . Yes. *Yes*, that's what I think."

"*Mystical* Mister Mitzvah!" Larry Adler says. "And a black belt fighter at the same time!"

Adam winces. "I'm no mystic," he says. "*And* no black belt. If I were, maybe I'd have seen that rock coming."

"But hey," Larry says, his voice growing guttural, "be serious. Hey! You took on three big guys half your age. You kept a girl from getting beaten, from getting raped. You tell me—am I right?—you broke that s.o.b.'s arm. I guess you know what you're doing. So, Mister Mitzvah, you think God was with you in that fight?"

"God's with us all the time. God's in this studio. If we make a place for God, God's here."

Calls start to come in. *How do you know when God asks something of you?*

Do you hear God's voice?

Suppose someone wants to help. This Mitzvah Foundation—where can we send a check?

My daughter in California needs money for a divorce . . .

"I'm glad that's over," he says to Larry Adler as the end music plays.

"Oh, yeah? You think it's over? Oh, no. It's not over." Adler grins and pumps his hand.

And the cry by Moses will become the lead in the *Herald's* story the next morning. Now he's besieged by reporters, local, some national. If he says nothing, they pump up the story by reshuffling old details; if he speaks, they quote him out of context, turning him into "The Boston Prophet, Adam Friedman. . . ." It becomes a tag—"the Boston Prophet" in the *Herald* but then in the *Globe* and on local TV news.

It begins when he gets home from Larry Adler's interview. He finds a man and a woman waiting on his porch. The guy sitting on his porch swing is in his thirties, wearing torn jeans and a shirt open to the third button, pink, with big flowers. Hawaii, Adam thinks. The woman is another story altogether; she's not with the guy. She's young, seems pretty. She's on her feet, walking back and forth, then smiles and waits for him. Adam wants to look into her eyes, but she stares down at the decking of the porch. The man looks disturbed, as if he's trying to look comfortable; his swinging is jerky, self-conscious, his face florid. Adam's wary. He can't predict: is the guy about to attack him or ask him for a handout?

"I was listening on the radio. Hey, you're okay, m'man." He rocks on the rattan swing that Adam and Shira found in an antique shop in Brighton and tied to the roof of their Camry for the ride home. He moves over to leave room for Adam, but Adam stays on his feet. "You're mucho okay."

Adam nods. "Good. I'm relieved. Here I thought I wasn't so okay." A handout.

"No. You're okay, all right. So if you've got God on your side, all I want from you is fifty bucks for lottery tickets—and a number to play. Fifty bucks, we split the winnings. What's fifty bucks if I just spend it? I don't even get dinner and a place to sleep. But if we hit it with a ticket . . ."

Adam laughs. "Think I might be lucky? If I'm so lucky, then two bucks should do it for us. Right?"

"Yeah, well, how about twenty?"

It's a cloudy afternoon, muggy, feels like it's going to rain. The Paroissiens' dog is barking behind its invisible fence. Adam is amused by the guy's chutzpah and ingenuity. "How about ten?" He reaches into his wallet, keeping a weather eye open, and hands the man a ten-dollar bill. "Good luck to us. What's your name?"

The guy stands up and shakes his hand. "I'm Tim Wright. I'm Tim, right?" he jokes, probably for the ten-thousandth time. "So. What's your birthday, Adam?"

Adam laughs. "You want it for a number? That's great, Tim. I'm October fifteenth," he says.

The man kisses the bill, folds it away, and sticks out his hand and shakes; he goes off with ten dollars and a number.

The woman—young, lean, pretty, in a skirt and a little blouse with the navel and a navel ring showing—has been waiting patiently; she looks at him now and waves, as if he were fifty yards away instead of three feet. And right away he knows. "You're the woman by the river."

"I figured I should thank you. You're in the book. I'd've phoned, if you didn't turn up soon."

At first, Terri's voice is flat, not committing her to anything. She snatches glances, shrugs, looks serious, as if he were her father. Clearly, she wants to impress him as serious. She seems so young; baby face, open eyes. He should call her parents. *McEvoy* should be easy to find.

"I'm glad I could help," he says. "You work in Boston? You a student? How did you get in a bar at your age?"

"I'm legal. I just look young. I'm twenty-two. Jesus, I was so scared. See, those guys met me in a bar, we sat around after the bar closed, and—don't tell anyone—we smoked a joint together, you know, and drank some more. I thought they were okay. We were laughing. There was nothing . . . sinister. I was with this other woman, but she left with somebody. They said it was so late, they'd walk me back to B.U.—they didn't want me walking back alone. One of them had a car, but he was too tanked to drive. I wasn't sure about them, but we were all kidding around. Then they got me by the river, and I don't know if they planned it or what, but they pulled me down."

"Cops still have no leads?" He asks, though he knows. He called the detective in charge of the case this morning.

"You kidding?"

"You're very, very lucky."

"And I'm real grateful, Mr. Friedman. I'm no moron or anything, Mr. Friedman. I go out drinking sometimes, but not like that. At B.U. I've got a 3.6 average. I work in the B.U. bookstore part-time, I take courses all summer. So please. Don't think I'm a bum. You still hurting?"

"Not much."

"You were so *great.*" She draws out *g-r-e-a-t* in a long, sliding-down tone, flatness gone, then covers her face with her hands. What's the gesture mean? She doesn't want to be seen? Or is she going through it again behind her hands?

"I've never been 'great' the way you say it. Like *cool*. I'm pretty much the opposite of cool."

"It was very cool, the way you fought those guys."

"I guess maybe it was. Except for pulling out that cell phone, middle of a fight. That wasn't cool. Can I get you a cup of tea?"

"Sure," she says. "Sometimes I drink tea, too," she laughs. "Black tea, okay?"

"I'll be right back." He goes in to make tea, leaving her on the porch swing. He'd be uneasy taking her inside, as if Shira might look at him strangely, as if he fears letting in lawlessness. Yet all her gestures are subdued. Except for short skirt and skimpy blouse, Terri's playing the lady. She rocks on the wicker porch swing that hangs from a beam. Her skinny knees are crossed, her toes pushing the swing. He makes tea, remembers Cal wanted just black tea, too, and brings it out to her. Her hair, auburn, fine, is tied back in a barrette. Strands keep coming loose, and she pushes them away from her face. The gesture sends a pulse of tenderness through him, makes him want to touch her hair, to take her in. "Want honey?" he asks, sitting down beside her.

"Yeah. Thanks. Nice house," she says. "A house like this, like in the country but it's right near Harvard Square. You're real lucky."

They sit looking out at the mangy front garden. He hasn't done a single thing to it this year. The gardens were Shira's. He doesn't like to look out at the mess, but he can't even clean away winter debris. They stir honey into their tea. "Where do you come from?"

"I grew up in the country. New Hampshire. Outside Concord. I don't mean you're lucky in everything. I read in the papers. I mean about your wife."

"Be honest, okay, Terri? Do your parents know?"

"My mom knows. That's where I've been since it happened."

"Right. You were on the radio together. And your dad?"

"My father? He doesn't live with us."

"I don't mean to bug you. . . . That's not true. I *do* mean to bug you. It worries me. Talk about lucky. You know what a close thing that was?"

"Right. That's why I came. So . . . thanks," she says again, but dismally. Her eyes are wet, though she's smiling. He burrows down into the look. He believes she's here to thank him. But here she wants him to think she's a good girl—it seems evident she wants him to think that— so then why does she dress so . . . loosely? Her eyes go soft, look into his eyes, then look down. Is that just self-consciousness? Are these just the clothes she always wears, the look she always comes on with, and he— well, he comes from a different cultural moment, so it seems strange?

Having saved her, he feels this bond with her. Strange, a bond with a kid like this. He's glad to have her here. He's aware of a desire to take care of her. Is it that she's pretty? Suppose she were homely. Would it be different? Yeah, it might, a little. He's ashamed that the ring in her navel, the dark cleavage of her blouse, keep catching his eye. But he's suspicious of always being so suspicious of his heart. If he looks down and down into his heart, he's certain it's mostly that he wants to do right by her. "I feel good about it, Terri. It says somewhere in Torah, 'You must not stand idly by the blood of your neighbor.' I think it means you've got to do something to help. I know it wasn't exactly me. I was just enacting God's plan," he tells her.

"You think so? Mr. Friedman? Really? That you found me? God's plan?"

"That's what I mean. Want some more tea? I brewed a pot."

"That's exactly what my mother thinks. I mean, what are the odds, somebody come along that early in the morning—somebody who could take on three young guys? I live with a couple women in a place on Bay State Road, and they can't believe it—cause you're so much older. Not *old* but you know. My mother says she read you were thanking God. She's big on God. She wants to meet you."

He laughs. "Well, I do thank God. I especially thank God those guys were drunk. I'm no street fighter." He walks her down the porch steps. "Terri? You stay out of bars, okay?"

She laughs, they shake hands, he waves at her from the porch. When she leaves, the house feels kind of empty. He reads. He walks to the Square for a solitary dinner. All this excitement, and when it's over,

Shira is still gone. All the summer energy of Harvard Square—the young and their desires—just makes him sad.

He returns early and slips a World War II spy movie into the DVD player. But in the middle of the commando drop behind enemy lines, the phone rings.

Ruth is calling. A different war. He stands in the kitchen and to stay calm against the attack on its way holds the phone cinched between shoulder and ear and washes a couple of dishes.

"So, Adam, how does it feel to be so famous?"

He's more wary of Ruth than of the girl. What's her agenda? He says as he has said too often lately to more friendly listeners, "I did a *mitzvah*. Anyone would have tried. I'm fortunate I was trained and they were drunk. That evened things up." And adds, "I still got beaten up, Ruth."

"You did a marvelous, marvelous thing. Four savages—"

"Three—"

"—And what it says in the papers—I knew you considered yourself religious, somehow, but the papers are making you out very Jewish. They're calling you 'Mitzvah Man.'"

"It's kind of a joke."

"Why, I didn't know you thought of yourself as a Jew."

"That's enough insults for one phone call, Ruth."

"Who's insulting? I'd like us to be friends. But tell me—you don't think of yourself as a prophet, do you?"

"Hell, no."

"Because Leo tells me it's absolutely not kosher to think of yourself as a prophet."

"I'll keep that in mind. Thank Leo for his concern."

"I know you mean well. But frankly, Adam—"

"You don't know how I love it when you begin 'Frankly'!"

"—Frankly," she repeats, "I worry for our Lisa's sake."

"Be well, Ruth," he says, and he hangs up.

· · ·

He's still in pain; all his muscles hurt. Popping an anti-inflammatory, he lies in bed and makes up smart, nasty retorts, angry at himself for letting Ruth get to him. He prays the Shema; the pain quiets. Almost asleep, he hears an ambulance siren by on Kirkland, and he's awake. He reads; at midnight he prays for Shira's soul. According to a Hasidic tradition Rabbi Klein has taught him, for eleven months the mourner prays for the soul of the beloved; after that it's the purified soul that intercedes on the mourner's behalf. Closing his eyes he half-hears a partita by Bach that Shira was playing the week she died. Her soul? It's already pure, it has always been his teacher.

Her dying has left a ragged hole in him. It's not new, this hole. It's that previously he hadn't needed to know about the wound—Shira was such a magician in making him feel complete. With Lisa home, well, he's a father; the role gives him substance—though these past weeks, even with Lisa present, he's felt sometimes he'd fallen off the world. Now, in this empty house, it's worse.

There's no one to speak to about the ruined space inside. Not Jerry, not Ben, not Rabbi Klein. Surely not Lisa. He's chatty with her; they laugh about the idiots who write the stories about him. The fight has temporarily filled him up, but it's unreal, busying him but not making whole his soul. When reporters stop pumping up the fight to fill screens and newspapers, he'll have to fill his life, heal his life. The foundation will help, keeping his attention on other people, off the wound.

Nearly asleep, he prays: Dear God, mend me or send me courage to live broken.

This morning he's scheduled an interview with the *Herald*, the Boston paper that has kept pushing the story. The martial arts community loves the fight. This morning's interview—fifteen minutes, he's been promised—will deal with his training. Ben has sent him the clipping from *The Week*: the tiny story is told under the heading

GOOD WEEK FOR US OLDER GUYS

A guy forty-five with a little martial arts training stands up against three big young men to stave off a rape. Actually, he's had more than a little training. He's usually been at one dojo or other at least once a week since college. Ben's note: "I hope you're not banged up. Remember that night at Chase? When you took that big ape down?"

Adam hears unexpressed concern in the note: *That's two fights—I'm worried about you.* Over coffee the next morning he's about to pick up the phone to call Ben and Margaret when the reporter comes. A young man, Carl Henley, strong handshake. He himself trains in aikido. He's the age of the guys he fought. Henley has brought a photographer. Adam says, "Why do you need another picture?"

"Well, what we'd like," the young man says, "is you in your white uniform striking a pose or two. That okay?"

"Not even close to okay."

"Well, okay, okay. Maybe," the young man says, "we're better off in street clothes. Just what you're wearing will be great. Tee shirt. Hey. What about that special tee shirt I read about?"

"Absolutely no martial arts pictures," Adam says. "How about a photo of me in my study—how's that? Will that do?—providing—" he lifts a forefinger, "providing you let people know about our foundation. . . ." He starts to explain.

And just then the doorbell rings. Relieved to get away from Henley, he opens to find a young man in a pin-striped suit and garish floral tie—he figures him for another reporter, and he's about to excuse himself and shut the door on him when the man meets his eyes. "You—oh, you're the guy from yesterday."

"That's right. Right. Tim Wright. I'm your investment partner."

"Investment? What investment we talking about?" He steps outside with the man in the suit.

"The money you gave me for the lottery. Remember? The ten dollars. You remember, right?"

"Of course I remember. Tim Wright. Ten bucks. Wait a minute. You telling me you won?"

"Well, not huge. The Daily Numbers Game. We made four thousand bucks."

"Come on!"

"We did. Here's your split. You've got a foundation, haven't you? Well, okay."

"That's great. You're not kidding?"

"No. No, not kidding. Check out the number in the papers. Four digits. Your birthday. Of course, I played it a few ways—month first, day first. I used your birth year, too—I found that in the papers. We made four thousand bucks. Look!" He turns in a circle, posing like a fashion model. "I bought this suit so I can look decent at a job interview. The rest we're splitting."

Standing behind him on the porch is the reporter from *The Herald*, notebook in hand. "Mr. Friedman here, he gave you a winning number?"

"He gave me ten bucks and his birthday, so I used it. I played it a bunch of different ways. I told him I'd win for us. Oh, the guy's in touch. Definitely in touch. You know what I mean?"

Henley waves to his photographer. "In touch. Will you explain that?" And the man explains—explains how he lost his job and went downhill and then his wife took off with their daughter. "And then I heard this guy on the radio. The guy's in touch with God, that's the thing."

"Please!" Adam says. "You're not going to write that!"

Henley stops writing, looks at Adam with shoulders hunched, palms up, like, *What can I do? It's part of the story.* Adam groans. "I won't make you into Jesus Christ, okay?"

"That's something," Adam says. "I'd definitely like to avoid that."

"He's the Mitzvah Guy," says Mr. Winning Ticket. "The Mitzvah Man. Mr. Friedman—how do I look?"

"Great. Really, Mr. Wright." And to Henley he says, "It's a family joke—'Mitzvah Man.'" He doesn't say that the family—Lisa—doesn't consider it just a joke. Nor does he. When he looks up this clear summer morning, standing in the shade of the porch, and he softens his gaze, he

knows it's true: holy energy enwraps him. It's everywhere, not a postu-
late to take on faith but run-of-the-mill reality you breathe into yourself. It's not *nature*, and no more than gravity is it an abstraction; as an
idea gravity is explanatory theory; as *experience* it's the pull on our bodies. There it is, in spite of wounds and hollow places. It's soothing to be
in God's Presence. *I give thanks before You.*

"My daughter's joke," he says. He laughs to think that here he's
standing in morning sun on his porch feeling a Presence that suffuses
all of them, all four of them—this man with the winning ticket and
himself, he feels, are both wounded; the reporter, the photographer,
Shira, not gone, part of this, too. See, it's like listening to the blood in
your ears. It's not there until you hear it the first time; then it's easier and
easier to access the hum. But this isn't something heard; not something
seen either, exactly. Felt as in touch? No. He wants to share the experience but he can't—and he'd better not. If he speaks about this, there'll be
trouble. Anyway, he has no words. The gap between awareness of the
Presence and expression reminds him of Psalm 19, read in services
every Shabbos morning. *Hashamayim mesaprim k'vod eyl. . . .* "The
heavens declare the glory of God and the firmament tells of his handi-
work. Day following day brings praise, and night after night speak wis-
dom." But then it says, paradoxically, "There is no speech and there are
no words; their sound is unheard." Always present, always praising, but
unheard. Right now. Here. He must be silent, too.

"How do you look? Great suit," Adam says. "But please, Mr.
Wright—"

"Tim."

"Please, Tim. That tie, Tim, I've been noticing it since you knocked
at the door. We've got to change that tie."

"Too loud?"

"Purple flowers! What is it with you and flowers? Want to get a serious job? Ditch the tie. Wait here." He goes upstairs; on a rack Shira herself installed when she found he was hanging ties on a hook, he finds a
nice conservative tie he's tired of and hasn't worn since he worked in
downtown Boston.

Returning he hears this reporter Henley talking to Mr. Winning Ticket. The photographer snaps a picture of Tim Wright handing a fan of bills to Adam. Adam complains, "Oh, come on!"

"It's a story," Henley pleads. "Come on, a story! You know I can't just bury a story like this. Now, Mr. Friedman, let me ask you something. When did God start speaking to you?"

15

At music camp Lisa is getting looks. The kids are talking. All the time, the kids are talking. When she gets to the computer late in the evening, her inbox is stuffed with emails. Her friends from school, even Annie, are all flurried up, gossiping, sympathizing, pretending to sympathize. Her so-called friends at camp love it, this story; they talk about it over lunch or waiting for Ms. Panzica to come in for the lesson in music theory. They're so thoughtful, so concerned— the rats.

She's dying to talk to someone who really, really understands. At camp she has Maisie and her pianist friend Anthony, who's so sweet to her—nobody else. One Sunday evening, after the once-a-week special dinner the camp takes pride in—each table gets a small roast turkey, and she feels nauseated looking at the dead birds and can't eat a thing—she calls Talia Rosenthal to ask about Dad; it's good to hear her voice. Talia says, "Your dad seems okay to us."

"Really, really okay, Talia?"

"I mean it, dear. He's busy with his foundation. His friend in New York—Ben somebody?—"

"Ben Licht. He's real nice."

"He's a lawyer? He's helping set up the foundation. Along with a local lawyer. It turns out to be a long process, applying for tax-exempt status. You know what that means?"

"So people can give money and take it off their taxes as charity."

"Right. Your dad came over for dinner earlier this week, and Lisa, dear, truly, he didn't sound so peculiar. He's working hard. Oh . . . he talked a bit too much about God's grace—nothing else unusual. There've been stories on the news and in *The Herald,* they blow it up—you know? Your dad has become . . . an icon of magical power. Lisa? Are *you* okay?"

"Okay, I guess. . . . You know."

"No. That's the point, dear. I don't know."

"Sometimes everything feels so weird. Here. To be here away from things."

"You need to come home?"

"Maybe. No. *No.* Talia? I wish he'd just shut up around those news guys. You don't know what it's like. You know what they've been saying at camp? According to a bunch of my so-called friends, he fought off four or five men with guns and said God gave him the power. I called Dad—he says he never, never said that. I *know* he never said that. But I keep hearing this stuff. All I want is to play music and be at camp the way I used to."

It gets so when she's not playing music, she hides out with a book or a sketch pad. She's begun being furious at everybody in advance. If they talk about it, she hates it; if they don't, they're pretending. Suppose she's making too much of it and they really aren't pretending.

But she's playing well. She's sure it's because of her mother's instrument. But when Miss Cole puts her in First Trio for the concert, is it because she's good, or is it a way to comfort her?

That Friday night the trio plays awesomely. Next morning in the big, sunny dining room made out of a parlor and a library when it was a summer estate for a rich Boston family, she gets lots of nice comments; then one of the girls at the cool table, a blonde wearing a tee shirt with "Smart Blonde" across the front comes over and puts down a print-out from a *Herald* article she found on-line. The girl puts a hand on her shoulder and reads as Lisa reads:

MITZVAH MAN BEATS LOTTERY

The story tells about an unemployed hi-tech manager, down and out, who got a ten-dollar bill and a lucky number from Adam Friedman and won thousands of dollars. "'Man's got the magic. I knew it. God tells him. I bought a suit and kept some cash, but I gave the Mitzvah Foundation its share,' Mr. Wright said."

"I can't believe what a cool guy your father is," the smart blonde says. But her voice is telling this to the whole camp, and Lisa can smell the hostility. "God! A real, live superhero. Knocks out four, five guys *and* beats the lottery? Are you kidding? Is that cool? He's spooky, your dad. Isn't her dad spooky?" she asks the whole dining room.

Lisa wants to turn and punch her, but she smiles and shares the laugh. "He's something."

"Omigod. Amazing." The girl pats a condescending pat, exchanges looks with a table full of girls, walks off grinning, holding her flute case.

And next morning another girl tosses onto Lisa's table another print-out from the on-line *Herald*. The girl says, "I can imagine how hard it must be for your dad. Have you seen this?"

POLICE KEEP FOLLOWERS FROM MITZVAH MAN

The story tells of people who've found Adam Friedman's house, who wait for him to come outside or return home. The police have had to help. When he walks down the street he's followed by one, two, three people, not all ragged, some of them well dressed, asking for help from the Mitzvah Foundation—though the foundation is not yet established—or just harassing him for lottery numbers. "'Everybody wants a number from him,' one of his friends told *The Herald*. 'Or they want his advice. Or they want a job for a husband or a scholarship for a kid. He has his hands full.'"

Lisa's friends take on the job of supporting her, defending her, cutting the girls who think it's funny, who think *she's* funny to have such a father.

"Oooh. The daughter of Mr. Prophet, Mr. Superhero." This is called out to her from across the lawn as she walks to practice.

Maisie and Anthony are with her, and they yell, "You stupid idiots!"

Anthony has become unbelievably important to her. She remembers first rehearsals of the duet—working through the first movement of Beethoven's Spring Sonata—she thought he was kind of a jerk—not, say, like the romantic engraving she photocopied in color from a book on nineteenth-century music and put on her wall at home—Chopin at the piano looking up at George Sand mooning down. But it turns out Anthony's so funny when he gets comfortable, and this summer, she needs funny more than anything. After she came back from taking care of her dad, they'd slip off for walks along the pebbly beach and hold hands. Sitting on his music bag and windbreaker they toss pebbles into the water, and, as she leans against him, over her shoulder his long piano fingers touched her breasts.

Anthony has saved her this summer. And Maisie, too. Omigod.

It's always been important for Lisa to stay until the last concert, then the last day at camp, a Sunday of hugs and tears, exchanges of email addresses and telephone numbers, but this year, in spite of Maisie, in spite of Anthony, whom she kisses and kisses the next to last night in a closet between their bunk rooms, she feels so out of camp culture she decides to call her dad to please, please come get her early, as he'd said he would if she asked.

So next day, after lunch, she slips away down the gravel road to meet him at the camp entrance. She's hugged Miss Cole goodbye, let Ms. Panzica kiss her cheek, circle-hugged with Maisie and Anthony leaving all three of them in tears. And when the white Camry, dirty with road dust, slows to make the turn into camp, she waves it down with wild semaphore hands, and she and Dad hug and hug in the middle of the road. He looks so good to her, even if he is wearing a yarmulke, which worries her a little. They drive back to her bunkhouse, where duffel and backpack are waiting by the door. Almost everybody's at practice. Anthony, cutting practice, is sitting on a bunk, reading. "Dad, I want you to meet my friend Anthony—he's the pianist I told you about." She takes Anthony's hand as if to help him up.

"I've heard a lot about you, sir," Anthony says. As he gets up, she looks Anthony over to see him as someone who never played duets with him: a skinny kid with a froggy voice. She finds tears coming to her eyes.

Her dad shakes his hand. "I know how kind you've been to Lisa. You dig?"

"'Dig'?" Lisa groans. "'Dig' is retarded. Nobody has said 'dig' for half a century."

Anthony shrugs, unable to answer. Then he puts an arm around her shoulder, and right in front of Dad, they hug very hard and bang each other on the back to make it funny.

"Goodbye, Anthony. Goodbye."

"Goodbye, Lisa."

"Goodbye, Anthony."

Anthony lives in San Francisco. But who knows? Will they see each other? Maybe they'll see each other—they've traded email addresses. Now a brief, sweeter embrace.

"So here's a story I don't know how to tell you," her dad says on the drive home.

"I know all about what the papers said."

"No. This is different. It's a little freaky."

"Oh, *Dad*." She closes her eyes as the car turns onto the highway. *Freaky.* The last thing she wants is one more freaky story; she wants to sleep, wants to hear that the buzz circling her father is settling. If she's going to listen to stories, let it be stories of her mother and her father, like when they met. Talking about Mom would comfort her very much. The absolutely last thing she wants is *freaky*.

"It's nothing terrible, honey. I know the talk bothered you at camp. The newspaper stories. You think I can help what those assholes write?"

"Dad! You've got an impressionable, young girl in the car." She pokes and laughs. They head down the coast; thick morning mist on rocky promontories, quiet water.

"Sorry. Anyway, this is different. It's about David. You remember David Eisen, the boy who had—or has—leukemia? Uri, Judith, David, Marjorie?"

"And?"

"Aha, it's going to be one of those 'And' days, huh?"

"No. I'm sorry. I mean, go on, okay?"

"So I went up the other night to talk with Judith about pledges. I can see she's worried about David. He's still in remission, but he has so little energy. He's not eating. She's scared. You can imagine."

"God, yes."

"So I went in to blab with him a little, kiss his head with the skimpy hair the way I do. Uri and I went in. David was in bed watching TV. He'd been out of school a couple of days. I sat on his bed. He's always pretty nice to me even though I'm an adult. Actually, sick kids, it's true, they come to have a good, straight relationship with adults. So I sit and I sing a corny old Yiddish song I know, and it turns out Uri knows, too. We sing it together. 'Roshinkhes mit mandeln.' He's smiling, David, and I look at the light around his head, David's head, and I notice it's not even."

"Dad? What light around his head?"

"Oh, it's something that's started happening, honey. Maybe after the concussion. Maybe it has nothing to do with that. Light. Faint. Just a pattern of energy hovering around people. Translucent. It's not that big a deal. Anyway, David's energy looks weird. Dim. Irregular. I look at him and I know it's not my eyes, a trick of the light. So I put my hands to the sides of his head, and I ask Uri, 'Do you mind if I just sit here with David a little?' He said sure. So I sat and I swear to God felt energy in my hands—or between my hands and David's head—a tingling. And I said what Moses said when his sister Miriam got leprosy—actually, *tza'arat*, remember?—for bad-mouthing Moses. Please God, heal her please. *El na refa na la.* Only this is a boy. So I guessed it would be *El na refa na lo,* but if I made a mistake in the Hebrew, God's not a grammarian, thank God."

She laughs on cue. But she's getting more uneasy. They pass a string of cars, each with a kayak on top, then a pickup with four more kayaks. For a moment she wonders where they're going and blanks out his story. But then he continues, and she's with him.

"The point is I sat there and felt warmer and warmer, and their apartment isn't air-conditioned. My hands got real warm, and David shut his eyes—I think he understood I was trying to heal him, trying to be a medium for holy healing. I know, I know it sounds fake—divine healing. I *mean.* But I sat there, and when I looked at the light around David, it seemed different."

"Different?"

"More regular. Calm. I kissed his cheek. I've gotten to love that little boy. Anyway, when I left, Uri thanked me, Judith thanked me, but I was half-afraid they'd think I was off the wall and never let me in the house again. But here's the thing: I get a call last night. David is eating. David's been to the doctor and his markers look good. He's at school today. He's got energy. I don't know what to make of it. You think he would have gotten better on his own? Or I gave him hope and he did the rest? Or did my intervention really do some good? It's not *me.* I know that, for godsakes. But was I a channel? Look, honey: strange things are happening all around me."

She squeezes his hand on the steering wheel. "Dad? Don't tell *anybody* else, okay?"

"Like a newspaper?" he laughs.

"Or *anybody*—like someone who might tell someone who might tell a newspaper." Lisa squirms in her seat. They're driving home along the sea, and the sea is calming. The traffic isn't heavy. A violin piece by somebody she can't remember keeps playing in her head.

"These emanations. I . . . see light hovering around people in the street. I feel them."

"Feel what?"

"All the work they do to keep pain at bay. I don't know what to make of it. Emanations."

"Maybe it's what you said—it's the concussion. Or maybe it's just what the eyes do if you look a certain way? My point is, Dad—"

"I know, I know, I know—I shouldn't make too much of this. Right?"

"Exactly. Please."

Her father pulls the car off to the side across from a gray-vinyl condo community meant to remind you of the houses of ol' Maine rugged fisher folk—a kind of upper-middle-class Disneyland Maine. He sits back, holds her hand. "There's more. When we get home, Lisa, honey, you should know, there'll probably be people on the porch, in the cul-de-sac. Cops keep coming by and chasing them, but they come back, and I don't press charges for trespassing. If I did, they'd just stand across the street waiting. The thing is, the thing is, something's been happening to me. Like, *I know what's going to occur.*"

"Dad?"

"Shh. Remember Moses asks to see God's face, and God tells him, 'No man can see my face and live'? But God lets Moses see God's back. He tells him something like, 'Hide in the cleft of that rock and I'll pass by.' And God does, and shelters Moses from seeing. And then Moses sees God's back. Now what does that mean, *God's 'back'*?"

"Dad? Can't we talk while we're driving?"

"Yes, in one minute. So. The people who come to me, they think I see the future, but that's not it. *I see God's back*, I see God's jet trail, I see what's happened, and the future may be embedded in that. Or it's like I'm feeling the blow-by of a giant tractor-trailer or maybe a 747, and I'm sucked into the future. I'm carried on this blow-by, riding the turbulence." He takes a big breath and pulls out into traffic.

"Dad? You're not saying you see God."

"No. But maybe I'm riding God's wings."

"Omigod. Dad? Are you taking your pills?"

"As a matter of fact, I'm not. Your mother's been such a comfort. I'm less depressed." He rubs his hands together. "So! You want to stop for ice cream, honey?"

Shira's become a comfort, a blessing, not just occasion for grief. *May her memory be for a blessing*, we say. Now he *gets* it, how that can be. She's *with* him. Not as snapshots of the past. How can snapshots or old, static narratives bless? It's her ongoing presence. He shuts up about this. If he said, "We feel . . ." or "My wife and I took a walk by the river today," they'd lock him away, but that's what it amounts to. He asks himself: is he companion to a ghost? No—and how is a ghost different? A ghost has her own agenda. Shira doesn't go this far. She's present in his blood, in the air he breathes. She doesn't get to argue with him, and oh, she was a great debater, the living Shira.

Yes, he grieves, yes, yes, sure he grieves, the world is colored sepia or gray—especially at night, when what's present to him is not Shira but Shira's loss. The crushed Shira, the gone Shira. He'll pour himself a little drink: *Here's looking at you, kid.*

Well, but he's looking at everyone these days. First off, he has to keep his eyes wide open because he's likely to get approached at Whole Foods between the produce and the fish: "You're Adam Friedman, aren't you? The lottery guy who saved that girl? Listen. I need a lottery number. Four digits." He's buttonholed at the frozen foods by someone begging for the winning horse at Belmont. As if he knew a thing about horses! "Here's three names. You tell me which one is likely to win. Please, Mr. Friedman. I won't hold you to it. If you're wrong, I won't get mad."

You're half-mad already, he wants to tell the guy. But he throws up his hands and shrugs apologetically. The guy's aura can't be seen against the fluorescent-lit shelves, for places, too, have energies and can interfere with the reception. He sees best in a quiet room against a painted wall. For instance, in the small sanctuary at his synagogue. Against the pale golden walls of the little room at the eastern end of the synagogue, lit by clerestory windows of clear glass and the dim glow of incandescent lights hidden behind soffits, the hovering outlines of pulsing energy of the other members of the morning minyan are apparent. This leads to something extraordinary.

At dinner one night, he tells Lisa what happened at morning minyan. "We were just finishing the *Barechu*, you know, when we first pray as a congregation, and we were still on our feet when I noticed Alan Koren—Jules' dad?—and it was as if I could see what had happened to him, it was as if I'd been through a film, I saw the whole thing."

"Saw what?"

"Not just energy. In my mind's eye I saw him walking out of a building, a gym I think, and suddenly he's keeling over, and then the ambulance is taking him away. I saw doctors working on him. I didn't see what was *going to* happen; I knew it as if it had *already* happened. You could say I rode the past into its future. I don't know what I was tuning in on—maybe his breathing or his skin color? The way he moved? And I think I saw something in the energy surrounding him."

"And what happened?" He hears the wariness in her voice.

"I waited till we'd repeated the Mourners' Kaddish and were unstrapping *tefillin*, and I went up to him, and I said, 'Alan, don't ask me how I know, but you absolutely need to get yourself to the doctor's—I mean right now. Please.' And he looked at me and grinned. He said, 'I've heard about your—' and he didn't know how to finish, didn't want to insult me by calling it *peculiarities* or something. We've known each other for years. 'But really,' he said, 'I'm fine. Okay?' And I wanted to ask him would he at least let me work on his energy, but that would have sounded totally off the wall, so I said, 'Alan, you can do what you want, but I'm certain about it.'

"So he smiled at me kindly like I was wacko and walked away."

"You're not going to tell me—Dad?—that he got sick?"

"No. What happened is he began to feel uneasy. Like, *This is stupid, but what if?* So he cancelled a meeting and went to see his doctor. And the doctor did whatever he does and next thing you know Alan's in Mass General getting an angioplasty. And guess what? He was clogged up like crazy. He could have had a major heart attack. They're keeping him overnight. But he'll be okay. He's got to change his diet and exercise. He called me right away, called me to say thanks."

"Which means not only did you see—"

"—but I was able to intervene. Yes. That's it. Here's the analogy I came up with—you've heard this before: an outfielder in baseball, he hears the click of the bat on the ball and must see something, but hardly anything—a quick wisp of ball. And at once, instantly, way before he sees the ball in the sky above him, he starts running like crazy, he's not even watching where the ball is going, he puts his glove out, looks up and catches what would have been a double or triple. Is he magically seeing the future? He's riding the trajectory and velocity at the click of the bat, and he intervenes, he changes what's going to happen."

They're at the kitchen table, a vegetable soup sitting on a wicker trivet between them, a French bread alongside; Lisa leans over and kisses his cheek. She doesn't say anything. He doesn't know if she's stunned and moved by what happened or just doesn't believe him or thinks it was an accident or if she's patronizing him or maybe feeling sorry for poor, dim-witted Dad. Or all the above. At last she says, "Dad? What was it for *you*—the click of the bat and the wisp of ball?"

He can't say.

News travels around the synagogue the way *challah*, broken off a loaf at *kiddush*, the Shabbat sanctification, is split and split again, lets everyone have a bite. In fact, the kiddush on Friday night, the kiddush on Saturday morning, are responsible for a lot of the spread. Then there are emails and telephone calls. And the story puffs up: Alan nearly died; if he hadn't gone to the hospital that very morning. . . . And news is, he saved someone else, also sick, perhaps with cancer. Now the story floats from somebody to a friend on the *Globe*. A request comes to Adam for an interview; by now he's wary and refuses.

But the number of people who hang around his house, who follow him up the street, who wave at him in Harvard Square, has grown. How long before the glitz dies away? He spots a man in a baseball cap in the bushes across the street, and he gets a bolt of fear—sees a tripod, sees the man lean forward over a scope. It's just a birding scope, snooping. Then there are cameras and video cameras.

Enough already! He's uneasy for Lisa. Fourteen—to lose her mother when she's handling the turmoil of ordinary metamorphosis. She doesn't need crazies or people crammed with avaricious visions of success, visions pumped out by TV or by *People* and *Cosmopolitan* at supermarket checkout counters, doesn't need them coming up to her on the street.

But the healing is something else—how he wants to heal! Judith brings David with her sometimes, and look—maybe it does no good, maybe it's just a placebo, but now Judith believes in him, so David believes, and Adam holds David's head in his hands and they kid around, and while David tells him a joke—he likes telling jokes—Adam feels a tingle of energy and imagines a calm flow through himself and the boy. Judith is sure David has changed, has been getting stronger. He's at school every day now, she says. He plays with the other kids.

But yesterday morning, walking Lisa to the T at Harvard Square, he saw men and women on their way to work, saw summer students on their way to class. In the moment of meeting the eyes of strangers, before turning away, not wanting to affront, frighten, do damage to the defenses people need, he saw—*saw* is, after all, metaphor; he might as well say *touched* or *felt* or *smelled*—how thick with pain the people were, how brave they were hiding all that pain. He was drawn to comfort, but he knew that it was beyond him. Parents are dying, bills need paying, how can I go without health insurance? There are divorces; there are humiliations. It's beyond his powers.

Someone at synagogue has talked to someone who's talked to someone; Adam gets a call asking would he like to run a workshop on spiritual healing? Me? Hell no, he laughs. He gets a real kick out of it. "Joan—do you really think," he says to Joan Schwartz, who after all is just being kind, "we can heal this city, this country, this world, one aura at a time?" He didn't add: *Or one check at a time?*

I need your good sense, he says to Shira.

·   ·   ·

father? Well, look how pregnant she is, and this is July 1964. So that baby in there, that's you. So your dad wasn't away. He was with her."

"Very good. Very good! Let's look for earlier that year."

They keep going. Fading photos, black and white most of them. "Here's your dad, here's Grandpa, with palm trees and a belly. Your dad was fat!"

"I know."

"Anyway, look, the palm-tree picture is labeled 1963. So your uncle s wrong. Right? Your mom was pregnant with you when he came ome—the next year."

"I think you're some detective," Adam says. "But of course, there's nother possibility. Suppose they began an affair and then continued it ter my dad was back home."

"Okay. Maybe." She thinks about this. "But that's *not* what Cal was ing. Right? So we can be pretty sure, right?—that he's just your uncle. 's probably not my grandfather."

"Okay. But we won't tell him. Okay?"

"You are so amazing, Dad." She hugs him around the neck. "That's dad!"

"Why am I so great, kiddo?"

"Don't be dumb. You're so amazing because you're not freaking out ut this uncle and your mother. Right? I can't believe it. You aren't , I mean. Wouldn't most people get mad?"

Oh, honey, it's so long ago. And the guy's so old. What good telling " And he can't say to her, *Maybe I'd prefer it if Cal were my dad.* say because it's shameful that part of Adam would rather have a t s.o.b. as a father than a good, but dim, soul.

e flashes back to one of the terrible fights between his parents. old was he? He can't remember. Cal was coming for dinner. His r began shrieking and his father slapped her—or no, not d—touched her with his fingertips like the quote of a slap, but she ed down to the carpet and he, his father, said, *Come on, get up,* Adam—*You saw! I hardly laid a hand on her.* Then his father gen- d her to her feet and helped her into the bedroom; they closed

It's August. Every morning Lisa goes to a special progra
land Conservatory. She can come home on the Red Lin
pick her up. He drives her to a friend's house, or she ar
cian come home to practice. Or he takes her to her t
Samuels' house, and listens to her chant *haftarah*. Ma
would be good for her to have a dog—maybe that wo

He takes her for a walk by the Charles: right over
the fight took place. Adam, in fading Mitzvah Man t
whole thing, parodying himself as martial arts he
poses, playing iron-jawed hero against Neanderthal
ing focus and getting clobbered with a rock. They l
Anderson Footbridge over the Charles, bridge betv
the B-School on the Boston side of the river. Th
river; two sculls sweep by, one, with a B.U. crew, b
in a motorboat with a bullhorn. At the Harvard
crews are putting sculls into the water. The pain
wraps an arm around her.

Every few days, Cal calls. This has become Cal
to talk—for longer and longer. *Did I tell you l*
pets? Stories about Depression Chicago, stor
mother." "She was one beautiful woman, you
Adam goes through his boxes and albums o
when he was a kid, from before he was born
on the glass coffee table in the living room.
enough to come into their living room and
sits next to Adam, plucking photos out of t
get a better look.

She's the one who makes the discovery
born? You were born in 1964, right?"

"1964. October 15th. Right."

"Look. Some of the photos have printi
lab? So okay, this is your mom, my grand

the door, and through the door Adam could hear her sobbing—not unusual—but *his* sobbing, too. Then Cal was at the front door, and everything was normal, the old phony charm of the Big Guy got to work. He'd brought a bottle of single malt scotch and they all sat down and drank, and he, too, Adam had a sip. He remembers hating the smoky scotch. So he couldn't have been a little boy or he'd have had no idea what kind of whiskey. Or is that a later emendation?

Was that fight about Cal being her lover? Or about Cal the big shot humiliating his father day after day? *He keeps us as poor retainers. Shleppers! Can I invite anyone to this house?*

A photo of Uncle Cal in Stetson, wearing his characteristic smile—one side of his mouth tilted up, the other down. The lone Jewish rancher of Fifth Avenue.

It's dusk; outside a lone man waits a respectful distance from the house. Soon there'll be tour buses and a hot dog stand!

He looks again at the photo. An old picture, but it's telling him something about the present.

He calls Cal. The answering machine picks up, but Cal interrupts when he hears it's Adam. For starters, he says, "Uncle Cal, I just want you to know how glad I am we're finally in touch. You've always been terrifically important to me."

This isn't what he's called for. Why has he called? He has only a vague idea.

But within moments, he knows. He walks through the house holding the portable phone. He looks at Lisa watching a movie on TV, wanders into the kitchen to make sure the oven's turned off. "Cal? You're going to laugh, but I find I'm worried about you. Just now I was looking at an old photograph and hearing your voice in my head, and something came to me. A picture in my head. You looked young when you were here. You sure don't look in your mid-seventies."

"What're you talking about? I hit eighty next month."

"No kidding! Cal! We should have a birthday party for you. You want me to make a small party for you in New York? You give me a list. I'll take care of everything. Please." Even as he says this he knows there's nobody to ask. When did Cal ever have good friends? He's asking half out of kindness, half out of meanness.

"There's nobody gives a shit if I live or die, kid," he says with a melo-dramatic quiver in his voice. "My pals are all gone—into graves in Queens—or living graves in Florida."

"Suppose I come down to New York and the three of us celebrate."

"What is this? I know you don't need my money. Anyway, I told you my dough's going to Sloan-Kettering. What then? You thinking about your foundation?"

"I understand your being suspicious. You're right—it's not about money. It's this: I was looking at your picture, picture from when I was a kid, and all of a sudden I saw something in my mind's eye. Something bad. Have you been to the doctor recently?"

"What if I have?"

"Cal? You're pretty sick, aren't you?"

"So maybe I am. Say! How the hell did you know? I look that sick?"

"No, no. Not at all. I don't have to be a genius. Sloan-Kettering, after all, is a cancer institute." But that name was only confirmation, not how the knowledge came to him. "Uncle Cal, you have a tumor?" Adam doesn't have to ask; he knows it as if it were growing inside his own chest.

"Yeah, yeah, as a matter of fact. Say, what is this? Yeah, a malignant tumor. A lousy spot on my lung that's getting bigger. It's exploding, the fucker. They say they can't operate on my son of a bitch of a lung. I'm starting radiation again next week. But it won't do a goddamn bit of good. See? Some lousy birthday present."

"*Again* you say?"

"I had the thing two years ago. Some lousy ordeal. I thought they caught it. Well, screw it. You gotta die from something."

"Cal. You mind if I come and see you this weekend? I'll leave Lisa with friends."

"Now that's a goddamned dumb idea. I'm not dying next week. Hell. If you want, okay. I'm not gonna be a shrinking violet. But don't expect me to be much goddamn company. . . . So? Are you coming? When? When are you coming?"

Adam tells Lisa: Cal is sick, he's going down to the city to see him. She can't stay with Talia and Jerry because the Rosenthals are at the Cape. She could stay with her friend Annie Morrel—but she wants to come along. Adam books a room at the Westbury and lets Ben and Margaret know they're coming. On Friday afternoon they take the Acela down to the city.

One of Lisa's assigned summer readings is a selection of Shakespeare sonnets; they read them aloud as they rock along at eighty, a hundred miles an hour, looking up words in the notes. "Let me not to the marriage of true minds admit impediments," she reads. Then, looking grim, she adds: "He doesn't say anything about the impediment of a drunk driver."

"Oh, but in a way he does, honey. In poem after poem he's aware of loss—especially aging and dying. They didn't have the problem of stolen cars and drunk drivers. But it was common in Shakespeare's time for people to die young. Life expectancy was just over thirty years old. Not many people lived as long as Uncle Cal. And you know what? That's what most of the sonnets start from. Loss. Listen," he says, and thumbs through the little Signet paperback.

When I have seen by time's fell hand defaced . . .

"Shakespeare's thinking of loss a lot. A *lot*. Let me read just the end of this one to you.

Ruin hath taught me thus to ruminate
That time will come and take my love away.
This thought is as a death, which cannot choose
But weep to have that which it fears to lose.

"You've got to hear the music of it. But first—do you understand?"

"Kind of. I think. What's *ruminate*?"

"To think, to chew over. When he thinks, 'I love this woman, and I'm going to lose her,' then even now, even while he still has her, he isn't able to enjoy loving her."

"Did you think about losing Mom?"

"No. I thought we'd live a million years—or at least till you were grown up and had a family of your own. I didn't know—I didn't take it into me—how vulnerable we were."

They take a cab uptown and have Shabbos dinner with the Lichts. Summer Sabbath—it gets dark so late. The dining room table, polished mahogany, is laid with crystal and silver. They wait for Jennifer, but she doesn't come. So they bless the candles and the *challah*, and Adam, placing his hand on her head, blesses Lisa. Ben asks what about the foundation and all this publicity? "It must get pretty obnoxious," Ben says.

"Yes! *So* obnoxious! Ben, I have some sad-looking people standing at the corner waiting to ask me for a lottery number. Religious fanatics hand me literature. Worse. Some ask me to hand *them* literature."

"It costs something, being a big hero," Ben says. "But it'll help raise money."

"Oh, you cool it about my superhero status."

"We're gonna buy Dad a Mitzvah-mobile." He likes it that she's being funny, razzing him, not upset by the foundation and her superhero creation.

When Jennifer finally comes in, just before Adam and Lisa are about to go back to the hotel, Adam sees Lisa light up. Jennifer has eaten and has stopped home just to pick up something, but she sits with them. At first Adam simply admires her, her youth and beauty. Dark eyes, black curly hair worn loose. He notices again the big gap between her and Lisa: young woman/young adolescent. Because the room is lit dimly by candle, he can't help seeing the shimmer of her energy against the pale ochre walls. Is it that fringe of energy or something in her eyes that worries him? For he is worried. The more he looks at her, the more worried.

Jen says she's going out.

"Can I come?" Lisa asks.

Jen sighs, "I'm afraid not, Lisa. But I'll be around tomorrow."

"Say, Jen. We haven't had a chance to talk, you and me," Adam says, hand on Jennifer's shoulder. "Mind if I take you to the elevator?" He knows it's a little peculiar; he's relieved no one says anything. Jen goes back to her room to get something; Adam follows her and knocks.

"Yes?"

He stands in her doorway just looking at her till she turns away. He speaks very quietly. "Do your parents know yet about the trouble you're in?"

"What are you talking about? Who's in trouble?" She busies herself at her dresser.

"You are, Jen, I know it. I don't know what it is. But I know it's terrible trouble, it can ruin your life or at least deform it. I can make guesses, but what it is, that's not important. You're scared—I can see that. Look—for now I'll keep it private. See—you have a choice."

"A choice?" She sits on the edge of her desk, swinging her purse, and cocks an eyebrow, as if what he said amused her. He knows better.

"You can change whatever's going on, or you can go down the tubes and have to change it later when more damage is done. Please, Jen. Here—" He goes to her desk and writes on a scrap of paper. "If you want to talk—absolutely between us—here's my cell. It's up to you, Jennifer. This is a big decision."

She stares at him, stares at the paper, takes a big breath, mumbles, "No. My parents don't know."

He nods and walks her to the elevator and says nothing, goes back inside, asks Margaret and Ben how things are going for Jen, and when they say fine, fine, he offers details of the fight by the river so Ben can enjoy razzing him. Then he and Lisa go to the hotel. "Okay, Dad. What's going on with the secrets?" Lisa asks in the cab.

"Sorry. It has to remain private."

"You saw something, Dad?"

"I saw something."

"Suppose it's not real. Suppose it's all in your head."

"I'm beginning to trust what I see."

"Something bad?"

"Not good."

"About Jennifer? She looks okay to me. Well, I guess you were right about Cal."

16

They ride up to Cal's in an elevator of polished brass and mirror wall. The door opens to a floor of two apartments. Cal is waiting at the door, wearing an embroidered silk paisley robe out of a 1930s' high-society film. Adam puts an arm around him and kisses his cheek. Lisa gives him a polite hug and carries the bag to the kitchen to slice and toast the bagels and put the sturgeon, smoked salmon, and cream cheese on a platter. "I hope it's okay bringing Lisa," Adam says. "She's going off to the Met in a few minutes to do some sketching."

"As long as we don't talk in front of the kid," Cal says out of the side of his mouth.

When they finish breakfast and Lisa leaves, sketch-book and phone in her backpack, Cal seems to deflate, looks debilitated, old, an old man, gray in the face. Cal stumbles to an easy chair by the living room window. He seems to have lost bulk; Adam thinks of him as big, though he's never been big. Adam's father was a big man. The power of an icon inflates its size. Now, he's no icon—a little old man. His shoulder bones push up the silk. There's dust on the radiator, the expensive furniture is unpolished. The armrests of the antique chairs are seedy. Adam remembers a guy who worked for Cal after his divorce, guy named Joe, who did everything—cooked, drove him around in the Cadillac he turned in every year for a new model, kept the house straight, took care of upkeep and repairs. Then they had a maid who came in twice a week. What happened to Joe? What happened to the maid? The apartment's a mess. On every surface—tables, chairs, bureaus—piles of papers. Bills, junk mail, financial documents. It's as if someone died here months ago and the place has been growing paper and a layer of New York grime. There's a smell of onion, of garbage. "Cal?" he says, "I think you need someone to help out around here."

"I don't want no goddamn strangers coming in and losing my things, stealing my things. Turning everything upside down. I know where everything is. Who am I trying to impress with a fancy apartment? The fancy, antique crap is from the broad I was married to. You remember her?"

"You want us to give you a hand?"

"You know, kid, trouble is, you and me, we got together a little too late." Cal's voice has a music in it. The sentimental music, if it had words, would say, *I'm a tough guy, these are battlefield wounds, don't cry for me.* But of course, the music wanted you to cry. "Now, it's my own goddamned fault we never got to know each other. I admit it—I was a major horse's ass. Fact of the matter is, I figured you were pissed at me because of how your mother bad-mouthed me."

"I *was.* She *did.* Was she wrong? She wasn't wrong."

"See? You see?"

"But still—you were a big deal in my life, Cal. A powerful guy. Smart. A success."

"Sure. I'm a big deal now you know I'm your biological father."

"No. Always. So I'm with you on this. Your sickness. If I can make things easier, I'll make things easier; if I can help, I'll help." Adam leans over Cal, puts hands on his temples.

"Now what the hell you doing? You're pretty weird."

"I'm comforting. It's something I've learned. It won't hurt."

"You're full of tricks," he says, but he doesn't take Adam's hands away.

Adam holds Cal's temples, eases his hands away half an inch, an inch, and feels energy flow from hand to head, head to hand. But it's not the way it happens with the boy David. With Cal it's faint, the light around Cal's head thin. As he moves his hands down along Cal's chest, if there's any flow at all, it's so slight he's not sure it isn't just imagination. Can he help energy flow to Cal? He closes his eyes and concentrates on his hands.

"How long you gonna keep this up? What the hell is this?"

"Shh."

His hands grow warm; they pulse.

"Come on, c'mon."

His hands grow warmer. But he feels no flow; he sees nothing around Cal. He whispers, "Master of the Universe, bring healing to this sick, sick man. *El na refa na lo, El na refa na lo.*"

"That's Jewish talk? Hebrew? Yiddish? What—are you praying for me? You know, junior, I don't believe in it. What do you need that old-time crap for? My pop left Odessa to get the hell away from that stuff."

"Shh."

Cal shushes. He lets the hands work him over. But then he cackles: "Ha! My pop swore he saw young men on the ship from Europe taking those prayer boxes you strap on your arm and tossing them right in the water as they passed Miss Liberty. He didn't have to toss his. He'd dumped them a long time before. But pray all you want. I'll tell you what I *don't* want. I don't want you sitting in the goddamn hospital room watching me die. You get me? Sitting by my bed wiping the spittle off my face? I've seen what that looks like. I'll hire a nurse for that."

Adam stops, balked. He says, "Cal, you're not dying yet."

"I thought you knew everything. I'm dying. I'm dying."

Adam goes back to work, holding his uncle's head in his hands. He feels warmth but no flow. Cal's eyes are closed. He wears his tough, one-sided grin, but slowly, the grin slips, the skin sinks, his breathing deepens, slows. He dozes. Adam holds his hands on his uncle's head, while Cal dozes.

After many minutes, Adam places his fingers on his uncle's skinny shoulders.

Cal rouses. "You all done?"

"Yeah."

John J. Clayton

"I think I fell asleep. Don't take it as an insult. Well, I gotta say, I'm feeling pretty good, pretty good. That was some rest. And I'm breathing okay."

"I'm glad," Adam says, though he knows he's being soft-soaped.

"So: we understand each other? About my end. I don't want no nonsense. It's my goddamn end, not yours."

Adam plants a kiss on the bald spot in the middle of Cal's head. Silently he blesses.

"Hey!"

Lisa calls Jennifer, hoping to meet her in the afternoon, but Jennifer puts it off. She's a little wrecked from last night. "How about brunch mid-day tomorrow, babe?"

"I'll have to ask Dad."

"And maybe your dad can come, too? I'd like it if he can come."

"What is it with you two? What did he want last night? He wouldn't tell me."

"Nothing. He just asked how I was doing."

"So how are you doing?"

"I don't know. Can your dad be trusted?"

"Trusted? Sure. My dad can be trusted. I don't know what's going on with him sometimes, but trust?—I trust him a lot. I trust him completely. You know. He's 'Mitzvah Man.'"

Jen doesn't laugh. "He's cool. He knows things," she says. "He really, really knows things."

"Like?"

"I mean . . . well, it's freaky. So. Ask him about brunch, okay? My parents are busy tomorrow. They're going to a wedding. Old people getting married. Second marriages. We could go for brunch."

Lisa loves secrets. But at the same time, she's disappointed. It's okay she's younger, okay Jen's the leader. She doesn't mind that. But it's hard to hear that Jen's real interest is in seeing Dad. What's the big secret? Is Jen pregnant? Does she want to talk about having an abortion? But to be trustworthy herself, not to gossip, she doesn't ask him again, just asks about brunch. "Maybe I should leave for a while tomorrow so you and Jen can talk." Saying this has a spiteful edge; it's meant to provoke denial—*No, no*—but her father nods. "Yes. Maybe just for a few minutes. I'll give you a high sign. And of course I'll tell you about it when I can, honey."

Tavern on the Green is this great restaurant in Central Park, wonderful on winter nights, when outside the glass walls of the restaurant the trees are laced with little white lights; wonderful in summer, when it feels like part of the park, feels as if Renoir should have painted it. She used to love coming here when they spent a vacation weekend in New York.

Outdoors at Tavern on the Green next day she excuses herself from the table and takes a long time in the bathroom. Well. Not exactly—she crouches, keeps a trellis or a tree between herself and Dad and Jen, peeks around waiters and patrons without being seen: a spy, like Jen. She's in tears, Jen—Dad pats her hand. They've been secret lovers; she's pregnant with his child. She knows this is absolutely totally ridiculous. Then what? For sure it's connected to sex or drugs.

She sits down. She has to ask, "What's the matter, Jen?"—because Jen's eyes are red and there's no way to ignore it. And her dad says, "Jen? You want to talk about it with Lisa here? Is that okay?"

It's weird to see her unravel, this totally gorgeous young woman in an ankle-length dress of peach-colored silk, silk with a sheen that captures your eyes as it moves, as she moves. To see her cry behind her sunglasses—and even behind sunglasses not meet your eyes—gives Lisa a very different feeling about Jen—makes Lisa feel older, stronger, makes her want to help.

"It's so stupid, okay?—just that at school," Jen says, "I'm with these kids who take risks. It's like taking risks shows you're not just a protected rich kid. Of course, that's all we are."

And Jen stops. As a risk of her own, Lisa takes hold of Jen's hand, and Jen lets her, and she goes on. "So it's like Outward Bound, except instead of climbing a fifty-foot cliff, you go to weird places in the city to catch music and you do drugs. I mean, when we're home. And as far as

Mom and Dad know, I'm in Connecticut for the weekend at a friend's house, but I'm here, down on the lower East Side, and you wouldn't believe all the people out at three in the morning. And there's like apartments to go to, and you know. We never did heroin."

She pauses to catch her breath. She holds her face in her hands, seeming to take comfort in the food smell from her fingers.

"So. No heroin," Dad prompts.

"Right. But there's coke and ecstasy and meth. Meth! I tried meth once, and that was real great so I tried it again, and after just a couple of nights, I was dead in the down times. And the up times were shorter and less of an up. It's cheap enough that like I could handle it at first out of my allowance and then I used more and got scared I couldn't keep it up, I mean the cost, and I knew it was going to wreck me. It was already wrecking me. I was either wired or ragged, wired or ragged. So . . . I started to take money from my mom's purse. She never knows what she has in there. Well. They've been so wrapped up in their 'issues,' they don't know anything. But I felt terrible. Your dad, Lisa, he came in and spotted it right away."

Dad says, "It's a great time to change things, because there's still time before school starts. We've been talking about Jen's going for treatment. A few weeks in residence. There are a number of good places. Of course, it means bringing in her parents, and that's scary. So we're talking."

Lisa's not really surprised about Jennifer and drugs, though at her own school, there's gossip but nobody she *knows* does anything like that, but she's shocked at her father taking this on by himself. Shouldn't he have gone right to her parents? God, yes. It's *so* out of bounds. She knew what he'd say—that he wanted Jen to have the chance to do it on her own. Still . . .

She asks, "Jen? So have you talked to your parents yet?"

"Obviously not," Jen says. "Or they wouldn't be at a wedding today, would they?"

"Sorry."

"You want me there when you talk to them?" Dad asks. "I'll do that."

"No. Not really. They'll call you. I'll bet they'll call. I'll tell them you spotted it."

"Good. I'll be waiting for their call. You understand, I didn't know it was meth, Lisa. I didn't even know it was drugs. Well . . . and in fact, it's not just drugs, is it?"

"Oh, please, Mr. Friedman. It's a whole lot of things. It's a couple of weird people it would be boring to talk about. There's what we do in empty apartments. I know what you're going to say. Like, I'm angry or something, right?"

"I'm not a therapist. I just feel the trouble you're in."

"So you think I should go to a therapist, right?"

"If you get treatment, doesn't that have to be part of it? . . . Jen, Lisa, you want to take a walk in the park? It's such a gorgeous day."

On the train ride home Lisa determines not to ask him about it unless he brings it up. But when he doesn't, she does. He's looking out the window, and she turns his chin to her and says, "Dad, I want you to talk about it, and don't say 'about what?' It's not about privacy and secrets, it's you, what's going on with you. How could you take the chance? If Talia found out something like that about me, wouldn't you expect her to call you?"

"It felt right. You'll see, they'll call tonight."

"But Dad . . ."

"Lisa? Isn't it clear? We were doing God's work this weekend. This was part of God's plan for us."

"Dad!" She's scared again. "Dad! Suppose she does something awful."

"She won't."

"Dad? You listen. I hate it when you start that God's-plan business. It freaks me."

The question at the beach: God's detritus. Look. Sometimes she thinks *God* is just a word that makes people feel better. Or a word for goodness. But Dad says, if you limit God to goodness, you're not talking about God anymore. But what about what Moses saw as God passed? The "attributes" of God she hears on High Holidays in synagogue. *God, Who is compassionate and gracious, slow to anger and abundant in loving kindness and truth.* What about that?

Sometimes, she prays; mostly she hides herself in that cleft in the rock and shuts her eyes.

On the ride home she wonders if he can read her thoughts.

There's a voice-mail message from Ben waiting when they get home. Her father calls back, and she's about to leave the living room but he waves his hand at her and she comes to his side; he puts an arm around her, and she listens in to his part of the conversation. He soothes, reassures, laughs. First Ben talks to him, then Margaret. Then Jennifer. "You'll see," he says to Jen. "I'm proud of you, honey. I'm sure your parents are proud. For your courage. Well, thank God, thank God." Lisa doesn't enjoy hearing his word for *her*, "honey," being handed to Jen.

"God's plan, Dad," she mimics when he hangs up. "Why? Just 'cause you saw something in Jen and did something about it." She half-knows what really bothers her—more than his saying *honey*. It's *suppose he can read me the way he read Jennifer.* She's a little afraid to catch his eyes.

Next day and the next, and the next, till a week before Labor Day, every morning, as they sit at breakfast together, she listens as he tells her his dreams. "They're so turbulent. Full of terrible images. But when I wake up, they're gone. Dark, dark dreams, honey."

His dreams scare her; the last thing she wants is to listen. But this morning at the breakfast table—a jumble of flowers from Talia's garden in a glass bowl between them, sunlight filtered by the trees streaming into the breakfast room—he tells her another dream, tells her terrible details. "This time I remember clearly. There are young people in a car. A girl is doing the driving. And she panics, loses control, there's a crash, the car is smashed against a pole or a tree."

"How awful," she says. "You think it's about Mom?"

"I don't know. I guess."

But next morning it's the first thing she sees in *The Globe.* Omigod.

Two sisters. The girl was driving illegally—she had only a learner's permit and was driving without an adult present—and at night. The younger sister wasn't wearing a seat belt. They were just a few blocks from home in Peabody, north of Boston. They were their parents' only children.

"Dad! Dad? Listen."

She reads him the story. Her father closes his eyes and says, "Dear God, keep these children in your loving attention. Keep their parents whole." He looks at Lisa. "Though they'll never be completely whole. We know that, don't we?"

"It's awful. But Dad—you *saw* it."

He shrugs. "Maybe. Don't tell anyone about this. Okay?"

Lisa watches him when he's not noticing. Now she's uneasy in a new way.

Next morning at the table he says, "I've had another dream. Very strong. Listen. There's a big man with a very big hat on. It's a side street at night. A man grabs him and knifes him, and he falls down, and the man takes his money and runs off. I can feel the knife. Even now."

Next morning, she searches *The Globe* for the story. And yes, a stabbing, there was a stabbing—a Sikh, a wealthy businessman, walking to his hotel in downtown Boston, was stabbed, murdered. "It's the turban, Dad. The hat in your dream."

"I don't know what to make of it. A turban—it isn't exactly a hat."

Next morning she listens to his dream. "I was attached by tiny wires, like Gulliver in the land of the Lilliputians, attached to the planet itself, the swirling earth. I was tied tightly, so as the planet vibrated, the earth, as it shivered, it kind of *sang* . . . and my body vibrated to its tune. It's as if I were the soundboard of a planetary piano. . . . I can see what this dream is telling me."

"Sure, I get it, too. Like you're tuned in."

"I'm not asking for it, Lisa."

"Oh, you're asking for it all right."

"Funny."

. . .

John J. Clayton

This morning he doesn't tell her anything. She makes coffee for them—
she's begun to have half a cup in the morning to keep him company—
and she hears him moving upstairs. Floors creak in the old house.
"Dad?" She walks up the narrow, carpeted stairs to bedrooms and study.
"Good morning . . . Dad?" She watches him stumble into his study; he
sits down and holds his head between his palms.

He says, "I'm trying to remember exactly. Shh." Then—"Maybe it's
nothing."

"Another dream? Dad? Hello, Dad?"

He nods, he meets her eyes. He looks awful.

"Another dream, Dad?"

"In this one, the earth was breaking open. You know what
microbursts are?—we've been getting many of them lately. Not just in
my dream. There were wild, localized storms, fierce microbursts, and
the earth was breaking open, it was bleeding, and life—life was being
extinguished. Oh, Lisa! If it's a prophecy, how terrible!"

He's afraid to go to sleep tonight. Maybe it's true—he's connected to the
vibrations of the planet. We think our dreaming is personal. Suppose it's
not. No more dreams of cataclysm, please, dear God. When he thinks of
the myth from the Zohar—holy light too intense for the created universe, splintering off into the *kelippot*, into evil, requiring *tikkun*, repair,
to restore the original holy unity—he doesn't imagine such catastrophe.
Repair work, yes, fixing the road so that the *Moshiach*, Messiah, can
come to us. But the nightmares he's had are of terrible evil, utter disaster.
*Talk to me, Shira. These dreams aren't your doing. I need your sweetness
now.*

Their Edwardian house is old-fashioned, two stories, the staircase
narrow, the rooms small. They're like a maze, leading one through
another back to the first. The unifying principle in the house is books—
books and music. Any room you enter, shelves are crammed with
books, tables are piled with music, Shira's as well as Lisa's. He sits in the
room they call the library, though every room is a library, lights a candle, sits in his leather reading chair, looks past the candle, out toward

the dark behind the house, where there used to be a garden. Maybe there will be again. It made him cry a few weeks ago to see Lisa on hands and knees planting Talia's Japanese iris bulbs. She's trying so hard to bring back beauty; actually, she's the beauty. He strains to see Shira in the dark glass. Suppose this is what it means to be held in God's hands. Not comfort. Suppose he's experiencing the pain the planet is going through. Like Isaiah, like Jeremiah.

It's not something he'd admit to Ruth, but suppose. *Suppose.* He half-remembers words of Malachi. Adam goes to the Hebrew-English Bible sitting on one of the shelves of Jewish books. Malachi, last prophet in the *Tanach*, the Jewish Bible. . . . A role, not a name: for doesn't Malachi mean *My messenger*? It's a brief text, with words that found their way into Handel's *Messiah*: "Who can endure the day of His coming, and who shall stand when He appeareth? For he is like a refiner's fire." "C'aish M'tzaraif"—translated in Adam's *Tanach* as "smelter's fire." The fact that Adam doesn't want his dreams, as Isaiah, Jonah, all the prophets don't want theirs, doesn't mean he's a prophet. Prophets feel unworthy, I feel unworthy, ergo, I'm a prophet: fallacy of the undistributed middle.

But what if?

God is like a refiner's fire. When Habakkuk complains, "How long, O Lord, shall I cry out and you not listen? Shall I shout to you 'violence!' and You not save?" But look at those not saved in Rwanda, in Darfur, in Poland. God doesn't answer Habakkuk as He answers Job, facing Job with His glory and power. God says, *Worse is coming.* "I am raising up the Chaldeans, that fierce, impetuous nation. . . . They are terrible, dreadful; they make their own laws and rules. . . . Like vultures rushing toward food they all come, bent on rapine. . . ." But, God says, *they'll get theirs.* "All surviving peoples shall plunder [the evildoers]—for crimes against men and wrong against lands, against cities and their inhabitants." Habakkuk says, "I heard and my bowels quaked." He, too, sees the earth failing. But "though the fig tree does not bud and no yield is on the vine . . . yet will I rejoice in the Lord, exult in the God who delivers me." What sense does this make? What good will this delayed salvation do for the millions of corpses, for those who wish they were corpses? What happens when the ice caps melt and the waters rise? When storms intensify? How will we be delivered?

Adam thinks: You need no God-inspired prophet to know we're setting ourselves up for destruction, and not just this country. Nation after nation. The resilient and fragile earth. We're dis-creating, desecrating, God's world. What are we pulling down upon ourselves by our violence, our greed, our narcissism? One way to express what's happening and what's coming is as *God's wrath*.

Remember the *Tanach*—the Book of Judges, the Book of Kings. God sends a prophet; the people follow. They're saved. Then they forget the covenant with God and degenerate into evil. They're warned. They resist repentance. No matter how many times it happens, God experiences betrayal, betrayal as if by a wife (he's thinking of the Book of Hosea). *You broke our covenant?* The evil pulls down God's wrath on everyone. But a remnant returns and are saved.

This time, what salvation of what remnant?

Or *is* this time so special? Each time must have felt special, the end of almost everything.

He grows sleepy. More dreams, this time of Shira. Shira hasn't died after all. Moses intervened. "They" performed an operation, and now bandages nestle her face as she wakes from a coma. She looks so young—as young as when they first met, when he first loved her. Younger, her skin soft as if with baby fat. She's smiling, radiantly—or is she amused by his worry? Nothing to worry about, she tells him or, rather, she communicates this without words from her hospital bed.

Now there's peace in the house for a couple of days. He has no particular dreams he can remember. He attends a Sunday concert to mark the end of Lisa's summer program at New England Conservatory. She performs a Brahms sextet. Of course tears fill his eyes. Shira, of course, has gotten in without an invitation. She sits with him, inside him, they *kvell*, rejoice in pride over Lisa together.

He goes to see Rabbi Klein. "Rabbi, my daughter calls me Mitzvah

Man. It's a joke, but it means I feel I'm in God's hands, directed by God, if you'll excuse the presumption. That's not the same as a prophet. If I'm tuned in, it's so I can do God's will. I feel the suffering around me, so much, and sometimes it's given to me to offer relief. If it weren't, I'd go crazy feeling the pain. And I can do so little. Every day, torture, murder, hunger, disease. Indifferent wealth, indifferent power. Destruction of the earth. So I help someone—while all around me are the ones I can't help."

"We can do only so much. But," says the rabbi, "we're all *mitzvah* men and women."

"Exactly! We find what it is we're personally supposed to do in the world. And that's plenty. As if God has given us a personal *mitzvah* to accomplish. You taught us the story about Rabbi Zusya—that he said, 'When I die, God is not going to ask me why I wasn't Moses. God is going to ask why I failed to be Zusya.'"

Ruth calls, "terribly upset." *Her* rabbi calls Adam. He's "dismayed" at this talk of Adam as prophet.

"I'm dismayed, too," he tells the rabbi.

"The era of prophecy—"

"—is over. Over! I know." Over or not, he can't walk out of the house now without being stopped by someone wanting a tip on the stock market, on a horse, on the pennant race. Or worse: he's beginning to collect followers. Mostly ragged folk. Some sit cross-legged on the sidewalk in meditation, some chant. They bow to him when he goes out; they follow to touch his sleeve. He worries, especially for Lisa's sake. But it disturbs him, too. Then there are the merely curious, who drive into the cul-de-sac or stand, endlessly, across the street with field glasses staring into his windows. His face has become too familiar. A Cambridge police lieutenant warns him to watch out for crazies. "Please. Remember John Lennon."

Remembering John Lennon, he begins slipping out the back door, through the gap in a neighbor's fence, waving in case his neighbor, Dr. Allyne, is looking, past the Semitic Museum and down Divinity Avenue to Kirkland, then, looking over his shoulder, off to Harvard Square. But he doesn't like to leave Lisa alone in the house. For looking back, he sees his followers encamped.

Jerry, calling from the Cape, warns him, too. "You're best off, man, just keeping a low profile. Keep down; keep invisible. Low profile, man. My mom used to say, 'You open your mouth too much, someone's going to shove a fish down your throat.' That sounds damn uncomfortable. Look. Why not get out of town till the excitement fades? Spend a week out at the Cape with us, the two of you, will you? We've got room in the studio out here. Lisa can do some drawing and painting. I told you—she's got a gift. That's my field, and I'm not bullshitting you."

"That'd be great."

"It'd be great seeing you, too, you mournful old prophet. If you keep off the God stuff, we could have a great time taking long walks on the sand roads. Dan and David will be there some of the time. Evenings, we can play charades or chess. Why not, man?"

"Okay. Maybe we will. We will. I'll work it out with Lisa."

They slip out the back way and walk down to the river. There's a photographer snapping pictures at the Harvard boathouse; two crews row out, return to the dock and the young man takes pictures. He asks, "Lisa? You want to visit the Rosenthals at the Cape for the rest of the summer?"

"Absolutely. Cool!" She hooks her arm around his. "When?"

"*Soon*," he says. "Well, pretty soon. Soon as we can."

She shrugs, nods, deflated.

"No, really. I promise."

Oh, wouldn't he love to spend a quiet end-of-summer time with the Rosenthals?—who don't think he's either superhero or prophet. In his skin he remembers the salty air and the constant *shhh* of waves, increasing, decreasing. He wants to sit on top of the dunes and see the horizon line like a bow before him, rising sun like a flaming arrow on the water. But first there are things he needs to say, and Jerry and Talia aren't the audience he needs to say them to.

even while mouthing God language, and bows down to idols. And the
risk now is so much greater than twenty-eight hundred years ago. Not
the destruction of a single city, precious Jerusalem or precious Boston,
but of a whole people, a planet. Geocide. Destruction of life—or degen-
eration of the quality of our lives.

"So with the vision we've been given, we need to speak the truth.
'Words of Torah always at his lips.' We all of us are prophets; all of us are
b'nai mitzvah, children of the commandments. Mitzvah Man, Mitzvah
Woman, we all of us need to speak the burning words of Torah—and to
act on them."

Lisa doesn't exactly understand, squirming there at the rear of the congregation, what her dad is getting at. It was so embarrassing to be
quoted! People whisper *yasher koach*, congratulations, as he walks
down the aisle back to her. Do they mean it? Mrs. Pomeranz holds her
by the shoulders and kisses both her cheeks. Then there are some who
know her well and won't look at her. This worries her. She goes up to her
dad and squeezes his hand. Is she being false? No. She's proud of him.
But what questions has he answered? All those big, big ideas he's spout-
ing—does he really think he's gotten himself off the hook? The hook is
digging deeper into him.

Next day she inches aside the curtains of her bedroom window to
look out at the three, sometimes four, sometimes ten people congregat-
ing near the house. It's really beginning to scare her. Dad is at Saturday
morning services. The phone keeps ringing; she lets voice mail answer.

The foundation, though not officially begun, gets ten, twenty letters
a day asking for help—to start a small business, to pay for dental sur-
gery, to put a down payment on a house, to help a family with many
kids pay for an education. And then there are the small checks—for
twenty-five, fifty, a hundred dollars—and along with them, long letters,
as if they'd known Dad all their lives. And then the prayers—as if Dad
were a guru, a wonder-rebbe, as if he could intercede with God and for
instance lift a child, victim of a drive-by shooting, out of his coma.
Prayers and simply cries for understanding, for answers—a mother

with two sons in prison asking what she should do to keep her third son safe. Every day, pain turns up in their mailbox.

And all he is, after all, is her father. Why is he supposed to sweeten everybody else's life?

17

Lisa has been holding onto a secret. It's—not like Jen's. It's this. When her father isn't around, busy raising money for his foundation among business friends from the old days in downtown Boston, or when he's safely squirreled away in his study, reading, she slips into her parents' bedroom and from her mother's side of the closet takes summer shifts, fall skirts, a white silk blouse she's always coveted. From the jewel box on her mom's dressing table, in front of the mirror with wooden frame carved in elaborate filigree, she takes her mom's pocket watch, takes pearl earrings, takes a silver pendant—a Jewish star hanging on a gold chain. She goes back to her room to try things on. Lisa does this a lot; sometimes she re-hangs the clothes where they were; sometimes she puts them in her own closet.

Her mother's pearls she's been wearing for a couple of months, but she never mentioned them to Dad, and he never asked.

There's no reason to do this secretly. If she said, *Dad, I'm taking Mom's earrings—I'll be careful,* he'd love it—of course—get goopy tears in his eyes and ask to see them on her. She doesn't want the attention—is that the point? It's embarrassing. It's also embarrassing to acknowledge to herself what she's doing. She looks through family photo albums for early pictures of her mother—Shira at sixteen. And standing before the full-length mirror, she puts up her hair in a chignon the way her mother wore her hair to a dance in the 1980s, or she lets it hang down long and loose, black and wavy, as it is in other pictures—*hippie-style*—that's what her mom called it.

She imagines her return to school in a couple of weeks, imagines appearing in a new hairdo, in an expensive white silk blouse. Power clothes from her mother—not that they were power clothes *for* her mother, just pretty things. But for Lisa, armor to keep at arm's length the kids' pity, a pity they delighted in, about Mom, their comments about Dad. She knows they'll all know, every one of them will have opinions, and she'll hate having to say, *Please, I don't want to talk about Dad.* Because then they'll think she's ashamed of him. And that's the last thing she wants them to think. Because she's not—just worried. Maybe, she thinks, Annie can say something to a couple of the girls . . .

She'll be in ninth grade, highest grade in middle school, lowest in high school. At Somerset, ninth grade is a transition year. You take classes with other ninth graders, but you do sports, drama, music, even language courses, with the high school. She's going to feel more exposed. What will the older girls be like? Not to mention the boys! No one had better make comments! She'll kill them. She thinks, maybe she'll forget soccer. Go to school, come home. Period.

Why can't she and Dad go to the Cape right now? There's so little time left this summer. The Rosenthal boys aren't her best friends in the world—Rob is too much of a big shot, and Danny is like a little kid. Still, they're okay to hang out on the beach with.

First there was his talk at synagogue.

And now there's Jennifer.

Jennifer has called, and after spending a few polite minutes with Lisa on the phone—and please, that's all they were—she asked to speak with Dad. He went into his study and hunkered down over the phone and mostly listened. *Uh-huh. Uh-huh.* He left the door open so as not to hurt Lisa's feelings, but she knew it was a private consultation; she got some dessert and read.

It's so weird. He's stopped living through her life, and that's good, but now he's gotten serious about being this Mitzvah Man. And she kind of started it. God! Helping!—Look at all the people he's helped. First Ben and Margaret and now Jennifer; then Uri and Judith and David; and the man with the heart condition at synagogue, and that girl he saved. And longer term, through the foundation, who knows? *I should never have given him that Mitzvah Man tee shirt. Because wouldn't it be nice if he spent some time just being a person? A father?* And she thinks, ninety percent just kidding, of staying out all night or smoking dope or drinking a bunch of scotch from their liquor drawer and getting sick all over the living room carpet so that for a change she could be the one he helped.

Still, isn't she proud of him? She is.

The usual weirdos are at the corner of Kirkland Place, squatting on the grass; pairs of them, trios. They've multiplied. They're mostly young people. High school age. *Her* age. But ragged, older folks, too. A couple are street people. There's a teenaged mother with her baby. She's flabby; she wears a loose cotton frock big enough to cover two of her. So weird. They stir, they stand up and actually bow when they see her dad. Bow! Oh! *That* she absolutely can't stand to see. He goes over and talks to one, talks to another, draws them together and talks for a minute, and then he goes inside with Lisa. What they seem to want is to touch him, to be touched; and when he pats, when he shakes hands, when he rubs an arm, when he addresses them, they're kind of satisfied. There's a guy, a college student, in jeans and a tee shirt—wearing his own homemade Mitzvah Man tee shirt. This gives her an idea. We could do that!—and make money for the foundation! Fantastic! She still has her original design. She could make a better one.

Does it make sense to sell Mitzvah Man shirts when all she wants is to live like normal people again? It makes absolutely no sense. Still . . .

She's the cook tonight. She goes to her mom's laptop and skims the hundred-or-so recipes in subdirectories—vegetables, meat, pasta. Some from books, some downloaded from the web, some from Grandma—Mom's own mom. And some she, Lisa, and her mom put together, and it's among these she finds the recipe for a simple Indonesian chicken with spicy peanut sauce. She remembers making it with her mom when she was nine, ten.

It's when dinner is just about ready and it's time to light Shabbos candles and say the blessing that she takes a call. "Dad?" she calls. "It's about Cal."

Adam takes the phone in the kitchen. It's not Cal himself—a woman calls, nurse or hospital administrator at Mt. Sinai Hospital, just up Fifth Avenue from Cal's apartment. "Mr. Friedman wanted to make sure you were informed. He asked us to say that it's not necessary to see him."

"Meaning," Adam says, "it *is* necessary."

"Oh, I'm afraid so, Mr. Friedman. He may not make it through the weekend."

He puts down the phone. "Lisa . . . God, you've made the kitchen so nice, tablecloth, candles. Honey? It's Cal, I guess he's dying."

And so they drive to New York in the morning, Saturday morning, and, dropping Lisa off at the Lichts', Adam finds a metered parking spot and walks up Madison to the hospital. Cal is in a private room overlooking Central Park, but he's curled up in the bed, sensor on his finger, IV trailing from his arm, a small oxygen mask over his nose and mouth. Cal looks half his real size. It's as if he has lost his body, as if it's just folds of sheet, his big head on a soft pillow.

The cancer in his lung has spread until even with the oxygen mask, his oxygen absorption is in the mid-eighties. But much of the time he's clear enough to look at Adam and it seems it's not just his eyes looking. Then he fades out. He sleeps, then his eyes flutter open, and he's trying to say something, but it's hard for him to breathe.

It's hard for Cal even to whisper, and Adam starts to say, Rest, rest, you don't have to talk. But really, what's the damned difference? Talk, talk! Say everything! You'll rest soon enough.

This, he realizes suddenly, is his mother's phrase. Adam remembers her working late into the night the evening before company came for Thanksgiving. Maybe the big man himself or Cal's business manager Marty or a friend was coming, and his mother would be on her hands and knees scrubbing the kitchen linoleum. Uch! Scrubbing, holding her chest to breathe. It was an act, he knew that, a way of saying, *Look, you see how exhausted I am!* But it worked. He felt lousy, he felt furious at her for making him feel lousy. He'd say, "Mom, rest, please, stop working so hard." And she'd moan her answer. "Rest? Don't worry, I'll rest soon enough." She loved to use the grave as the climax of her drama. Now that he thinks of it, she imagined her life through the lens of theater. If there were no such thing as death she'd have invented it for the third act. "Perhaps," she said at other times, "I don't deserve to rest. I must have done wicked things in my life."

Meaning, *I've done nothing wrong, so why is God making me suffer?*

Now, it's as if this room with the lovely big windows over Central Park, a room that looks like an upscale modern hotel room—it's as if this private room were *semi*-private, as if in that one bed are both Cal and his mother. He remembers his mother, dying so quickly at the end. Seven years ago already! Eight. In the cranked-up hospital bed in his old bedroom, the window washed as he couldn't remember ever seeing it, she said, "My son, my son. . . ." It saddened him—that even at the end she couldn't stop acting. "I'm dying, my son," that phony *my son* business! *Yes, you are dying. Please, say the simple truth, at least now.* Not that there was some particular truth he wanted from her. Just that she not play the old melodramatic role at least now, at least at the end.

She kept his father out of the room so she could spend time alone with Adam. His father just grinned and shrugged, accepting this last whim. But then she called, sang, for her husband, "Norm, Norm, come back. You have plenty of time to read newspapers *after* I'm gone." Unfair, but it seemed to wash off his father. He came in and sat by the bed and patted her hand. "You don't seem to realize. . . . ," she said. "Oh, sweetie," he said, "just cause you got me beat by a couple years, don't think you're all that special."

"No, I'm ordinary. I'm an ordinary woman. That's why I married you."

"That's not what I meant, sweetie. You want me to read to you?"

"No, my dear, just sit. My son will read to me."

She's in this bed with Uncle Cal. In fact, so is Dad—Cal's brother Norm. They're all in bed, the dead and nearly dead, a ménage à trois. Peculiar—Adam finds he wants to stroke Cal, this monster of his childhood, rub his bony shoulder through the johnny. "Are you comfortable?"

Clearly enough he mumbles: "With all this morphine, who the fuck wouldn't be?" Then for a very long time nothing, silence. His eyes are closed, Adam thinks he's slipping away into a coma and death, but Cal whispers, "Glad you . . . make it. Gotta have somebody watch the nurses or they'll ignore you."

"Nobody ignores you, Cal."

"What do you know? They'll steal you blind."

"Nobody's gonna steal from you, Cal."

"That's right. . . . Christ. I'm so fucking tired," he whispers through the mask. "Jeez, and I got to pee. So bad. I don't care so much about dying, I can just pee."

"It's what happens when you've got a catheter in you. There's nothing to pee. It feels that way," he says, remembering his father's dying. *I'm gonna pee all over the bed*, his father had said. Go ahead, it's okay, it goes right in the bag, he told him and now tells Cal the same. "But it must feel lousy." He doesn't look forward to it when his time comes. "Squeeze my hand," Adam says.

"Say—I got a son. Ain't that something!" Cal says this—or something close to this. "Sonny boy," he says. "Jesus! Son-of-a-bitch!" He reaches out a hand.

When Cal touches his hand with fingertips, Adam expects the hand to be frosty cold; it's soft, warm from the IV and the oxygen. But instead of the love of a father, or someone who imagines himself to be a father, Adam feels fear and confusion pour from Cal, feels it as clearly as if there were an IV connecting them. Helplessness. Bravado gone.

It's strange to him his mother couldn't get away, even at the end, from the sad role of righteous victim, while Cal, who'd played a big, fat, flamboyant role all his adult life, seems simple now, helpless, bodiless, almost without a role. There's no invisible Stetson, like a Texas halo, hovering over his head.

"Hey! You believe in this white-light crap?" Cal whispers after many minutes.

"It's there all right," Adam says, as if he's seen it. "You close your eyes, you'll find it."

Cal's eyes are already closed. After awhile he whispers, "Well'd you look at that. . . ."

Adam closes his own eyes; he actually dozes. Cal goes out, comes back: his eyes slit open, then the weight of the lids shuts them again. Adam feels him like a second body. He sits up, chants the Shema very quietly and thinks he hears something from Cal's throat. Maybe, maybe not. A nurse comes in and straightens the plastic tubes, goes out. Adam looks up at the oxygen absorption digital screen. It keeps sinking into the low eighties.

Now, with no warning, a high-pitched sustained song from the machine monitoring Cal's pulse. He's gone, and a nurse hurries in. "You're not going to try to bring him back, are you?" he asks, but she ignores him. *No*: no frantic call for a machine to shock and restart the heart. "You'll have to step outside," she says, and he does. But here's the thing: he's brought Cal along with him into the corridor. This is slightly scary. How long will Cal stay with him, in him? It's a weight.

He's permitted back inside the room. In the bed, washed, wires and tubes gone, is a sculpture of a human being, bust of a calm, wise soul, head braced by a pillow, with none of the anger and greed and boastfulness of the man himself. But that man himself, puffed up as if by a mantra: *No one's gonna fucking put one over on me, Sonny Boy*—that tough guy, American sport, make-believe cowboy, urban rancher in ten-gallon hat, seems to be inhabiting Adam. Adam kisses the handsome old-man head. As he walks away down the corridor to the nurse's station, he takes Cal's old stride, asks about cremation arrangements in Cal's voice. It's the way Cal used to lengthen out vowels, their tone slipping down a third or quavering like a cello shmaltzing the vibrato.

·　·　·

That night they eat together at the Lichts', Lisa, Jen, Margaret, Ben; and Adam tells stories of Cal. He demonstrates Cal striding big-time down the street, Cal talking to the men who sold rugs and carpets for him. "The guy used to sound like a Baptist preacher. He'd get the sales people at one of his stores together at eight in the morning and he'd preach at them. He'd hold his vowels—like this—"We're gonna sel-l-l-l one ama-a-a-zing shit load—you'll excuse th'expression, gentlemen—of kiss-my-ass c-a-a-r-peting today."

"Poor Cal," Lisa says.

Ben asks, "You're not going to sit shiva, are you Adam?"

"No. No, but I'll be saying Kaddish for him. There's no one else to do it." He looks across the table at Ben. The hanging light over the table reflects off his big steel-framed glasses. It's funny. Though Adam's been through another death, he and Ben have been smiling at each other a lot tonight. The guy has such kindness. What a good man to have as a friend. "You know," Adam says, "Cal wrote it all down—no funeral, no service, just cremation. Which seems pretty sad. But in my memory," Adam says, "he's vivid." Memory, he calls it, though it's more than that. He feels the man in his bones.

Jen looks at him whenever he looks some other way. He knows she wants to talk, and when Ben clears the table and Lisa and Margaret are doing dishes, he raises his brows, gestures to Jennifer, and they go sit in the living room. "So tell me," he says. "Are you okay?"

"I'm pretty okay."

"But you're not in rehab."

"Well, we looked into programs, but they all require months and months. I didn't think I needed that long. I may still take a year off and do that. But right now," she says, "I'm here. We call it the Broadway Alternative Retreat Facility—the BARF."

Margaret comes into the room and sits by Jen on the sofa and wraps both arms around her. "It's been hard," Margaret says, "but very moving—for me; for Ben—for Dad. For you, too, Jen?"

Jennifer nestles. "Actually, it's been a kick in the head. But," she adds, "a bearable kick."

Margaret says, "I cancelled meetings, held off potential clients, did some drafting, sketched, I spent time showing Jen how I begin a design for an apartment. It hasn't been all bad."

"It's only been a few weeks. God, I can't believe it. It feels a lot longer. I knew I was being watched."

"Oh, I didn't watch you."

"Oh, yes you did. . . . Mom was like my nurse. That's cool. She talked to a couple of doctors, friends of ours, and eased me off the bad stuff, gave me some tranquilizers when I was bouncing off walls, and it's been like a drag but not, you know, unendurable."

"Thanks for thinking of me as 'endurable,'" Margaret kids.

"Oh, Mom."

"I think it's wonderful," Adam says. "Wonderful, Jen. Wonderful." Tears come to his eyes.

"I don't know about wonderful . . . but I think we kind of did it. You wouldn't believe how much sleep I got. The idea of meth makes me sick right now. I kept thinking about you, Mr. Friedman." She has her eyes shut, and now she looks right at him, into his eyes, into his heart, and it's hard to take. "I heard your voice in my head all the time. You know? And Mom and I got the way we used to be. Right?" she asks her mom. "Instead of hating each other. You know? And Dad, well, he'd check on our progress and make a game of it, bring us fabulous food—great steaks and lobster—or give me an 'award,' like when I was a kid. It was okay being a kid for a change."

"Wonderful," Adam says. "It makes me feel so happy for you all."

"But *now* what? If I go back to school, the same kids will be there, and it's not like I can just ignore them."

"We've talked a lot about this," Margaret says.

"I mean, I'll be living with them. So. I'm a little scared. I mean, the people I'm talking about, they're not going to push me around or anything. But they're my friends. I'll be with them."

"So are you thinking of living at home?" Adam asks. "Going to school in New York?"

"Exactly. Maybe. I don't know."

"But Jen, you know," Adam says, "there'll be kids like that everywhere. Any city school—public or private—any boarding school."

"Sure. I know. Of course I know that. So anyway, Mom and Dad talked to the headmaster. You know, it's not like a terrifically druggy school. It's not. It's a good school, a fantastic school, and as a matter of fact I kind of love it. But what happens when I get back?"

"Say more. What you think it's going to be like. Imagine a situation . . ."

Lisa comes in. And Ben stands in the living room doorway. "This has been good for all of us," he says. "That's the funny thing."

"Some funny," Jen says.

For all of us, Adam repeats in his head. *I need a Mitzvah Man for me.* It's so clear to him the way being Mitzvah Man has protected him from grief. Who is he without the costume?

But maybe, he thinks, driving through Connecticut with Lisa the next morning, still feeling Cal inside his bones, he needs Cal's arrogance to get him through this peculiar time. He talks to Lisa in Cal's voice. Finally, she rolls her eyes at him and he stops.

"You're really good at it, Dad. But please just be you, okay? And you're *not* going to grow another beard, are you?" she asks. "Please, Dad. If you don't want people to think you're some nutty prophet, please, no beard for mourning. Okay?"

"Promise. No nutty prophet. Promise. Businessman. Mitzvah Man. A quiet, private life."

But at home privacy comes hard. The followers watch the house from the corner; they continue to bow when Adam comes and goes. He agrees with Lisa. They should be anywhere else, at least until school starts. So they call Jerry and Talia, and they pack for the beach.

Just when the bags are packed, a telephone call comes from the

DSS—Department of Social Services. Among other things, it oversees protection of children from abuse and neglect.

Someone, it seems, has filed a report. The woman, a Mrs. Connor, can't say who filed it. He sets up an appointment for this Mrs. Connor to come over the same evening. "I don't know who's making trouble for us," he says to Lisa. "My guess is your Aunt Ruth. Or maybe someone I offended politically in the newspaper? On the radio? Maybe someone felt angry or threatened?"

"Dad? See? Haven't I been nagging and nagging? I'm sure it's my wonderful Aunt Ruthie. Can I call her up and yell at her a little?"

"It'll just make things worse."

"You've got to be careful from now on. Right?

"Right. Watch me." He goes out to the corner and calls out, his hands a bullhorn. "Friends! Friends, please come over here a minute." He waves them close. Four, seven, eleven of them including a baby circle him right below the porch. He knows Lisa's watching through an open window. "I need you all to go away from here. It's absolutely essential. If anything I've said has touched you, please, please help me now."

Someone asks about terrorists. Someone else calls, "Do you really hear from God? What do you hear?" Someone says, "Hey, Mitzvah Man! Mitzvah Man!"

He spots Mr. Lottery Ticket, the man in spiffy suit and Adam's own tie. He's not been a nuisance, this guy—he's stopped by a couple of times, he knocks and says hello, hello. Now Adam finds him at the edge of the little crowd. The man pushes forward. "Leave it to me, Mitzvah Man." And the guy calls out, "Friends of this prophet, please listen to our guy, listen to the Mitzvah Man." And like a shepherd he opens his arms and gently sweeps the others away. Then he turns. "Hey, Mitzvah Man—I just stopped by to tell you. I got a job. I got me a job. You're my boy!"

It's not just these people who are in pain. But because they're there especially to see him, because they look at him, he can feel their pain more than that of most people, who wear defensive masks to hide it. . . .

Marks in every face I meet, marks of weakness, marks of woe. Of course, it's the defenses against those marks that cost so much work and pain. The silent screams of sufferings and then the strain of keeping silence, of appearing composed in hell.

Hurrying back inside, Adam clears books, teacups, papers from the living room. He keeps looking outside. The corner is clear, thank God, when Mrs. Connor drives up in her blue Taurus.

Mrs. Connor is a lean, athletic woman in her late thirties, plain-faced, heavy-jawed, but attractive in the strength of her walk, her posture. Lisa has dressed up in a skirt and her mother's white silk blouse. Mrs. Connor wears a neat gray suit. It looks uncomfortable. She looks as if she'd feel more herself in a track suit. "Can I get you some tea?" he asks. She barely answers. She hunts through her briefcase for the folder. He feels waves of irritability—from himself, from her?

"Now, Mr. Friedman, here's what's at issue." Sitting on the only uncomfortable chair in the living room, she leans forward and interlocks her fingers over her notebook. "We've gotten reports about your family situation."

"And you can't say from whom?"

"I'm sorry."

He can see she's trying to be firm and kind at the same time and ends by looking uncomfortable. Feeling what she's going through to keep up ramparts and battlements, he wants to comfort. "Please, Mrs. Connor, that's all right. I understand. Go on. Listen—can I get you some tea?"

She ignores this. "We're required by law to follow up. DSS would like to know about the stability of your household for a growing girl. There have been reports questioning the stability of your home, Mr. Friedman. No one has claimed you're an abusive father. But, as you can imagine, there can be various forms of abuse and neglect."

"Absolutely."

"And there's been some concern about the home you've created since your wife's death—about your ability to provide a normal, safe home for her."

"Reports, hmm? But ask anyone. Ask our rabbi. Lisa goes to a fine school, she continues her music. She has friends. What else could any-body want?"

"Dad's great," Lisa says. "Absolutely great. Just . . . passionate. Which is cool. Right?"

"I'm sure. We have to ask. It may feel like an intrusion, but once a report's filed, we're required to investigate. Lisa? Tell me about what it's been like for you since you lost your mother."

Lisa tells, very simply. And avoiding, of course, the weird stuff from the beginning of the summer; avoiding, for example, his use of a Camry as a guide, pointer of a ouija board. She tells Mrs. Connor about camp and conservatory, about her father's kindness, about the way the news-papers wrote a load of false, stupid stuff. "They want to make him some kind of prophet. But he's just a father. Dad and I have been okay. We get sad. Of course we get sad. But Dad's awesome."

"Thank you, Lisa. Now, if I can just speak to your father alone?"

Lisa goes off. From her room they can hear her violin. Adam knows she's playing to feel calm—but more than that, to show Mrs. Connor the kind of home this is. And, he's sure, to invoke the spirit of her mother.

Adam finds Uncle Cal inside himself, feels him now as he speaks. And that's helpful, for the guy has power, and Adam doesn't feel so pow-erful in his own right. In fact, he feels scared. "My top priority, Mrs. Connor," he says in the musical drawn-out phrases of his uncle Cal, "is to give Lisa a solid growing up. My girl has lost so much, losing her mother. I know you don't really want to wreck her—to try to take her away from me? I know I can count on you for help."

Mrs. Connor spreads out her folder and notebook on the coffee table and leans forward, her hands folded on her lap. When he speaks in this Cal voice, he notices, she glances up quickly, changes expression; so he determines to make his speech as ordinary as he can.

"We're not talking about your losing her. We're really not, Mr. Fried-man. Not," she adds, "at this point. Certainly not for any extended period. No. But we're looking for some assurances. Here's what we see. We see a cult figure. Cult figures can turn dangerous. Tell me, were you prescribed medications?"

"I have a feeling you already know the answer. I was. To deal with the grief at first."

"We'd feel better if we knew you were continuing to take what was prescribed for you. We're charged to speak to your therapist during the initial ten days of investigation. Does Lisa have a therapist?"

"No."

"I can't tell you the sources of this report, but can you understand that DSS might worry about a man with dreams of violence? And not just dreams. It's accurate, isn't it, that you got into a fight. You could have been killed in that fight. We're aware of your bravery that morning. But it makes DSS uneasy—the fight, the dreams, and this talk of prophecy."

"Not my talk."

"We have reports about some very disconcerting public appearances."

"Is it my sister-in-law Ruth who's filed this report?"

"Can you understand the effect of your public behavior on a sensitive teenager?"

"Can you understand the effect of your visit on a sensitive teenager?" This is the moment he realizes he's changed, his voice has changed. It's no longer Cal's phony twang, nor his old businessman charm. He hears a new voice, voice of someone he is only beginning to be acquainted with, a good guy, solid, stronger than he's ever been. At this crazy moment he thinks, *What if this were the man Shira married?*

"DSS is going to need to keep an eye on you. No one's talking about taking your daughter away. That's always a decision of last resort. But we very much want to see stability in this household. For Lisa's benefit. Do we understand one another?"

"I think so, Mrs. Connor. The media has turned me into a story. I'm not a story. I'm a businessman with a serious interest in establishing a charitable foundation. Let me tell you about it." And he goes to the glass-fronted secretary that he inherited when his father died. Inside he finds a large scrapbook. "I want to introduce myself to you." And he shows her clippings from his years in business. His awards. The marks of success he felt smug about at the Chase School reunion. They belong, in a sense, to someone else; it's no longer *his* success. He's someone else. But she doesn't have to know this. That someone else is out of the picture. "You can be assured, Mrs. Connor, you can be assured I'll do everything I can to keep things normal. To keep a low profile. To keep the damned newspapers away. You can bet," he says, "I intend to make a stable home."

She's silent for a minute. She borrows the album and puts it on her lap to give her time to think. "Very good," she says at last. "I'm pleased. And so as to claims of being a prophet—"

"But I've never made such a claim."

"We understand you wear a special shirt claiming to be a—" she consults her notes—"'Mitzvah Man.' Do you think of yourself as a special person—a person favored by God?"

"No, Mrs. Connor—that's a family joke. A gag. A *mitzvah*—it just means one of God's commandments, incumbent upon all Jews. Many are for everybody, not just Jews. Like loving your neighbor. The tee shirt is largely a joke. It refers to our foundation—the Mitzvah Foundation. The "Good Deed" Foundation. We're offering help to people in small doses, person to person. For college tuition, for medical help. But the shirt—my daughter gave me the shirt as a joke."

"A joke. Well, that's fine," she says, and takes a deep breath and smiles at Adam. "I'm very glad we understand each other." She stands, arranges her papers. "Say good night for me to your lovely daughter. Oh—" She says this as if it were by-the-way, but Adam knows it's not. "I noticed a couple of suitcases by the door. Are you traveling anywhere?"

"Just to the Cape. Visiting family friends."

"Within Massachusetts. That's fine. We do understand one another." Enough to shake hands.

Upstairs, Lisa's in tears. He sits next to her on the bed in this room that's scarcely begun to change since she was a child, ten, say. He rubs her back. His fingers remember rubbing Shira's back through the same silk blouse. "She scared you, didn't she, honey."

"I guess."

"Sure, she did. Don't worry, I'm not going to let anything happen to us. I'm not. We'll be okay."

"You keep saying that. And things get worse and worse."

"I'm trying, honey."

"Dad, there was something so spooky about it. It felt like one of those movies about conspiracies. It doesn't feel possible that someone was just worrying about me. Even Aunt Ruth."

"We'll keep a profile so low," he says, "that a snail won't see us raise our heads. Okay?"

He stands at the top of a high dune watching Lisa sixty feet below toss a disc around with Dan and Rob. The three of them get along pretty well. The wind keeps whisking the disc away. Ocean's coming in, and the disc peels off and skims a wave and one of them has to swim for it. Adam's feeling clear. He's rejected requests for two phone interviews. He's called up Celia, the woman who used to clean for them, and set up a regular schedule. The house has to be brought back to order. He's called people he knows in software and called back a headhunter who called several times over the past year. He knows it will look better if he has a position; he'll appear more ordinary. Then if he wants to do "charity"—well, no one will be upset at that.

And the foundation is going strong. Cal must have changed his will during his last weeks; for he's been notified by Cal's lawyer that a great deal of money in investment funds, at this point valued at over three million dollars, has been left to Adam's Mitzvah Foundation. So there'll be enough money to enable him to fund the foundation long term, employing only the interest for small business loans, and direct aid for medical expenses and education. And if people find out about the legacy, it's sure to bring them more.

He shuts his eyes to savor it: all the families he can help!

Of course, he thinks, there's no end to pain. You can pour out succor like cement, fill up the hollow places ground out by grief. There's no fill-ing the holes; water runs right through. Is that really true? You look around, you hear the cries, and, yes, it feels that way. But no, it's not true; for instance, now Judith and Uri don't have to worry about paying for David's medications. That means something; he's done something real.

So am I talking about myself? A hole at the bottom of my life? And no way to fill that?

The wind presses steadily against his open shirt, and it flaps backward like wings. He can lean against it and not fall. He's seen hang gliders lift off from this dune and hover over the beach, and in his mind he's doing that now. Lifted by the wind, held like a kite by gravity.

The line of whitecaps coming in to shore seems urgent, purposeful.

As it churns toward shore, the line of waves, like the line in a graph, on an electrocardiograph, brings messages. He's not equipped to read them. What does the line say, keep saying?

Not to mention the wind in his ears. He can feel the singleness of field: wind//ocean//sun. Information coming from wherever he puts his attention, this information is the same, one, unitary, as the Lord our God, the Lord is One. All One, Whole. Found in every fractal: the Whole. Looking at the churned water he seems to see patterns. Looking at the sky bleached out this hazy afternoon, he sees so many spots of light rising and falling—angels descending, deeds rising, that's how it seems. We act with purity on the sluggish earth and our actions lift and transmute into . . . *what* in the other worlds? They turn into angels. A flow rising, a flow descending. One: the warm sand under his feet same as the energy in that disturbing, seductive, metamorphosing ocean and sky.

When you feel that unity, isn't that enough?

He is tied to the sand by gravity but he feels his life rise up, or no, something within him lifts, a column of pure energy, bubbling through his body, it cowls and lifts his body, dizzying him, making him a little giddy. But he rides it.

He is held by the wind, grounded in hard sand, and in his ears is the music of wind. A high call. Almost a voice. Not almost; it *is* a voice. Psalm 19. *Eyn omer v'eyn devarim. . . .* There is no speech and there are no words, yet their voice goes throughout the earth. . . . So listen. If God isn't here, God is nowhere, and loss takes over the whole enterprise; the hole at the bottom of the self that can't be filled. But for sure there is Presence. He's grateful. Words in the wind—all right, he knows they're not just outside him; they're a union. Voice in the wind, translation he brings to the wind. But Voice, beyond his ken, is surely speaking. *Boston*, it says, doesn't it say? *Boston, violent city*. He's trembling now in the wind. *City that doesn't know Me*, it says—or he manufactures.

"What do You want of me?"

Boston, it seems to say. And he understands exactly what this means. It's not that Boston is worse than any other city, more violent, more filled with pain or evil. But it's where he lives. And the other day, when he was on his way to visit an old crony, the CFO of an import-export firm near Government Center, the suffering around him became a miasma, like bad Boston air on the muggiest day of summer. He felt urged to stand on the steps of King's Chapel and hold up his hands to the people walking by. To say what? That all their worry, their rage, their pain, was charging the air, making it hard to breathe, polluting the spiritual city?

What does God want of him?

"Please. I'm doing my best—isn't it enough to be Mitzvah Man?"

He shakes his head. I won't go to Boston. I'll take my pills, I'll get stronger pills, Lisa doesn't need this, it's the last thing she needs, I'll stop my ears. And he does. He puts his fingers in his ears. And if the whitecaps breaking in a jagged line are also speaking to him, that line he can't read.

Oh, please, please! What do you want of me?

Below, Lisa and the two boys are sitting in a semicircle talking, their legs outstretched and feet touching, arms bracing them behind.

I'll take my pills.

What do You want of me?

He turns away, walks the dune crest trail, crestfallen.

Lisa has spotted him at the top of the dunes. She throws the disc so that it curves in the wind and Rob can leap for it and bring it in. She wishes Jennifer could be here with them. It's so great she's kind of okay. And she's removed the surveillance cameras. That was, Jen said, a real hard thing to do. But there's less she needs to snoop about now that divorce isn't in the air.

She likes knowing her dad's up there on the dunes, watching over her; he's simpler now, less full of God-talk. Maybe they can just have a simple life. Maybe school won't be a pain if she just doesn't let it be. *If I treat it as normal, maybe it'll be normal. And Mom will be with me.*

That woman, the monster from DSS, omigod she was such a scare. Still, she's glad the woman came. The scare was good for Dad. It's bringing him to his senses.

Not that he's wrong. He's not been wrong. He knows things. He dreams things.

The next day, day after that woman came to visit, Lisa got him to drive them to the cemetery in Waltham, to the plot, still with no stone for a few more months. "We'll have to plan a beautiful unveiling for next spring," he said.

She nodded. Then she said, "Mom would be so happy to know we're going to live—you know—a private life. And the house will be the way she loved it. Right, Dad? And people will forget that prophet stuff. We'll be okay, won't we Dad?"

"We will. Of course we will."

"A dumb, simple life."

"Right. A simple life. Not dumb. Your mom would approve."

Simple. Celia will come back to help them clean, and they'll make a chart and clean some of the house themselves. She'll bully him into it. All she'll need do is look into his eyes and say, *Dad, it makes me so* depressed *living like this.* Maybe that's manipulative, but it has to be done.

She knows her mom would approve. It's a joke between them, her and her mom.

For she's been talking to Mom a lot. And little signs come back. A pile of Lisa's music blew off the table the other day, and a sonata by Bach for solo violin skidded out of the pile and across the living room floor. Can that be an accident? No way. Her mom's very favorite. And then in Tower Records yesterday a CD including that same Bach sonata was at the very front of a stack of new arrivals.

She's almost sure. She dreams of Shira so often. And then the next day there'll be a sign. In a store window, the title of a book; in a florist's window, her camellias. Little jokes from another world . . .

It's nice sitting on the sand with Dan and Rob, tickling toes. If it were just Rob, they couldn't sit like this, touching feet, sun heating them, wind cooling. It would make them self-conscious. He'd be staring weirdly at her. With Dan, they feel comfortable together.

She wonders: Is her mom watching now?

They'll bake in sun and have to cool off, diving into the surf and taking in waves. And tonight, like last night and the night before, she'll feel the rocking of the waves when she's in bed, and she'll dream of waves rocking her. So simple. Good end to a sad summer.

He appears on time for cocktails. The Rosenthals have invited a couple from Truro, and the couple has brought along a weekend guest, a young woman—no accident, a set-up, he's sure. They sit on the brick terrace; it's sunset, the sun glows. Lisa's in a giddy mood. He gives her a sip of white wine from his glass, whispers, "How you doing?" She doesn't answer, leaves the terrace behind Rob, laughing. Talia and Jerry's house doesn't face the sunset, but faces a hillside with high yellow grasses and green beach grasses, a hillside that gets beautifully washed by the last sun. He offers a platter, hummus and crackers, to the young woman. She's assistant to the head of development for B.U. They talk about his foundation; she offers a couple of suggestions for raising money. He can tell she's impressed by his venture—or wants him to think she is.

He knows it's just a question of time. The Voice will return, voice he heard at the top of the dunes. That Voice, its demand, which he doesn't understand, is more urgent, more real than life on this brick terrace. It will return.

If he has to, he'll take his pills.

What's most important, after all? No matter what the Voice asks.

She wears a simple white cotton dress with spaghetti straps, this rather pretty woman in her mid-thirties with long, straight, red hair—dress and hair as if she were a young girl. He has to admit—that gets to him. Fantasies of starting all over. That is, looking at her he thinks, *I could begin again*. But at the very thought, the sweet erotic glow that was playing through him dissolves. Sadness fills him up.

"What do you *do*—I mean besides raise money for your foundation?" she asks him.

Isn't there, when you come down to it, a hardness about her face? And the boring question! He remembers visiting London with Shira, remembers being warned off asking that question: *What do you do?* "It's not perceived as quite polite, you see," his London friend warned. Here in America, it's the first question anyone asks. And what does he say?

"I've been asked to fill a significant role in Boston," he says, "but I'm pretty sure I'll decline—it's more than I can handle. I expect just to take a job at some IT company. We've had a loss, Lisa and I. Perhaps you know that."

She's heard about their loss, he's sure; she looks down at the brick, she nods. He imagines she's waiting for him to continue, but he doesn't follow up; and so she doesn't follow up. He's afraid to look at the golden sun on hillside grasses for what the light might tell him. He goes over to the table and pours himself another drink.

"You took some long walk this afternoon," Jerry says, handing him a platter of smoked fish. "How was it?"

"Great," Adam says. "A beautiful walk. Music of the waves, you know. Very pleasant. All I saw was a couple of seals. Nice and boring."

"Right. Quiets the mind," Jerry says.

| 18 | On a Sunday in mid-October, two weeks after Sukkot, the week-long festival when you're supposed to build and eat and study in temporary structures, structures through which you can see the stars, Lisa dresses up at the old, slightly battered dresser mirror in high-necked white blouse and long black skirt to go visit Dad. She listens to her mother's voice in her inner ear: *You look so grown up. . . .* And even though she's put the words in her mother's mouth, it's comforting. She's got a room to herself here at Uncle Leo and Aunt Ruthie's—a boy's room, plain, walls with the pin holes from childhood posters, with adolescent photos of Red Sox players and a faded blown-up poster of a bearded rabbi who gave a talk in Boston. This is Nathan's room; Nathan is at some big-deal yeshiva in New Jersey. The room retains his odors. In the mirror, she looks to herself as boring as old Nathan. Tall, skinny, drab, with retainers. In black and white.

Lisa has been living here a month now. It's the first Sukkot she's ever helped to build and eat in a sukkah, the temporary shelter. Everyone on the street built a sukkah! This was the first time she's ever heard Aunt Ruthie laugh and laugh. Those are the only good things about living here. Her dad was still with her for Rosh Hashanah and Yom Kippur; then, before Sukkot, checked himself into McLean's Hospital for a "work-up." Every day she takes a long subway ride from Brookline to her school in Cambridge. That was the deal; she agreed to come only if she didn't have to go to a Jewish day school where everybody knew lots of Hebrew and she knew just a little, where everybody was completely used to Jewish customs and she wasn't. Sure, they always lit candles for Shabbat, she and Dad, and Mom before the accident, and yes, she was studying for her belated Bat Mitzvah. But she didn't know much. And then—forget those vain things—silly worries, really—what about friends? Friends were the chief thing. There's Sophie, there's Annie. She'd been afraid kids at Somerset would give her a hard time—with her father gone off the deep end. But they didn't.

It's kept her sane, her school.

Black and white. A long row of pearl buttons. Her hair is tied back neatly. It's such a severe look that, catching sight of it in the mirror, she almost giggles. She mugs seriousness into the mirror. Nobody's ordering her not to dress up in colors. But she feels that today a sober look is called for. A Decorum Costume. Black and white in the mirror. So absolutely boring, the way she looks. To soften the look she puts on her mother's string of pearls. Still—all black and white.

It reminds her of when Ruthie takes her to synagogue—the sea of men's striped black and white full-body talises she can look down on from the women's balcony through a gap in the screen, the *mechitsa*. Barely attending to the distant service, she watches the sea of men in black and white shift and flow. Aunt Ruthie's lips move with her prayers; she doesn't stay with the service but is on her own page. Some of the women huddle and laugh together; Ruthie swivels to give them a quick, severe look. Lisa has the impulse to "accidentally" yank off Ruthie's helmet wig. She doesn't. She peeks down through the gap at the rabbi and the other men up on the *bima*—the *bima* is not a low platform at the end of the sanctuary—what she's used to—but a high stage with a railing, set in the middle of the high-ceilinged room. Only the ark is at the end. Most of the men, what she can see of them, are bearded; it's hard to see anything but talises, striped black and white.

It's Sunday. After brunch Leo drives her out to Belmont in the Chrysler minivan. The car feels so huge for just the two of them. He asks her about what girls her age are listening to—what music. She

John J. Clayton

barely knows. She mentions names of singers she's heard but wouldn't recognize if she heard them on the radio. And what about movies? She names some titles. She wants to be nice to Leo. He's awful kind. He doesn't care at all about the music or movies. It's his way of saying, Lisa, I'm not your enemy, you and your dad. And she knows he's not.

Ruthie—well, she's another story.

Ruthie thinks she's saving me. Oh, sure.

It must have been Ruthie who filed the report and kept bothering DSS until they came to investigate. Ruthie hasn't said she called DSS. The one time Lisa mentioned it, Ruthie gave her a blank stare. After Dad did what he did last month on the radio, it was Ruthie who volunteered to "rescue" Lisa until her father became stable.

Lisa talks to her as politely—and as little—as possible.

Leo turns in at the gates and up the long drive, commenting on how pretty the grounds are. The day is chilly; there's a vague, pale sun through the mist. The great deciduous trees have lost a lot of their leaves and most of their color except for some oaks, still musky red. There's a smell of wet dirt and tree. "Did you know," Leo says, "James Taylor was here once?"

She says, "Uh-huh. Dad told me. And Robert Lowell, Dad said."

Parking, he looks at the brochure he's been using for directions. "Over there, down that path," he says. Suppose I come back for you coupl'a hours. Okay? I'll go do some shopping."

"You're not going to come in with me?" And it's weird. She wants to see Dad alone; but she wants the support of this big galoomp.

He shakes his head. "Look: if your dad wants to see me, I can see him when I pick you up. I'd be happy to see him. Either way, I'll be right here. Two hours, sweetie, okay?"

Mostly, she's thankful. She gets out, smiles and waves, and the minivan pulls off.

Her dad, in khakis and a windbreaker over an open blue shirt, is standing on the portico of a big white building leaning against one of the columns. "Dad!" She forgets about decorum and charging up to him, hugs him. "Dad?" she whispers, looking around wildly, "are you supposed to be just *out* like this? I thought you were kept—"

"No, no, don't be a goose. I came in on my own, I can go out on my own. This was my decision, honey. You know that."

"I know, I know, but I thought once you *made* the decision—"

"No, no. Honestly, they're not treating me like I'm crazy and dangerous."

"Oh. Good. Great. So I guess you're having to talk to a million doctors?"

"Let's go take a walk." As they walk the curving paths past perennial borders clipped back for winter, past neat lawns, residences, offices, with the corner of her eye she sees him looking her over. It makes her straighten up, a lady, then breathe and relax to show him she's easygoing, not burdened by his situation.

"Leo's been great," she says. "Maybe you'll see him when he picks me up?"

"Sure, if you want." Now he stops her and stares. "Ah! You're so grown up I can't believe it." They're silent. She listens to their shoes clomping on the path. "Did I tell you, honey? It's all straightened out now. My medical insurance covers most of this. Nothing but the best for us superheroes." Then, solemnly: "Lisa? I'm sorry. I'm really, really sorry I opened my mouth."

"I guess you *had* to." To show this isn't meant critically, she takes his arm. "I mean it. Had to."

"How is it going at Ruthie's?"

"Fine, I guess." She mock-gags, holds her throat, stops and grins. "Well. Acceptably. Dad? I mean it. I see it now. You had to, you just had to."

When they came back from the Cape six, seven weeks ago, she could see he was brooding. The night before school started, she made her last nice dinner for a while—a veggie lasagna and a great salad. Once she was back at school, he'd take over. They ate at sunset on the back deck, the sad remains of their sad garden to look at. From Kirkland the noise of cars and trucks, from overhead the whine of jets on their flight paths. She laid the wrought-iron table with a white cloth and put out real napkins and wine glasses with sparkling grape juice. "This is really something," he said and started laughing, laughing, laughing till she began to get spooked out. "No, really. I'm so lucky. . . ." So—were the tears welling up tears of luck? Not exactly.

"What's the matter? Dad? What?"

"It's kind of a torture," he says, playing with fork and knife, putting it down to take a big breath and answer her. "To feel I'm bid to speak and then not to speak."

"Dad? So you can speak to me."

He half stands and leaning over, kisses her smack on top of her head. "And I do," he says, sitting back down and eating his lasagna. "But I feel I'm hiding."

"Like Jonah? Just kidding. Dad? If you have to speak, just be kind of cool. Okay?"

"I know. Oh, I will. *If* I speak. Cool."

She has the feeling he'll be anything but cool. Even in his telephone call to Larry Adler—sitting in the cracked-leather chair in his study, watching him at his desk, Lisa overhears his end. Yes, he tells this Larry Adler, he'll agree to take part in another call-in show, he'll talk about his dream-prophecies—but in return, Adler needs to let him speak about his larger vision.

"I'm not even sure what I need to say, Larry. I'll know when I get there."

There was a spot on the call-in show the following Tuesday.

Lisa finds herself spying on her father. When he's on the phone, she puts her hand over a receiver somewhere else in the house and listens. When he's out of the house she looks on his desk and finding notes he's scribbled, attempts to read them. Her stomach is upset a lot. When they're home together she knows just where he is in the house. It's hard to focus on her homework.

The day before the radio show, Lisa telephones Talia. "Will you let me come over so we can listen together?"

"Of *course*, honey."

"You don't mind?"

"We'll have tea and listen. A couple of ladies having their tea and listening to the radio. We'll have a good time."

"So, I'll explain to Mr. Melman and get out of school a little early. The show's at four o'clock. So I can come over?"

Jerry's at home, too. He sprawls on the couch; Talia sits cross-legged on a cushion. Lisa is curled up in a soft, velvet-covered easy chair, sipping tea. She tries to focus, consciously, on the things in the Rosenthal house that usually make her feel happy. Not today. She stares at the stereo.

"Frankly," Jerry says, "I wish to hell your dad had stuck to tennis. I'm damned uneasy about what that madman father of yours might say. This Mrs. Connor. . . . We wrote a letter to DSS. Did you know that? Saying what a great father, etcetera, etcetera."

"Dad said you did."

"Well. We'll see. You know I'm kidding about 'madman.' But why does he have to go on the radio, damn it?"

"I guess he doesn't want to be like a Jonah. You know—run away when he's called?"

"Oh. Oh, Jesus Christ." Jerry turns on the radio.

A commercial, Larry Adler's theme music, and another commercial, and another. Adler begins. "We've got a hero on the show today, folks, a real live hero. You sent me a lot of emails telling me how much you liked having him on the show." Adler introduces Adam: a successful businessman, folks; a black belt. The fight. "Adam Friedman is Mitzvah Man, superhero of the good deed. Adam, how about telling folks about prophecy? Just lay it all out there, Mitzvah Man."

Lisa, Jerry, and Talia groan. "Yeah. Just lay it out there," Jerry laughs. Lisa puts her cup and saucer on an end table and covers her face with her hands.

"I'd like to talk about patterns I see in our world."

"Well, go right ahead, Mitzvah Man. Ladies and gents, Mr. Adam Friedman. Our local prophet."

At the Rosenthals, they're not laughing. They stare at the patterns in the carpet and sip tea.

"What I see . . . isn't simply, what are we to do about this problem or that. About Iraq, let's say. Should we pull out our troops now? How can we change our energy policies? Can we turn the country towards alternative sources? Of course we've got to do that or we'll destroy ourselves. And we're practical people—Americans—we think that way. And what do we do about genocide in Darfur or malaria and AIDS all over Africa? Those questions matter a lot. I'm not saying they don't matter. They're huge. We need to do *teshuvah*—to turn from destruction, from corruption, to turn to God. But what I *see*—and, Larry, isn't it what anyone can see?—is *all* these things at once—a terrible, dark pattern; we're threatening to tear the fabric of life forever. We've called up destruction. It's like invoking demons. For what we've done, we'll all pay. No wrathful God has to willfully punish us. We always enact God's will, even when we rebel against God. And there's no undoing it by spin or by clever diplomacy . . .

"The consequences of our greed and violence are upon us. Our oil hunger is enriching murderers. With AK-47s children are forced to fight children for control of diamond mines. Women are raped, men are murdered, land is taken from people, and we—we let it happen . . ."

Adler interrupts: "So, Adam, would you say you're a prophet of doom?"

But Adam keeps going. ". . . And storms—storms grow more violent, water levels rise, and on the other end of, say, a cell phone call— *that* close to us—demons pull out fingernails and pock their victims with lit cigarettes before decapitating them or shooting them in the back of the head. More cities will be bombed. Is this new? We may have reached a tipping point into something new. More violence, until the delicate fabric of our infrastructure is torn; worse, until we give over our freedom. This time, will there be a remnant, a holy people? *You shall be*

holy, for I the Lord your God am holy. Can we turn? Is it so late that all
we can do is mourn the losses in advance?"

"But isn't this just what the old-time prophets told us?" Adler asks. "So what do you think—you think this makes you a prophet?"

"The prophets have given us the eyes to see with: Isaiah, Amos, Jeremiah. They've taught us to see. To see the connection between unholy behavior and its effects. Not on the guilty individual. On the community. On everyone. They also taught us about turning back to God. Me, I'm not special. I just see through their eyes. . . . And Larry, what about you? What about *your* eyes? The collecting storm—doesn't it give *you* bad dreams?"

"Let's see what the folks at home have to say about this."

In the living room, Jerry moans a long out-breath. "Ohhhhh. . . . I gotta tell you, Lisa, your dad, he's gonna sound a little bit off the deep end to the ordinary folks at home. All right—even to me—and don't get me wrong, I absolutely love the guy."

"Still," Lisa says quietly, "he happens to be right, doesn't he?"

Talia says, "Lisa . . ."

After a series of ads, a caller talks about the Bush presidency, another about "our lying, liberal press that's weakening this country," another about the "the Rapture," the fundamentalist belief in an end-time in which Christians will be taken into heaven and cataclysm and final battle will occur on earth. "I don't believe in that kind of heaven or that kind of end," Adam says. "And our choices aren't between pure right and pure wrong. Whatever we do in Iraq, in Darfur, we'll bring more suffering upon people. Whatever happens in Israel, people will suffer . . ."

Maybe none of this would've caused Dad trouble, Lisa thinks, if he hadn't added, "We *are* God's judgment. We are bringing that judgment into being. It's not something out there, up there, coming down upon us. We're it. We're God's judgment!"

"So are you saying," Larry Adler asks, "that you're like God? Is that what you're saying?"

And there it is, no matter how her father denies it, and he does deny it, again and again. Adler wants to hit his listeners with a jolt of excitement. *A guy who thinks he's God.* Obviously he doesn't care one bit whether it makes any sense—or what it does to her dad. Now, more callers, and the show is over.

"Your dad is a damned smart man," Jerry says. "God, how I wish he'd learn to shut up."

"If you think about it," Lisa says, "he's not saying anything wrong. Not really. He's not." Then she looks at Talia, whom she believes in so much, and at Jerry, who's the most sensible person she knows, and they look back at her with solemn faces. "Well, he's not. Is he?"

That was three weeks ago. Half an hour after she got home from the Rosenthals and started heating up the stew he'd made for them the night before, Aunt Ruthie called. She didn't hear the program herself, but a friend did, and their friend spoke to their rabbi, and do you know what the rabbi says? "Your poor dad," Ruthie sighed. "I feel sorry for him. Don't you?" She left big gaps between her sentences. "Lisa, dear? He's disturbed. It's grief. I know. But. You have any idea what he's been saying on the radio? Seriously disturbed." During each pause Lisa tried to get a word in. At once Ruthie interrupted in a louder voice, until Lisa gave up. "Yes, Aunt Ruthie."

Three days later a call from DSS, and she has to take a day off from school to go with him and speak on his behalf, on *their* behalf, at a "family group conference" run by DSS in their local offices on Memorial Drive by the Charles. It's such a total drag. DSS keeps them waiting half an hour; it's like sitting in a hospital waiting room. Pale, lime green walls; a large bulletin board with notices stapled up. Overhead fluorescents, which she absolutely despises. There's a leftover smell of ham or something probably heated up this morning in the small microwave in the corner. Lisa pulls out her sketch pad. "As long as we've got to wait, my dear Dad, sit still and I'll draw you. I'll pretend I'm a sidewalk sketch artist, okay?" He sits for her. "And don't talk, okay? Shh. You can look down at your book, okay?"

He sits for her, his eyes looking sad. She feels more sad for him than for herself.

"Mr. Friedman? Lisa, dear?" Mrs. Connor stands in the doorway in a suit, a black suit. Her hands are folded in front of her. It's meant to show how calm she is. She leads them to a cubicle with no window. Someone, some nice administrator, has put a Breugel's *Harvesters* on the wall to provide warmth. The painting makes Lisa want to cry, first because inside she's thanking that decent person for trying harder than you have to. And second, because when her mom took her to the Met, they'd stop in front of that painting and her mom would find a huge sigh and let it out. Lisa lets her eyes be soothed by the peasants in a golden field. Her mom is asleep under the tree. Mrs. Connor's supervisor, Dr. Lewin, plunks down a cassette recorder. "All right if we record this?"

Her father nods.

"That's a 'yes'?"

"*Yes*," he says in a formal voice, aloud for the tape this time. "Yes."

Dr. Lewin, a tall, graying man in his fifties wearing maybe the ugliest checkered polyester sports jacket Lisa has ever beheld, says, "At this meeting DSS is acting for the most part as facilitator." He smiles at Lisa; his teeth are crooked, omigod they need orthodonture. *Here, have my retainer, Dr. Lewin.* She can't help comparing them, Dr. Lewin and her father. Uch. "Our hope," says Dr. Lewin, "is to avoid a formal charge, a Care and Protection Petition, and a formal court hearing in Juvenile Court. We have certain allegations to discuss, and we all have a common interest—I know that's true in this case—in making sure that Lisa is living in a stable home, making sure that you, Mr. Friedman, can take care of her. All right? All right, Mr. Friedman?"

She expects he'll tell them what a good father he is, where she goes to school, what she does when she isn't in school. Which is okay. Administrators, she's sure, love violin lessons. But *then*—then she's absolutely sure Dad will open his mouth and not shut it till his foot is all the way down his throat. Dad told her they had a letter from the Rosen-

John J. Clayton

thals saying Ruth Hochberg has a grudge against her father, that this is a case of a family quarrel, not neglect or abuse. So—a letter from the Rosenthals and also from Rabbi Klein and also from the Eisens—from Judith and Uri. Now she waits for a wild, embarrassing, prophetic speech. But Dad doesn't say much.

"If you feel I need therapy," he says, "I'll agree to it. I want us to work together on this."

"This is a great dad," she blurts out. "I don't know why you want to put him through all this stuff. Do I look abused or something? Just because he's got these ideas. Well, so what?"

"We know he's a great dad, Lisa," Mrs. Connor says. She's seated kitty-corner to Lisa, and now she puts a hand on her shoulder. "And he loves you a lot. We know that."

"I'm happy with my dad. Look. It's none of your business if he's . . . like a prophet."

"So do you think your dad is truly a prophet?" Dr. Lewin asks. "Inspired by God?"

Right away in the pit of her stomach she knows: if she says, Yes, he's a real prophet, his dreams tell him things, he sees patterns, God's patterns—if she says that, she'll be showing his effect on her, and they'll take her away from him. And if she says, No, I don't believe that, she'll be showing that even his own daughter thinks he's cuckoo. So she just shrugs.

Mrs. Connor puts her hand on Lisa's shoulder again; this time she keeps it there. The shoulder starts to feel hot, but she's uneasy about brushing off the hand. "Nobody at DSS wants to keep you from your dad," Mrs. Connor says. "You love each other. You're doing well in school. Lisa . . . you understand, this is rather an unusual case for DSS."

"Unusual," Lisa echoes.

"We usually deal with obvious abuse, terrible neglect. This is so different. But we're worried"—she turns to Dr. Lewin—"isn't that right, Dr. Lewin? DSS is worried that your father may not be providing a stable life for you."

"What's wrong with it? I think you're against freedom of speech.

You're un-American. My dad is so brave and smart." Now she can't hold it anymore. "He's Mitzvah Man. What's bad about helping people? What's bad about seeing the world as . . . filled with God or something?"

"Take the radio show for an example," Lewin says, as if she hasn't spoken. "Your father said that God is acting through him."

Adam thumps the desk. "No. Listen. You miss the point. God is acting through you, too. Through us all. This is ordinary theology. Not particularly crazy. The talk show host was trying to make me sound peculiar."

"Well, of course," Dr. Lewin says. "Of course. Talk show hosts get you to say things you don't mean. Most people are wary. So tell me: would you say you're really *not* a prophet? In the sense of *special*? In the sense that God has given you, personally, directions?"

Her father takes a long time answering. She can see he's coming to an answer. When he finally answers, it's in a subdued tone; Lisa can hardly make out the words. He nods his head to himself. "I have to say . . . I have to acknowledge . . . there's a neurotic component to my role."

Lisa keeps shaking her head. She can see this big supervising idiot's little hidden smile at her dad's admission. Oh, this smug nobody knows all about the real world. Sure! Well, thank God I'm not *his* daughter. *Officious!* That's the word. Exactly. Boy, the word helps. He's got a little power, this Lewin. Officious, officious! Mr. Officious. He nods and nods and takes his notes.

Mrs. Connor is saying, "Well. I'm glad you see that possibility. Yes. There are people in the street outside your house. Some of them sleep out there. Isn't that so? You talk to them. And these dreams—what about these dreams? I've been saying to Dr. Lewin—"

Dr. Lewin says, "And let's not forget that fight you had—you could so easily have been killed. How do you feel about the fight?"

"Your therapist says—" Mrs. Connor begins.

"What?—*that* fool," her father says. "My therapist is a fool."

"Your therapist suggested you continue," Mrs. Connor looks down at her notes. "Isn't that right? And he wanted you to keep taking your medication. But you're not taking it. Is that right?"

"Well, look, Mrs. Connor—if that matters to you, I'll take my antidepressants. It seems an intrusion, but I'll take your advice. Let's call it *advice*, all right?"

"That's hardly enough assurance for us. We're suggesting," she says, "you get a full evaluation. We're suggesting that in the meantime your daughter stay with her aunt and uncle."

"My aunt and uncle! Omigod! With them? But don't you get it? My Aunt Ruthie's exactly the troublemaker. And the crazy one. That's the real truth. This makes absolutely no sense," she says. She looks around the room, but there's nothing to calm her except the Breugel.

"They're your only local relatives," Dr. Lewin says, "and we've spoken with them. We're convinced they have your interest at heart. Lisa, suppose the other choice were a public facility?"

"You're trying to scare my daughter?"

"Please, Mr. Friedman."

"All right, what about a boarding school?" her father says. "That would be less destructive."

"No!" Lisa says. "That's even more awful, Dad—it's for the whole year if I do that."

"Lisa is making sense," Mrs. Connor says. "Now, your aunt and uncle tell us that if you stay with them while we settle certain questions, you can continue to go to your own school."

"So Lisa, what do you think?" Dad asks quietly. "Suppose I check myself into McLean's, suppose I have them do a psychological workup." He turns to Dr. Lewin. Lisa is jolted by the way he looks straight into Lewin's eyes. It scares her—it's so intense. People don't share looks like this with other people. "Does that make sense?" her dad says. "What do you think? If they find I'm stable—maybe neurotic like the rest of us but stable—will that be sufficient for DSS?"

After about an hour, it clouds over. Sad Sunday. Lisa and her father have been sitting on a bench under the tent of a willow, talking a little, her dad sighing a little; she's taken her mother's violin from her case and played for him. When the rain begins, she sees he doesn't notice, so she ignores the rain. But it starts really coming down. "Dad?" she says. He looks up out of a daze. His pills? "Come on," he sighs. "Your violin—it'll get wet." He holds her violin in its canvas case under his windbreaker and shepherds her back to the inpatient building where he has a private room. The lobby, the halls, are warm, with comfy old furniture; the staff people they pass are just people, not dressed in white. Entering his room, she sees a landscape in watercolor—maybe, she thinks, by a patient—because it's really good but with a kind of amateurish stiffness. Not that she's saying she could do better.

She looks around. Easy chairs. Papers and books lie in piles on a round wooden table between the chairs. "Is it okay if I shut the door? Is that allowed?"

"Sure. Sure. I'm not a prisoner."

She feels awkward with him here, as if just by being here, he's been changed, become a mental patient. It scares her like crazy. Deep in her stomach, deep in her chest. "Dad? When you said to that jerk you were 'neurotic,' what did that mean? Did that mean you were wrong about what you saw, about what you said?" She waves him into a big chair and sits across from him, her legs crossed, her fingers locked around her knees.

"*Neurotic* means—"

"Dad! I happen to *know* what *neurotic* means. I mean, what did *you* mean? What did *you* mean?"

"What did I mean?" He sits nodding to himself, elbows on the arms of the chair, resting his chin on upraised fingers. She finds herself wanting to imitate him, feels it would be really satisfying to sit that way, but she's afraid he'll think she's making fun of him. "It's so hard to explain," he says, "what happens to an adult. All your life, you build up layers and layers of defenses. The way a tree makes a lump sometimes around a wound, or the way when you break a bone, extra layers of new material grow over the break, you know?—"

"I don't get it. What kind of wound? Would you please stop saying

'You do this,' meaning anybody, and tell me what you mean for *you*?"

"Right. Give me time on this, honey. See, it's not just me. And I don't know what it is exactly. Down at the core of me there's a broken place . . . or an empty place, and all my life everything I do has been to cover it up. You build—okay, *I* built—protective casings around it. All the bullshit of personality. All the roles. Even 'Mitzvah Man.' So nobody sees this broken thing I know is there. That's what I mean. Look. I'm not even interested in the etiology—do you know what etiology means?"

"No. Sickness?"

"Cause, origin. Where it comes from. Even using that word, even that's a defensive gesture. It makes something simple, a brokenness, maybe from when I was a child, into something clinical, objective, medical. But I mean, so what if I can name the reasons? You know, it's not just me. I see it all around me, people posturing, putting on the dog, like that foolish shmuck—excuse the expression—that Lewin at the meeting at DSS. The way he speaks with a modulated tone of voice to give him professional stature. The poor bastard. . . . So maybe . . . God hasn't touched me. Maybe all that is just another protective layer. I don't know. All I know is, I've been scared good. That I could lose you? I'll do what it takes, honey. If it means not listening, then I won't listen."

"You mean to God?"

"Let's say I've been in God's hands—I mean in a special way, because we're all of us always in God's hands—then maybe God will have to be patient with me. Till you're away at college. That's just four years."

"Dad! Remember on Yom Kippur at synagogue the rabbi had me and Misha and Aaron read the story of Jonah aloud? Well? Jonah ran and hid. He wouldn't do God's bidding. Only in the belly of the big fish he prayed and was saved and then he knew he couldn't run? Dad? I couldn't say it to them at that meeting, but I guess I really believe in you. I do. You're a prophet. You know you felt called. So you can't wait four years to do God's work. If God is calling you?"

"Maybe God's timeline isn't the same as yours. Honey, one doctor here said I was suffering a 'situational depression.' Like grief. Like the suddenness of your mom's going. And she kept me on the straight and

narrow. She did. And maybe I had to replace her, and all the rest is just
cover-up. Maybe. Anyway, we're all prophets, we can all *be* prophets.
That's what I've been saying, right? Right now I'm staying calm and taking my damn pills so you can come home to me."

"Well, isn't that what I want? You think I adore it at Aunt Ruth's? But Dad, you've *got* to speak. Look—" Lisa stands up and turns from him and unbuttons her white blouse. Turning back, she shows him the Mitzvah Man tee shirt. Looking down, she sees it's a little faded. She lifts arms in a superhero stance. "See? And by the way, I found out how much it would cost to make 500."

"No, dear. It's not worth it. . . . Lisa? I think it's time to leave. Let's not keep Leo waiting."

"'Not worth it'? Not *worth* it? Dad! Is that what a Mitzvah Man says? Suppose Moses said at the burning bush, 'It's not worth it.'"

"I'm coming out of McLean's with a good report. And I wasn't dishonest in the interviews. Well. Not exactly. Just . . . not saying everything. Come on, now stop laughing." He joins her in laughing. "So here I am, coping with 'situational depression.' Yes, I know it means nothing."

"Well?"

"It means we're sad, honey. Means I'll be taking mellow-izing happy pills for a while. So what? I'm stronger than those pills. It's not situational anything, it's world-grief, and I can't stop, not completely. But," he whispers, "I can hold off for a little while."

She comes over to him and balancing on his knees, puts her arms around his neck. "A little while? Like four years? Mitzvah Man. My Dad. You're the Mitzvah Man." She kisses him and stands up, grown up again, fourteen going on thirty again. She hauls him up from his chair. "It's time, I guess. Dad? You'll come say hello-goodbye to Uncle Leo?"

19

It's two weeks later, again a Sunday. He's finished fixing dinner; it's cooking, releasing odors of brisket, onions, and herbs, and now he's sitting back in his soft papa chair listening to Dvorak. It's dusk. In a few minutes Talia and Jerry Rosenthal are coming for a tiny celebration — his homecoming, Lisa's homecoming—an early dinner, an early evening. The Rosenthals have to go to work tomorrow, and Adam has to look seriously for work. *Thou shalt not leave thy head in the sand*, he tells Lisa.

Six months ago tonight, Shira was still alive. Two days later, dead.

Lisa, her homework for tomorrow morning finished, is stirring brownie mix. Seems she's gotten tired of nagging him. This afternoon, every time she took a break from the essay she was writing, she stood arms akimbo at the back door as he was raking leaves or in the doorway to the living room if he was reading, and, three times, she announced something like this: "Dad? I've been thinking. It's just too important, your being Mitzvah Man. You've got to promise me—you can't give it up to be just normal." Then she'd heave a huge, dramatic breath, turn and go back to her homework.

Once he called after her, "Hey, I appreciate. You want me to know you believe in me. I'm really touched, honey. But enough already."

"Oh, blah."

The amazing speed of the human brain! For instantly and all at the same instant, he's hearing the music of Lisa stirring and he's smelling chocolate from the kitchen; he's wondering if he bought enough beef for tonight and feeling a dark wave from the future that's making him a little seasick. But he's seeing and smelling Shira's fingers, too, he's licking chocolate off her fingers. So this moment must be overlapping with the Sunday before he went to New York for the Chase reunion—that Sunday overlapping this homecoming Sunday.

Adam and Lisa are half-listening tonight to a trio by Dvorak. At one chord change he hears her tiny soprano shriek of delight. He calls from the living room: "Yes. Yes, beautiful."

Beautiful, but he makes a mental note to change to Keith Jarrett's Köln Concert when Jerry and Talia come. Jerry prefers jazz—which is okay with him.

So. Peaceful, inside and out. The peace of six months ago is here now, too: Shira offers him *her* chocolate fingers to lick, one at a time, while she looks in his eyes and smiles a promise. Peaceful now, whatever wave threatens. No one's camping tonight in the cul-de-sac outside or walking up and down under the street lights on Kirkland. When he got home Thursday from McLean's, he made a pitch; the three men, one woman, nodded as if he were their coach. One nutty guy with scribbled signs was taken away by the police; he hasn't returned. Just before Ruthie brought Lisa home this week, a few others came by and gawked at the house or knocked at the door for a lottery number. He waved them to him. *Please leave. I'm no better than the next guy.* And they left.

Peace. The smell of chocolate.

Mrs. Connor called to ask if she might stop by tonight on her way home from her sister in Somerville. That's okay by Adam. He'll introduce her to Talia and Jerry. She's grown pretty human, Mrs. Connor. Nancy Connor has begun to nod when he speaks and even smile at him over the notebook she holds on her lap for psychic protection. She has visited twice, and she looks different—softer. No beauty, but a pleasant face to face. She wore, last time, a knitted light sweater in pale gold. "For the leaves that haven't turned," she said, when he complimented her, and didn't she blush? Oh, she did. He thinks she kind of likes him.

Turns out she's an athlete. Last March, she told him, she ran the Boston Marathon. She's talked about her sister, stuck in a bad marriage to an alcoholic. Then, just before she left, she said, "I shouldn't tell you this, Mr. Friedman—"

"—Adam."

"Adam. I'm Nancy. I shouldn't tell you, but for the sake of family harmony you do need to know: it wasn't Mrs. Hochberg—Ruth Hochberg—who reported your family to DSS."

"It wasn't? It *wasn't?*"

"No, it wasn't. Though afterwards, she also filled out a report. And please don't ask where the initial report came from," she says, lifting her hand like a traffic policeman, "because even if I knew, and I don't know, that's all I can tell you, and I shouldn't tell you that."

He holds himself back.

Now Mrs. Connor puts her notebook on the table and sits back. "Let me put it like this. You've got me reading the Bible again, Adam. You see your effect on people?"

"The Bible?"

"The prophets."

"Really!"

"Yes. Now, you take Jeremiah. Jeremiah was thrown into prison. He was thrown into a pit. He was almost stoned to death as a traitor. He upset a great many people. Important people. He told the king to surrender to the king of Babylon, to become his vassal, because Jeremiah had a vision. But the king—what's his name—didn't listen—"

"—Hezekiah."

"—Hezekiah didn't listen, and Jeremiah barely escaped punishment. He would have been killed if he hadn't had important friends. It's good for a prophet to have friends."

"Yes. I see what you're saying."

"Nebuchadnezzar captured Jerusalem just as Jeremiah warned, and Nebuchadnezzar had Hezekiah's sons killed in front of Hezekiah and blinded him and took him back to Babylon as a servant."

"I see. You're telling me it's nothing new—I mean prophets being right and getting into trouble."

"That's right. Not new. Very old. I'm not saying you're a prophet. Nor that you think so. We have it from you and from your psychiatrist at McLean's that you don't think that."

"Of course not. I'm just a normal person who gets sad at the world sometimes. I try to make repair. Small repair." Suppose he told her what he sees. No, not *sees*. He doesn't *see* what's coming. Nor does he *hear*— hear, say, the voice of God. Rather, he *feels* what's coming, feels it as a mountain, a swollen sea, a terrible wave, a great beast: not visible but as if he'd found an additional mode of perception.

He can't say any of this. He can't say that he stands on his deck upstairs looking out over the roofs of Cambridge and feels in touch with the interweaving of the four worlds, the *olamot*. The destruction that occurs in this material world of action reverberates in the other worlds. This interaction is as real as Mrs. Connor's notebook. As below, so above. He feels the wounds in the fabric of all the worlds. He feels the way goodness, too, reverberates.

There's darkness. And there's chocolate and Dvorak.

Light in the living room tonight is dim; if he's Jonah, say, then maybe this is the belly of a great fish. If it's the belly of a great fish, accommodations have improved since the time of Jonah.

The king and people listened to Jonah. Nineveh wasn't destroyed. Jonah was the prophet who least wanted to speak; when he did and the people of Nineveh turned from their evil and God saved them, Jonah was bitter. Was he embarrassed? Did he want the city destroyed? God had to teach him how precious creation was. Worth saving.

And isn't it? Worth saving? Look at the evil, yes. Torture, murder, injustice. But what would they matter, what would death matter, if there weren't something worth saving in creation? Chocolate and Dvorak. Lisa. Judith and Uri's kid. A hundred people a day are executed in Iraq. Oh, my God, my God, these numbers. Symbolic numbers. Maybe 600,000 Iraqi civilians dead in the war, surely 800,000 Tutsi killed by

Hutus. The rising numbers of the women raped every year in Darfur. And the six million. How much worse can it get?

Adam sits in the plush papa chair Shira's father used to sit in. In his mind's eye, heart's eye, it's Shira who comes from the kitchen with chocolate fingers and presents them to him one at a time. He closes his eyes and says, "How good."

She's nudging him—yes—to go to the reunion. This memory-time must be a little more than six months ago, a few days before he went to New York and Shira died. He doesn't visualize what Shira's wearing; he imagines only her tender face, her bright eyes, the funny little ironic smile she handed him. She says—of course!—she *did* say this, he'd forgotten—"You need to come back to the world, honey."

"Oh? I'm not in the world? I'll show you later on tonight how much I'm in the world."

She squeezes against him; the chair is a little tight but big enough for both of them. "I see you listening sometimes, your head cocked to one side, when there's no music. I'm a little worried about you. You're hiding. Adam? I think so. I want you to get out more. You've done so well these past few years—I mean financially—it's not that you need the money. But why stay home?"

"Why go to a reunion at Chase? What a pathetic school that was."

She has one remaining chocolate finger, and this one she sucks herself while she thinks. "Adam? It's exactly because that school was so awful, so traumatic for you. You've never gotten past it. You've never assimilated it. I'd like you to go there and see it simply for what it was."

"It was just a lousy high school."

"No. Much more than that."

"Well, I would like to see Ben Licht."

Shira knew the brokenness in me, maybe loved me for my brokenness. She's in bed with him. It's dark, dark, he touches her. When he enters her he whispers, "You're my world, you're the world I want to hide in." And what was it she answered? *Well. That's quite good enough for tonight.* Something like that. She always looked so young when he was inside her, when they looked into one another's eyes. And the next day, or the next week, he went to New York, she went off to rehearsal.

"Dad?"

"Coming. I'm coming."

"I hear their car. Talia and Jerry's."

"Coming, coming." Isn't he still hiding? *Shira? You know it's true.* Hiding by avoiding his calling as Mitzvah Man? Well, yes. But also *in* the role of Mitzvah Man. There's comfort in being held in the hands of God. Psalm 27, the psalm prayed every day the month before High Holidays, says it outright. *One thing I asked of Adonoy, one thing shall I seek: that I dwell in the house of Adonoy all the days of my life. . . . God will hide me in God's shelter on the day of evil.*

"Coming, coming."

There's the hush of a secret wave approaching. When it arrives, he'll have to plunge. But in the meantime, he hears Lisa go to the door and open it for Talia and Jerry, and laughter begins.

About the Author

John J. Clayton, author of *Wrestling with Angels: New and Collected Stories, Bodies of the Rich, Kuperman's Fire, The Man I Never Wanted to Be,* and *What Are Friends For?,* has taught modern literature and fiction writing at the University of Massachusetts since 1969. His stories have appeared in *O. Henry Prize Stories, Best American Short Stories,* and the Pushcart Prize anthology. His collection *Radiance* won the Ohio State University Award in Short Fiction and was a finalist for the National Jewish Book Award.